The Quest of Frankenstein

The Quest of Frankenstein

by
Frank Schildiner

A Black Coat Press Book

Acknowledgements: Mary Shelley and Jean-Claude Carrière.

Copyright © 2015 by Frank Schildiner.
Cover illustration Copyright © 2015 Mike Hoffman.

Visit our website at www.blackcoatpress.com

Introduction

"Yes, he is dead. But what is death for one such as him?"
(Old Man Blessed to Helen Coostle
Jean-Claude Carrière – *La Tour de Frankenstein"*

In 1957, writer Jean-Claude Carrière [1] was approached by Editions Fleuve Noir to continue the adventures of Mary Shelley's immortal creature for their newly-started *Angoisse* imprint of horror novels. [2]

---

[1] Carrière (1931-) is an award-winning French screenwriter who has collaborated with such famous directors as Luis Buñuel, Jacques Deray, Jess Franco, Jean-Luc Godard, Louis Malle and Volker Schlondorff, to name but a few. His film credits include such masterpieces as *Belle de Jour* [*Beautiful by Day*] (1967), *Le Charme Discret de la Bourgeoisie* [*The Discreet Charm of the Bourgeoisie*] (1972), *Cet Obscur Objet du Désir* [*That Obscure Object of Desire*] (1977), *The Tin Drum* (1979), *Le Retour de Martin Guerre* [*The Return of Martin Guerre*] (1982) and *The Unbearable Lightness of Being* (1988).

[2] The popular *Angoisse* and *Anticipation* imprints of Editions Fleuve Noir were reviewed in our introductions to André Caroff's *Madame Atomos* series. Other Fleuve Noir novels published in translation by Black Coat Press include b G.-J. Arnaud's *The Ice Company*, Richard Bessière's *The Gardens of the Apocalypse* and *The Masters of Silence*, Gérard Klein's *The Mote in Time's Eye*, Kurt Steiner's *Ortog*, Pierre Pelot's *The Child Who Walked on the Sky*, and the forthcoming Maurice Limat's *Mephista*.

Carrière then proceeded to write six *Frankenstein* novels in 1957 and 1958, which were initially released under the house pseudonym of Benoît Becker.[3]

In his first novel, *The Tower of Frankenstein*,[4] written with some plotting assistance from Guy Bechtel, Carrière followed the footsteps of the Monster. The creature is christened *Gouroull*—one of the first words that he utters as he returns to life, the meaning of which remains a mystery throughout the series.

Unlike the more nuanced version of the Creature portrayed by Boris Karloff in the universal *Frankenstein* movies, depicted on the cover of the books by renowned French artist M. Gourdon, Gouroull is a ruthless, demonic thing, the very incarnation of evil. His yellow, unblinking eyes hide a cunning, inhuman intelligence. He barely speaks, but uses his razor-sharp teeth to slit his victims' throats.

In the novel, Carrière chose to emphasize the inhumanity of the creature: it does not breathe; his skin is white as chalk, but strangely impervious to flames; his strength and speed are prodigious; what runs in his veins is not blood but some strange, black ichor; and he has no normal heartbeat; even his thought processes are shown to be alien.

---

[3] The nom-de-plume "Benoit Becker" was also used by writer José-André Lacour who wrote six horror novels for *Angoisse*: *Expédition Epouvante* (*Expedition Terror*) (No.4, 1954), *Le Chien des Ténèbres* (*The Dog of Darkness*) (No.6, 1955), *Laisse Toute Espérance* (*Abandon All Hope*) (No.10, 1955), *Terreur* (*Terror*) (No.15, 1956), *Château du Trépas* (*Castle of Death*) (No.19, 1956) and *Le Souffle Coupé* (*Short of Breath*) (No.46, 1958). Other writers having used the "Becker" pseudonym include Stéphan Jouravieff and Christiane Rochefort.

[4] *La Tour de Frankenstein* (No.30, 1957).

BENOIT BECKER

LA TOUR
DE FRANKENSTEIN

D'après le célèbre personnage
de MARY SHELLEY : FRANKENSTEIN

M. Gourdon

ANGOISSE

Éditions
"FLEUVE NOIR"

Cover art by M. Gourdon

The Tower of Frankenstein opens in 1875 in the Ulster village of Kanderley. In it, a young woman, Helen Coostle, meets the old man Blessed, who runs a Frankenstein Museum in his tower. Blessed was ten when Victor Frankenstein and the Monster briefly stayed in Kanderley after they left Scotland, following the scientist's failed attempt to create a Bride for the Creature. Frankenstein and his Monster became Blessed's lifelong obsession; he eventually located the Monster's body in the Arctic and brought it back to his Museum.

Eventually, the Monster is returned to life by the evil Vrollo, a local hobo who hates the villagers and lusts after Helen. Vrollo thinks he can control the Creature, but instead, it ends up killing him. Gouroull then escapes when Blessed arrives with reporter Gordon Mallorey and the police. The Monster is believed to have perished in quicksand, but in reality has fled to the sea.

The next novel, *In the Footsteps of Frankenstein,* [5] takes place a few years later in the Scottish village of Plosway located on the Isle of Cround in the north of Scotland. This is the place where Victor Frankenstein tried to create a Bride for his Creature. Percy, a resident witch doctor who learned how to make zombies in Haiti, becomes the unwilling assistant of the mad Dr. Pilljoy. Pilljoy has come to Cround with Gouroull, hoping to succeed where Victor failed: he wants to create a new Bride and a race of monsters.

When Percy finds out that Pilljoy plans to drain the blood of a local widow, Mary, he rebels and is savagely murdered by Gouroull. But the witch doctor eventually returns as a zombie, kills Pilljoy and, with the help of other zombies he created—including Mary's late hus-

[5] *Le Pas de Frankenstein* (No.32, 1957).

band—Percy saves the widow and drives the Monster away.

The Night of Frankenstein [6] takes place in 1895 in the village of Gottwohl in the Swiss Alps, near Ingolstadt, where the Monster had once found refuge. There, the misanthropic Pastor Schleger, obsessed with Nietzchean theories, comes across Gouroull and plans to mate him with a woman in order to create a superman. But all the women Schleger kidnaps are terrified by the Monster and, enraged, the Creature kills them. Gouroull eventually rapes Ingrid, Schleger's wife, and ends up killing the Pastor and driving Ingrid to her death in the icy mountains. A local poacher, Molli, hunts Gouroull who is attacked by wolves and falls into a chasm.

The Seal of Frankenstein [7] takes place in 1924 in Austria. Doctor Markus is taking care of Ingrid at the Lunatic Asylum of Hallshofen. She survived, found herself pregnant and went mad.[8] The Monster returns seeking his child. During a carnival, he is unmasked by Markus, and kills him. The Monster then breaks into the asylum. The readers are never told for certain, but Carrière hints that the Creature's son is a deformed woodsman and serial killer interned in the asylum. The woodsman attacks the Monster, who kills him. Gouroull then frees the other inmates, sets fire to the asylum and escapes. Ingrid hangs herself in her cell.

---

[6] *La Nuit de Frankenstein* (No.34, 1957).
[7] *Le Sceau de Frankenstein* (No.36, 1957).
[8] The book retroactively moves the events of the previous novel to 1904. Frank Schildiner's novel would be located between *Night* and *Seal*.

Frankenstein Prowls [9] takes place a year later, in 1925, in the Black Forest, in Germany. Gouroull comes across an exiled Chinese doctor named Wou Ling and his blind ward, Nulla. The Monster, aware of his own hideous appearance, forces Wou-Ling to use acupuncture to alter his features, but in vain. Wou-Ling fails, and Gouroull kills them both.

The last novel, *The Cellar of Frankenstein*, [10] takes place about 15 years later, just before World War II, in Antwerp, Belgium. The Monster is still seeking to transform his appearance. He threatens an old Jewish junkman, Samuel Rohrbach, his young son Daniel, and Samuel's friend, an alcoholic doctor named Mossart. The doctor is, at first, eager to complete Frankenstein's own work, but ultimately realizes it is hopeless. The Monster kills him and locks Samuel in a cellar infested with rats. After trying to kill Daniel, Gouroull vanishes back into the darkness.

The popularity of Carrière's *Frankenstein* novels never waned. In 1972, French comics publisher Aredit, which also published translations of DC and Marvel comics, as well as comics adaptations of the *Madame Atomos* series, devoted issues Nos.16-21 of its digest-sized *Hallucinations* horror comic magazine to adapt Carrière's novels, right after doing their own adaptation of Mary Shelley's classic.

For completists, Jean-Claude Carrière's Gouroull has also appeared in the following short stories published in our *Tales of the Shadowmen* series: Matthew Baugh's *Mask of the Monster* (Vol.1), Christofer Nigro's

---

[9] *Frankenstein Rode* (No.41, 1958).
[10] *La Cave de Frankenstein* (No.50, 1959),

Patricide (Vol.8) and Frank Schildiner's *The Blood of Frankenstein* (Vol.10).

Jean-Marc Lofficier

Frankenstein Rôde in Hallucinations No. 20 (1972)

CHAPTER I

The grass was stomped flat by hundreds, possibly thousands, of booted feet. Deep ruts in the earth were visible everywhere, though the fog made that more of an impression than an actual view for the eyes. An inhuman stench filled the air, gunpowder, rotting flesh, sickness and fear, as if the mists were conjured from some circle of Hell rather than the war-torn lands of France.

The Germans had been on the march, determined to destroy their French enemies under the command of their controversial general, von Moltke the Younger. But the French, along with a corps of their British allies, were not folding and failing at the rate the Prussians strategists had predicted. The result was mass slaughter on both sides and the screams of dying men and horses added to the inhuman horror of the landscape.

Squatting and reloading their rifles, members of the heavily reduced 5th infantry regiment attempted to peer into the gloom. They knew the Colonel was determined to secure the nearby hill no matter how many men died in the attempt. The officer, Colonel Albrecht Gronau, was a tall, erect man who, though the son of a very successful boot manufacturer, held himself with the stylings of a Prussian nobleman. This caused him to wear an unnecessary monocle, speak with overt precision, and demand perfection from his men whatever the cost. He was openly despised, but beloved by the officer class who promoted him far beyond his capabilities.

"The little *lugner* is preparing for another rant," Sgt. Paul Kropp muttered, taking a swig of water from his canteen.

Lugner, or liar, was the regimental nickname for Gronau after the officer boasted about having connections to the Kaiser by blood. It had been quickly learned that their Colonel was about as noble as a street sweeper, having earned his place in the military academy thanks to his father's money rather than blood.

"*Ach*, he's ready to scream like my daughter when I tell her to get back to work," Olf Leer stated with a head shake.

A baker by profession, he prayed nightly for this war to end so he could get back to his family.

The *lugner* in question was berating his hapless aide, an undersized, mouse-faced boy named Peter Muller. Muller, an apprentice footman in a semi-noble house, was unsuited for military life and was assigned to be a batman to the imperious officer. The whole regiment pitied Muller, all the more so because he went out of his way to help the soldiers by keeping the Colonel's attention on lesser duties and away from the soldiers.

"Form up!" Gronau snarled, his voice deep and full of scorn.

Striking his gloves against his thighs, Albrecht Gronau stared at his men with open distaste. They were a pack of middle-aged men and boys, little better than half-trained tradesmen! But they were his path to a general's rank, and he would secure all the objectives given to him by his superiors and would be recognized as a leader among men.

Striding back and forth before the regiment, Gronau spun on them, his face now controlled but full of menace.

"We must take this hill, and we must do it now! General von Moltke requires this position in his move to destroy the Western front, and we will not disappoint that great man! Now, prepare yourself, for the Kaiser, von Moltke and God himself!"

Gronau was surprised that the men did not cheer his final statement. From all the military history he read, everything from Julius Caesar to Clausewitz, had said that men would cheer such sentiments. Still, so long as they were obedient, he had no worries.

"About face!" Paul Kropp ordered, smiling slightly.

The men would fight despite Gronau and his ambitions because that was why they wore their uniforms. If their winning this hill from the French would get rid of the pompous officer, all the better.

And so the march began, into the fog-bound land, the stench of decay even stronger as they moved upwards. But there was another smell filling the air, that of blood and the sickness that comes from violent death. This was a new sensation, making the soldiers uneasy as they marched into the gloom of the battlefield. Their hands tightened on their rifles and a few reached to their belts to insure their bayonets were in place for easy access.

Then the screams began, filling the air and causing more than a few men to slow their marching step and quake with fear. There was something primal within them that caused the men to sense that something terrible was ahead. Another scream rose above the sound of their march, causing most to slow and stop in place, their fear rising with each second that passed.

"Forward! We are the Kaiser's men and we do not retreat!" Gronau shrieked, pulling his saber out of its sheath and raising the sword above his head.

He knew he looked like a warrior of old, a Viking or a Teutonic Knight come to life to inspire his men to defeat their fear and overcome the enemy.

"Fix bayonets," Paul Kropp called out, knowing bullets would be next to useless at that moment. The men were full of fear and likely to shoot each other than any of the enemy.

The 5th fell into the routine of weapon drill, fixing bayonets and spreading out so they didn't risk stabbing each other. This relieved a bit of the terror they felt. They had been drilled mercilessly by Gronau and were able to ready themselves within seconds. Tensed and ready, the remaining members of the regiment waited for the order to charge.

"First rank, charge!" Gronau howled, waving his sword.

He waited and counted to himself, knowing the official time between rank charges was listed as 5 seconds between ranks. At the moment he hit five, he ordered the next rank in and started the count again.

It was then that the screams began again, rising in pitch. Gronau smiled, knowing his men were destroying the hated French, winning him the hill and his future on the General staff. Throwing caution into the wind, he ordered the remaining ranks to charge, joining in and screaming like an ancient warrior.

The mist seemed to grow thicker as the howls of agony rose in volume. Gronau lost his men in seconds, but swung his sword in front of him, prepared to slice anything in his path and show his bloody sword to all with glory. He smiled at the thought of decorations from the Kaiser himself, one day receiving a title like Baron, Count or even, like his idol Bismarck, Prince. It would be glorious!

It was then that the head of Paul Kropp struck him in the chest, sending his sprawling to the ground.

Albrecht Gronau stared in terror at the head of his lead Sergeant, the face twisted in a rictus of agony.

The Prussian Colonel backed away, beginning to blubber as a pair of enormous hands grabbed him by his shoulders and lifted him to his feet.

Gronau looked over his shoulder at the one who lifted him up, prepared to thank the man for his kindness. Instead, he dropped his sword and began to shriek in horror at the face before him—a monstrous visage straight out of his nightmares!

The being that filled Gronau with terror was a giant of a man, at least eight feet tall, with pale, chalky skin more reminiscent of the underbelly of a sea creature. His lips were an unpleasant black and the teeth that peeked out from beneath them appeared razor-sharp. His hair was long and dark, resembling the mane of a lion or the pelt of a bear more than that of a human being. But it was the eyes that were the most frightening aspect of his visage: they were deeply set, yellowish, and seemed to glint with an inhuman malevolence—a demonic intelligence that stared at the screaming soldier with the same regard as most would use to view an insect.

This was Gouroull, the legendary creation of Victor Frankenstein, whose tragic story was believed by the world at large to be mere fiction. But the truth was far more awful than even the secretive whispers told in the deep of night of a man who had created life from the dead. For Frankenstein's creation was a true fiend with an inhuman intelligence and purpose that only his alien mind could comprehend.

Gronau's fears were well-founded since the Creature was a true predator and all too often his prey was mankind.

Gouroull continued to watch the panicking human with a faint trace of amusement. The scent of blood and fear had attracted him to this hill in the middle of the battlefield, even more sinister than any other location in this land of death and destruction. It was almost as if a beast was tearing apart the soldiers, rending them limb from limb, in this one location. This had intrigued Frankenstein's creation, since the scent in all the other lands the humans were doing battle was quite different.

The death of so many men was intriguing, far more than the sniveling fool whom he had dropped and who was backing away from him. Gouroull knew something... no, someone... was present at this location and was capable of killing humans in an impressive manner. As one of the most dangerous beings on the planet, this interested him and he had to know what was causing these deaths.

The answer came a heartbeat later, emerging from the mists and causing Gronau to bleat with fear. The man striding towards them was just as impressive and terrible in his own way—another beast in human form. He was a head shorter than Gouroull, but the breadth of his shoulders was far wider and gave the impression of inhuman power. His face was overly long and wide; his nose was the size and shape of a spade; and his lips were too wide and thick for his gigantic face. Everything about him was massive and oversized, making him as frightful to see as Frankenstein's creation. He was dressed in a heavy black coat and slouch hat and stared at Gouroull, disregarding the jabbering German soldier.

Gouroull smiled, his teeth gleaming in his pallid face. He recognized the newcomer: he was a legendary killer who had been haunting Europe for some time. Known as the Creeper, or the Brute, he was said to be unkillable. His favorite method of dispatching his victims was to shatter their spines. Until now Gouroull had discounted these rumors as mere gossip, but seeing the Creeper standing before him changed his mind. This was a being like him, a born killer far beyond the rest of humankind. This would be an enjoyable test.

"I know you," the Creeper said, his voice a rumble that sounded more like two rocks clashing. "You are Gouroull."

Gouroull replied, "You are the Creeper."

They nodded; no more needed to be said. They both acknowledged this would be a chance to see who was the greater, the more dangerous predator in the world. They were alike in many ways, both born with inhuman strength capable of destroying anything in their path. Gouroull knew the Creeper was not a product of Victor Frankenstein's mad genius, but his enemy was far from a natural creation. And because of that alone, they would fight to the death.

There were no preliminary motions or circling about each other, looking for openings. Without a sound, both monsters charged forward. In less than a second, they were locked together, hands and arms fully engaged in a struggle for dominance. Two facts became instantly apparent to both creatures. Gouroull was faster, but the Creeper appeared to be a little stronger. Their methods of fighting were also vastly different. Gouroull used his power and invulnerability and sought to use his teeth to tear out his opponent's neck. The Creeper used his strength and seeming ability to never be harmed to crush his enemy's neck and spine.

Locked in mortal combat, neither moved, yet both strained against each other. To an outsider, it would have looked as if they were standing still, merely holding each other's arms and pushing with no effort, but nothing could be further from the truth. Both monsters exerted their demonic powers, with a strength so massive that it could tear apart any man or beast. Neither Gouroull nor the Creeper perspired, nor did their faces hint that this fight was pushing them beyond their limits. Their horrific countenances remained impassive, Gouroull's yellow eyes locked with the Creeper's dull black orbs. Neither of them blinked; they merely continued to struggle without a sound or even a breath of air.

Gouroull knew he had met his equal. The Creeper's flesh was not as unyieldingly hard as the one Victor Frankenstein had made for his creation. Nor was the Creeper as fast or agile as Gouroull, though these differences were only fractionally apart. However, he was more powerful, possessing strength that exceeded even that of Frankenstein's horrific creation!

Slowly, moving with glacial speed, the Creeper's massive arms began enveloping Gouroull. He started to squeeze, his massive strength seeking to shatter the iron-strong spine of his foe. Gouroull felt a wave of pain fill his body; yet, instead of gasping or shrieking in agony, as would anyone else, he slowly fought back. He lowered his head, seeking to bite down on the Creeper's throat and tear his jugular vein.

These were their favored methods of destroying their enemies and it was now a slow race to see which would achieve victory.

Gouroull's teeth were mere inches from the Creeper's throat, while, at the same time, his back began to creak and his spine was seconds away from shattering. Slowly each monster labored, attempting to defeat the other. This would tell them which of them was the greatest, since they appeared to be equals in every other way.

The idea that another in this world was as dangerous as they were was unacceptable; there could only be one creature considered the most deadly, and both were determined to hold that title.

Suddenly, the air about them became still, as if they had entered the eye of a hurricane and stood in a rare moment of calm. The silence was broken seconds later when a loud whistling could be heard, coming from every direction at once. But Gouroull and the Creeper ignored it, their battle continuing despite the war around them.

Albrecht Gronau knew the source of the noise and threw himself onto the ground, covering his head and beginning to pray for his life. Between the monsters battling and what was coming, he believed he had truly entered Hell itself!

A moment later, the entire hill shook, as if a giant fist had struck the land, causing the whole area to quake. Then, the explosions began, throwing Gouroull and the Creeper in different directions. The air was filled with the sounds of thunder as the mortars struck the area, making it appear as if the world was coming to an end. Where the shells came from would never be known— French, British, Prussian or Austro-Hungarian, it would never be discovered. But the bombardment threw apart two of the most dangerous beings that had ever existed since life began, tossing them aside with less effort than an elephant would use against a single insect in its path.

The mists thickened with the scent of cordite, burning flesh and scorched earth as the explosions continued relentlessly, destroying everything they struck.

Then the bombardment ended, concluding as fast as it had begun. Gouroull stood up in a lightning motion, large clumps of dirt tossed aside as he sprang upward, and searched for his enemy. The hill, previously a grassy mound that rose above a nearby river, was now a torn ruin, a lifeless hulk. Huge craters, some filled with bodies, were all that could be seen. Formerly a location used by painters and poets for inspiration, it was now a gaping sore, a horror-filled land of death. Life would never return to this place; mankind had stolen it from the land.

Albrecht Gronau stood up, shocked to discover that he was uninjured. The explosions were terrifying and caused him to weep as he prayed; yet, it seemed the Lord had determined he was needed to help the Prussians in the march towards victory. Looking down, he spotted the head of Paul Kropp in a crater and gave the dead soldier a textbook salute.

"Farewell, my comrade. I will remember you when I lead our people to victory!" he shouted, wondering if the Kaiser would elevate him to the nobility now or after he had defeated the French. Possibly it would take some time, but even God seemed determined to protect Colonel Gronau from harm when all around him were doomed. It would not be long before his name was mentioned in the same whispers as the late and legendary Prince Otto von Bismarck.

Turning to leave, Gronau started as the enormous form of Gouroull suddenly became visible to him again despite the fog. Before the Prussian could emit a sound, or even a squeak of fear, Victor Frankenstein's monstrous creation seized him up with one huge hand and lifted him by the neck. With a lightning movement, his razor sharp teeth clamped down on the German's neck, tearing half of the flesh away and killing him in mere seconds.

But the Lord had promised me that I would become the next Bismarck! Albrecht Gronau thought as he died.

Tossing the corpse aside, Gouroull once again scanned the land for the Creeper. But his enemy was gone. He doubted that the massive killer was dead. Like Gouroull himself, they were so easy to kill. For now, their fight had been halted by the hand of man, but he knew that, in the future, it would resume and only one of them would survive. It would be a glorious day, one of blood and terror.

Gouroull's teeth glinted as he smiled, thinking of that day in the future.

CHAPTER II

Bullets whistled through the twilight, sounding like angry insects rather than the messengers of death they were. The lifeless land was broken by rips in the earth where explosions had torn open the ground, killing anything they landed upon.

This area, known as "no man's land," was the gap between the lines where both sides fired their weapons, hoping to kill their enemies and advance into their zone. The scent of death was everywhere and only rats thrived, scurrying and attempting to devour the fallen body parts of soldiers, as well as other rats killed by mankind's instruments of death. This was truly a Hell created by humanity, worse than any describe by religions or poets.

Throughout this realm, Gouroull preyed upon both sides, amused by the humans' attempts to advance a few feet and claim this as a victory. The killing was mere sport, a method of passing the time as he searched for the Creeper, or something that could advance his larger plan. His enemy was still missing and there had been no traces of the massive murderer since their epic struggle near the Marne.

Additionally, something was pulling Gouroull to this zone to disease and death. It was not the presence of so many humans attempting to kill each other—that could be found anywhere in the world. No, there was a distant scent in the air that reminded him of Victor Frankenstein's laboratory and that, in itself, was interesting. Someone here was experimenting with the raising of the dead, defeating the Grim Reaper and flying in the face of nature. If so, that person was one whom Gouroull needed to meet. He had plans of his own, thwarted since his demand for a mate from Frankenstein had failed. Victor, a genius with alchemy and other methods of creating life, had initially agreed to his demands, but upon realizing that he would be unleashing a race of monsters upon the world, he had destroyed Gouroull's mate before she was reanimated.

No amount of revenge had satisfied Gouroull since that awful night; his plans to secure a mate had been hindered in the past. Humanity, despite being soft and weak, continued to thwart his attempts at creating another like himself. A few, like Doctor Pilljoy and Pastor Schleger, had attempted to aid him, but their experiments had all failed. Had he not been ageless, he may well have despaired of his lot in life.

A young writer had produced a volume telling his story, based on confidences gleaned from Victor's brother, but she had added a sadness to him that Gouroull had never felt in his life. He was no lonely creature desiring the love of humanity, but a predator who wished to create a tribe of similar beings that could fulfill his larger desires. But to realize his first step, he required the aid of a scientist with skills comparable to Victor Frankenstein's.

Leaving no man's land, Gouroull crossed the British lines without being seen. The scent was close now, not far from the front, but not in the lead trenches either. For a massive being, well over eight feet tall, he could move with a stealth that a jungle cat would envy. It was not that he feared the soldiers and their guns—such crude weapons could not harm his inhuman skin. At best, they would merely slow his progress. The soldiers were too spread out to overwhelm Gouroull by numbers. His reason was simpler: killing these men could cause the scientist whose presence he sensed to flee. That would slow his plan; therefore, the soldiers' lives were spared. If they died at the hands of their fellow man, so be it, but they were safe from Frankenstein's creation this day.

Leaping silently over the trenches, Gouroull glanced down at the little fortresses the humans had created. They were remarkably efficient, a deep cut in the land that allowed a small force to hold off a far larger unit. The problem was that both sides were beginning to use similar tactics, and neither had found a method to bypass the trenches. Warfare, at least in this conflict, would become difficult, a battle of attrition that would bring about massive loss of life. This amused Gouroull. He was the most dangerous being alive, yet the number of deaths at his hand paled in comparison to what this war between humans would accomplish. Men, despite holding themselves as higher beings, were essentially animals using tools to kill each other. Although animals was not a correct comparison—beasts were part of an essential chain of life, none of it involving the wholesale slaughter of others of their kind. Humanity was closer to the cave-dwelling savages who once inhabited these lands. They still behaved towards each other with a callous disregard that made them less than beasts, and even far less than the higher beings they proclaimed themselves to be. But only an outsider could see this simple fact, and no being was more outside mankind than Frankenstein's creation, the demonic horror known as Gouroull.

Blood, its coppery stench unmistakable, was everywhere as Gouroull moved about the British zone. This was a non-combat zone, far enough away from the fighting that only an accidental artillery attack could result in death. Yet, blood, disease and decay hung about, giving the area a grim stench. Frankenstein's creature was not given to poetic thought, yet this place felt as if the Specter of Death itself hovered above it. The *wrongness*, for lack of a better word, was a part of its soil; it as a slaughterhouse just as horrific as the front lines.

The stench rose higher and more pronounced, as if its source was centered in this one location: a long flat building, probably once a farm, lay ahead. Most of its windows were shuttered. Small glimmers of light peaked through the edges of the wooden slats, adding an unearthly air to the building. The bare yellow lights that were visible cast shadows about, highlighting the lack of life. This was indeed a land of the dead. Yet, the decay that hung about this place set it apart from the rest of the battlefield. Instead of sheer terror, this place breathed a sadness and a loss that were almost as a physical force.

Moving closer to the building, Gouroull peered through the slats and beheld a scene that would have made even the strongest men sick. Frankenstein's creature had spent many years learning human ways; yet, he was always amazed at their ability of being so cruel to each other, and the creative ways they used in such behavior. It was possibly the one trait of their kind that he admired, though he was able to surpass them and demonstrate that, here too, he was the superior being.

This building was filled with men, all of whom were maimed in body and mind. They were missing arms and legs; some had faces twisted beyond recognition; a few were bandaged so heavily that they hardly resembled living beings anymore. The stench of corruption hung over the chamber like a supernatural fog, a sickly sweet scent rising from the men's wounded bodies. Few would live, despite the attempts made to keep them alive, and they would succumb to disease caused by the poor medicine used to keep their shattered bodies whole. This was a house of death, a slow torture chamber that would lead most of its occupants to a forgotten grave in the scorched earth.

At the far end of the room were men wounded in mind and spirit, their bodies intact, but their minds destroyed by the horrors of the war. Some lay in bed, shaking, every creak of the wood causing them to shiver with terror. Others lay still, their spirit gone, their body an empty shell. A few wept or gibbered, tied down to their filthy cots to prevent them from harming themselves or others. These were the true example of how twisted humanity was towards each other, the mental destruction of their fellow being so complete it was nearly an art form.

Gouroull, despite himself, was impressed. He could still learn something from these lesser beings. Though they were weak in both body and will, their imagination was both fiendish and impressive. In his quest, Gouroull knew he still had much to learn from these creatures. That essential spark that humanity possessed allowed them to create wonderful works of beauty as well as methods of killing and torture that were, in truth, an art unto themselves. That was the reason he searched for a mate—and more, to gain that missing piece of himself and replace their race with his better version.

But this charnel house of human misery was not the scent that had drawn him. Though he would like to savor the horror for a little longer, the pull to this location was that of a laboratory, one very much like that of Victor Frankenstein's, based on Gouroull's memories. He had visited many labs in his long life, but almost all were missing that essential element that distinguished them from the one used by his creator. Victor's possessed a supernatural flavor, a mystic quality, as opposed to the standard scientific establishment. There was a place similar to that here; it was it that had drawn him there.

Stepping into the stygian darkness, Gouroull circled around the makeshift hospital and spotted a small light a short distance away. A cottage lay behind a small copse of trees, barely visible from the main house despite the short distance. A moment later, he was gazing through another slatted window, this time seeing a far more interesting sight than that of the dying, decaying men. Leaning closer, he realized that he may have found at last a method of obtaining what Victor had denied him so many years ago in Scotland.

The cottage was a laboratory, though one that looked as if it had been built on the site of a slaughterhouse. Dried blood, new and old, stained the floor; walls and other surfaces were drenched with it; a pile of human limbs were stacked in a corner. The scientific equipment was a makeshift affair, a jumble of old and new, with many pieces obviously adapted to new and unique functions by their owner. But everything was placed in a precise order; straight lines and sharp corners made the items resemble an odd diorama of an architectural nightmare. There was something otherworldly about this laboratory, as if normal medical and scientific theories and laws were suspended there, and the Creator had a different plan in this one small location. This was the same environment Victor Frankenstein had created many years ago, even down to the odd and repurposed items.

But it was the man within this unusual laboratory that interested Gouroull the most. The master of this chamber of horrors was a little man, just a head or so over five feet tall, with thin, blonde hair that was carelessly tossed across his scalp. He possessed the pale skin of one who rarely ventured outside into the light and the fussy mannerisms of a person always seeking to control his environment. He moved in quick spurts, perpetually making slight adjustments to everything he passed. He was dressed in a bloodstained tunic and seemed unaware of the dried blood splattered on his person.

Stopping before a bench with a human arm strapped on the top, the little man poked the disconnected limb gently with a silver scalpel. The arm flexed slowly, but then fell limp once more, so the little man repeated the motion twice. Nodding, he pulled out a leather-bound notebook and began to furiously write in it, periodically checking his pocket watch as he did so.

Gouroull knew at once that this was the man he needed to enlist in his cause; the sheer monstrosity of his laboratory was proof enough that he possessed a mind to rival that of Victor Frankenstein. The fact that he was experimenting on the dead merely confirmed this fact.

Moving to the door, Gouroull found it surprisingly unlocked and pushed it open. The little man turned around, his face a mask of fury as he peered at the intruder. His mouth was twisted with rage; he seemed about to snarl a curse, but stopped when he saw Gouroull standing on the threshold, eight feet tall, his twisted face hidden by the shadows. The little man continued to stare, pushing his round spectacles up his nose and looking at Frankenstein's creature with the same interest he had demonstrated for the unattached limb moments ago.

"I know of you," he said in a reedy voice, peering up and down Gouroull's gigantic form. "You are the creation of Victor Frankenstein, the greatest scientific mind of his age. Are you he?"

"Yes," Gouroull replied, his voice a low rumble, stepping inside and closing the door behind him to prevent anyone from interrupting their discussion.

The little man was possibly the answer to what he sought and it would not do to have anyone prevent their talk.

The little man seemed to bounce with joy as he rushed to a table stacked with books and papers. Pulling a battered book from the top, he leafed through the pages for a moment and returned to Gouroull, holding up a page to the light. It was drawing, done by Victor himself, of his creation—his most terrible creature.

"This is you! I knew it immediately! The genius of Frankenstein, still alive to this day! I have heard that you go by the name of Gouroull—may I call you such? My name is Herbert West and I seek the same truths as the great Frankenstein himself!"

Herbert West looked upon Gouroull with delight rather than fear and revulsion.

"Why?" asked Gouroull, wanting to know this human's motivations.

West seemed to understand immediately and closed the book with a loud snap.

"Humanity is slave to a master more terrible than any tyrant: death. Every day, we grow closer to this spectral monster and once he strikes, we are finished! Nothing is left but dust! The fools who abide by the laws of the Church and medicine pretend this is inevitable—a law of Nature. I say to this blinkered minds that death itself can be defeated, and that I will become its master! Look here!"

West lead Gouroull over to the table where the arm was strapped. Once again, he gently touched the limb and it flexed in response, falling limp within seconds.

"This arm was removed from Captain Cathcart eight days ago. It is still responsive and there has been little deterioration of the tissues! Imagine how my reagent will react once I perfect it upon the newly-deceased! They will live again and Nature will be slave to Mankind!"

Gouroull smiled, his teeth glistening as he stared down at Herbert West. The man shared the same egotism as Victor Frankenstein, as well as Victor's elderly teacher of alchemy, Doctor Septimus Pretorius. They all viewed their kind as far greater than all of the universe, and were shocked when that was proven not to be so in the end. But, like all narcissists, they could be used and manipulated into producing the result he wanted. Yes, West could well be the answer to Gouroull's plan.

"I need your help. A mate. For me," Gouroull rasped, remembering how he demanded the same from his creator so many years ago.

Victor had agreed in fear, but eventually had destroyed his mate, also out of fear. But West seemed more determined and twisted than Frankenstein; he would not shrink away from his creation. He was a fanatic, with the ego of a madman. He would be... useful.

West nodded and opened the book again.

"I have here the details of the process that Frankenstein used for your creation. It's not a direction I had planned on working on, since the ingredients needed are very unusual. I did some research and I know I would be unable to procure the necessary items. They are... exotic, to say the least."

"I can get everything," Gouroull stated, knowing this was the moment of truth.

West had the notes of Victor Frankenstein and could create a female version of himself. Not a stone or clay golem as they did in China, as he had learned, but a mate. But would he? No doubt, the scientist had his own plans. His own elixir was meant to defeat death. Would he be willing to create beings like Frankenstein's monster.

West cocked his head and seemed to consider the idea for a moment.

"Well, that would be an interesting experiment to attempt while I'm perfecting my reagent. If I provide you with stone bottles, could you obtain and save each of the ingredients? You will have to travel widely abroad. Frankenstein was given most of the items on this list by his mentor, Dr. Pretorius. You will have to go far and wide in your quest."

"Yes," Gouroull replied, unconcerned about the distance required. This little man believed he could recreate the alchemy of Victor Frankenstein, and, based on his current work, it seemed probable he was not lying.

West bustled over to a cabinet and retrieved the bottles he had stored there weeks before, when first occupying this cottage to pursue his experiments. Life in Europe, so far, had worked out quite well.

The cottage was the right size for his work and even had a trapdoor leading to a cellar which he used to rid himself of the useless bodies and limbs. But, best of all, had been the day when he had moved into the building and was putting together the laboratory. He had been visited by a man in a black robe, whom West mistook for a monk of some sort.

The "monk" hadn't said much, but had given him a truck of books formerly belonging to a man named Baron de Musard that contained many dark secrets of alchemy and vivisection, including the works of Victor Frankenstein, a genius whose work was different from

Herbert West's but had the same aim. Together they would defeat death and change the universe!

Handing the bottles over, West began to copy the list.

"I'll provide you with a few rumors I've heard about the location of some of the ingredients. If I'm forced to move back because of the Boche, look for me near the lines at the hospitals. Once you provide me with everything from that list, I will be able to duplicate Frankenstein's experiment and create your mate."

Gouroull took the list and the bottles and left without another word, leaving the bloodstained madman behind. Insane or not, West was the man for the job; he would search the Earth for the ingredients and then. he would have his mate.

This was a new beginning.

CHAPTER III

Captain Oswald Fielding-Jones of the Sussex Rifles smiled at his men and straightened his uniform blouse.

They were assembled before him, nervous because they knew a charge was coming across no-man's land. Many would die for another few feet of land. But seeing the noble, upright and brave officer always seemed to make them feel a little better. There just was something about the Captain that instilled confidence and made them all willing to follow his orders without question.

In the second rank of troops, the two dirtiest and most forgotten troopers slouched and quietly discussed the coming battle. They were among the few who had signed up on the regiment's original muster and they were old members of the brotherhood of soldiers. They were distantly related, but an explanation of how took several hours of discussion and arguing on their part, so few people actually cared to ask.

"Another charge," Pintel grumped, glancing across no-man's land and shaking his head.

He was a stocky man, broad-shouldered and brutish-looking, with a short thick beard and a shining bald head that he often wiped with his sleeve. Pintel was a slovenly brute of a man, but loyal to a fault. He'd survived ten charges across enemy lines with only a scratch or two as his reward.

"That's our duty, the classic counterpoint between personal desire and the needs of the many," Ragetti replied, watching the Captain as he spoke.

Ragetti was a full head taller than Pintel, but forty pounds lighter. He had a narrow face with a long thin nose and appeared to be more like a weasel attempting to be human than an actual man. His hair with straw-colored and stringy, and looked dirty even when he vigorously cleaned that tangled mop on his head.

"What the bugger's that supposed to mean?" Pintel asked, looking annoyed.

Ragetti shrugged and continued to watch the Captain.

"Dunno. Reckon I picked it up somewhere. Maybe when I was in school. Or maybe I read it in a book!"

"You quit school when you was eight-years-old. And you can't read!" Pintel snapped back, slapping Ragetti behind the head. "Stop talking like a prat!"

Ragetti rubbed his head.

"Well, it is, isn't it? We don't want to go and attack them Germans. But for the regiment and those at home, we have to go kill them. It's a dilemma."

"Just try and keep your head down and shoot anything that looks like a Hun!" Pintel hissed, seeing the Captain approaching.

Ragetti looked confused.

"What, you mean Johnson?"

Pintel started and looked at his friend and relation with confusion.

"Johnson? What's that bugger have to do with the run across no-man's land?"

Ragetti nodded at their fellow soldier, a tall, power-fully-built man whom they knew was a former iron worker from Wales.

"You said, shoot anything that looks like a Hun. His ma was half-German and he looks like all them soldiers we captured last week. Should I shoot him? I think the Sergeant might put me on a charge."

Pintel exhaled loudly and closed his eyes. Ragetti could drive a parson to drink with his questions.

"Forget what I said, just shoot the Huns when we get out there."

But Ragetti wasn't done yet.

"Those that are Huns or those that just look like Huns? I'm thinking only those that are Germans would keep me from the guard house."

Pintel rubbed a sleeve across his bald pate and counted to ten, trying not to slap Ragetti again in front of an officer.

"Yes, just the real Germans. Shoot them."

Before Ragetti could ask another of his endless array of questions, Captain Fielding-Jones cleared his throat and all of the men snapped to attention. It didn't matter that they were dirty, tired and hungry, the Captain was here and about to speak, and they hung on his every word.

Captain Fielding-Jones was a tall man with the narrow whippet frame of a long-distance runner and the angular face of a nobleman born to command. His mustache was dark and prominent and he carried himself with the calm self-assurance of a born soldier. Everything about their officer inspired the Sussex Rifles and they knew he led them from the front, fighting to keep as many of them alive as he could.

"Lads," Fielding-Jones stated, his deep voice carrying to every ear despite the explosions covering no-man's land, "we will soon be charging out against the German position and I know you are up to the challenge. Charge with all your might and remember that all of the Empire is behind you!"

The Sussex Rifles all cheered and began moving to their positions, waiting for the artillery to stop firing and the charge order to sound. On the far right of the line, Pintel and Ragetti crouched behind the wall and waited, knowing the guns would begin to quiet soon.

"The line's thin now," Pintel remarked, seeing a large gap between himself and the other men in the Sussex Rifles.

"According to Corporal Maitland, the regiment is down another 820 men after the last time we charged across to fight Germans. Though they wasn't Germans, they were Austrians that spoke German." Ragetti explained, having made friends with Corporal Maitland, the Captain's aide, when they were in rifle training before they were sent to the front.

"That means of the original 5000 or so of us, there's what, 1200 left? Rum thing, Ragetti. Really rum," Pintel pronounced. "At least, we got the Captain leading us now."

Ragetti was about to remark the odd fact that the majority of the regiment's losses happened after the Captain became the leader of the regiment. According to Maitland, the former leader, Colonel Ffolkes, had kept the losses far down, but performed more careful actions with the unit. He'd lost an arm a month back and, so far, no new commanding officer had come to relieve the Captain.

At that moment, the artillery guns slowly began to fade out, leaving a silence throughout the front.

The silence was jarring for everyone present, all the more so because of the lack of natural sounds one would hear when outside away from a city. But there were no birds, no insects, not even the tiny skittering sounds of small animals. The explosions that were so much a part of the regular life in the Great War, when removed, left behind a lack of life that was so profound, it felt overwhelming. Life was removed from this area of France; humanity had scorched the land and left behind a wasteland. The void pressed down on every man in the zone and, for a brief moment, there was almost a kinship between the British and their German enemies, an understanding of how horrific this conflict was for all those forced into this battle.

Then a bugler sounded and every man grabbed his rifle tight. Captain Fielding-Jones's voice suddenly rose and he shouted:

"Charge! All units, forward!"

Pintel and Ragetti rose up, their voices joining the charging shouts, their hands gripping their rifles so tight their knuckles turned white.

The Germans began firing, though the bullets never seemed to touch Pintel and Ragetti, who were later found by the remainder of the unit, holding a German position. Afterward, they would receive medals and be placed behind the lines, safe for the remainder of the war.

In the center of no-man's land, Captain Fielding-Jones looked down at the dead men littering the ground, their blood seeping into the earth. The scent of sickness, excrement and urine mixed with that of gunpowder and burning flesh. This stench was the embodiment of fear, terror in the purest form, and few men could brave this land of death and horror. But not Terrence Fielding-Jones—this was what he lived to see, feel and consume.

Dropping to his knees before Corporal Maitland, Fielding-Jones's long tongue snaked out and he tasted the drying sweat and blood across the dead man's flesh. Shuddering with ecstasy, his mouth opened, far wider than any human jaw could sustain, showing rows of huge, rounded fangs. His hands lengthened, seeming to grow more bone and sharp black claws burst forth from each digit. The oversized jaw crunched down on flesh and bone, shattering the latter as he began to feed on the dead soldier. Maitland was reduced to a few small bits in moments and Fielding-Jones crawled over to next man, feasting on his men and knowing he would be able to consume at least twenty before he was needed to rejoin the regiment.

Terrence Fielding-Jones was a ghoul, a member an ancient pre-human race who hid in plain sight and lived off the dead bodies of humans and animals. Many legends of vampires, goblins and werewolves came from those rare times humans caught sight of a ghoul feasting on the dead. Between the pheromones the ghouls could emit, enabling them to make humans and animals feel terror, love or any other emotion, their people were able to live in plain sight and even prosper. The Fielding-Jones family were high-ranking members of the armed forces, members of the medical profession as well as undertakers and owners of graveyards. The ghoul tribes were scattered around the world, but all had adapted quite well with modern society.

Terence Fielding-Jones was the latest member to lead troops to their death for the sake of the tribes. By behaving as if he was fanatical follower of the plans of the high-ranking officers, he could throw away many lives, feed, and still keep his men happy through the use of pheromones and clever talk. Bullets were of no interest to him—a ghoul could sustain a few hundred or more gunshot wounds before they were in any danger. He wasn't sure how long this war would last, but, for now, life was very enjoyable for a young ghoul.

It was then that he spotted the man watching him a short distance away. The figure was large and hard to see

in the twilight, but Terrence Fielding-Jones was unconcerned. He was stronger and faster than any human alive
and able to make them feel any emotion that he deemed
necessary.

Glancing up at the man, he sprayed a good dose of
terror, hoping to send him running off gibbering into the
German lines. Sometimes humans dropped dead with
fright, their hearts unable to sustain the sudden rush of
fear. This was a double benefit: the story of seeing an
inhuman creature like a ghoul was not spread and caused
fear to the location, keeping the region safe for continued feasting. And also, it provided more food for the
ghoul.

Spraying fear at the man, Terence Fielding-Jones
was surprised that the observer did not move a muscle or
even make a sound. Perhaps the distance was too great,
he thought. So, he slid a little closer and increased the
spray, hoping to guarantee a quick death and some more
food the feast. Watching the man, Terence blinked several times in shock; he appeared unaffected by the ghoul
pheromones, their most important weapon!

If that was possible, this man had to die, since his
immunity could spread and result in mankind discovering that an ancient race lived among them and fed on
them like a parasite. If humanity knew the monsters they
spoke of in fearful whispers were actually living and
hidden in their midst, a witch hunt would begun and
their people might be destroyed.

Moving forward, Fielding-Jones got a better look at
the man and knew that he was no common member of
humanity. He was huge, eight feet tall, and possessed a
chalky gray skin that looked inhuman. Then the wind
changed and the hackles along Terence Fielding-Jones's
back raised and he flexed his wicked claws. The man

before him was not human, not ghoul, or any of the many creatures he had met with over his years. There was a scent of death about this inhuman figure, but also a power that was almost a physical force.

"What are you?" Fielding-Jones hissed, his gigantic maw barely able to formulate the words. "You are no human or ghoul...what are you?"

"My name," the creature rasped, "is Gouroull. I have met your kind before—graveyard rats and parasites."

Fielding-Jones knew the name Gouroull—a legend that he believed to be mythical; a creation of science and madness; a monster created from the dead who rampaged throughout the world. He was spoken about by humans and ghouls with the same fearful reverence used for monsters that existed in the nightmares of the young and ancient. Yet, like the ghouls, this monster was real and seemed intent on some mission that only his alien mind could understand.

Recognizing a threat and knowing this monster meant to take his life, Fielding-Jones sprang forward, claws extended and teeth flashing. He struck Gouroull's massive frame and hardened skin with the power of a locomotive and the ferocity of a tiger.

Frankenstein's creature fell backwards, his heavy form hitting the dead earth with a loud crash.

Fielding-Jones knew that his foe was unhurt by the attack. The chalky skin of Gouroull was unpierced by the claws of the enraged ghoul, a feat unheard of in the history of the pre-human race. Legends told of their people fighting saber-toothed cats and dire wolves for food and often winning the battle. Even the massive mastodons were wounded by the weapons of the ghouls, yet this creature possessed skin far more hardy. This made

Gouroull a threat to ghoul tribes around the world, one that could not be allowed to live.

Tearing at the monster's arms, Fielding-Jones was trying to distract Gouroull long enough to employ his most dangerous weapon—his bite. A ghoul's teeth and jaws were more powerful than a shark's and their saliva was acidic, allowing them to consume even the toughest to digest matter. With a hiss, Fielding-Jones launched himself forward and clamped his teeth down hard onto Gouroull's exposed throat. The skin there, usually thinner than other parts of the body, was a favorite target of all creatures of the night, a fast way to destroy your enemy quickly.

Yet the skin of Frankenstein's creature was stronger than any other the ghoul had ever tasted. It was harder and seemed to resist the saliva acid Fielding-Jones used to make it more pliable and easier to consume. The British ghoul bit down harder, breaking the skin after much effort and anticipating the coppery taste of blood that would soon follow. Then would come the death throes, the slow painful end of life, followed by the feast. In this case, destroying this monstrous creature, the feeding would be done with joy. Frankenstein's creation was an abomination and it was the duty of all of the pre-human creatures in the world to destroy Gouroull.

But instead of blood, a bizarre ghastly taste entered his mouth. A burning sensation filled his body and he knew at once that this creature's blood was poisonous to life. But ghouls were stronger than other living beings; they were able to eat any material and process it in time. This would take longer, but in the end, it, too, would become food.

Just then, Gouroull reached out and grabbed one of Fielding-Jones's hands in a grip of iron, pulling it away from his chest with strength that dwarfed the ghoul's. Raising the hand to his face, Gouroull opened his mouth wider than seemed possible and stuffed the extremity into his mouth up to his wrist. Then he bit down. His razor sharp teeth sliced through the hardened ghoul flesh, removing the hand from the body!

Fielding-Jones shrieked in agony, pulling away from Frankenstein's creature, clutching his maimed arm. Gouroull lashed out, his heavy fist striking the ghoul on the side of the head, sending him tumbling off into the night. The giant then spat out the hand and wrapped it carefully inside the oilcloth packet West had provided. He remembered what the fussy little man had said when he had come to this item on the large and unusual list.

"Flesh, blood and talons of a ghoul. It would best if you provide me with at least two intact fingers. That way, I can harvest the material needed for the creation of your bride. According to Frankenstein, that was all he required, and no doubt I could make do with the same. But more would be welcome, of course. The method of removal is your choice. You should keep in mind that ghouls are notoriously dangerous to encounter."

West had demonstrated how the oilcloth packet should be used after the ghoul flesh had been obtained.

Gouroull scanned the battlefield for the ghoul, but the creature was nowhere in sight. He was no longer important—West's item had been obtained, and now only the next item on the list was important. Still, he disliked the idea of leaving an enemy alive, especially one capable of injuring him in a fight. The claws hadn't penetrated his skin, but the ghoul's bite was painful and its saliva had burned.

But, in the end, the creature's attack was too slow to be truly lethal. Turning his back, Gouroull headed towards the German lines, his next mission ahead in his quest to create his mate.

Fielding-Jones held his breath and listened as Frankenstein's creature left the area. Why that creature sought him out, he had no idea. Gouroull's mind was alien and terrible and a danger to all life on Earth. Limping towards his lines, he was determined to live and get his revenge. The tribes must know and work together to destroy the abomination that Victor Frankenstein had unleashed upon the world!

CHAPTER IV

Georg von Bodmann was a man with a vision. He knew he was different from his fellow men and that made him proud. Because he and he alone understood the true ways to power in this universe—paths to power that even his fellow nobles had forgotten about centuries ago. Georg von Bodmann was different than they—his eyes were open and his power grew on a daily basis.

Once he had been just a second son of a noble, if impoverished, family from Hesse. His eyes had been opened after meeting a distant relative, Baron de Musard. The Baron, an amazingly learned man, had opened young Georg's eyes and showed him that the true path to greatness did not lie with the military, but through the powers of darkness and ancient forces lost in the mists of time.

After being inducted as a warlock and a servant of the left-handed path, the world had changed for Georg. A few spells and sacrifices were performed and the results were pleasing; his father and brother died in the same car accident, and he attracted the eye of a wealthy heiress who had previously spurned his attentions.

From the moment that Ria agreed to marry him, and he was promoted to Hauptmann a short time later, Georg von Bodmann devoted all his life and energy to his secret studies. Publically, he was the model of a German noble officer, complete with a beautiful wife and five children who were all high achievers in school. But this was an act, one he learned from his friend and teacher, de Musard. The great man had taught him that a false face was needed if one was to rise to true power. The ways of the left-handed path caused fear and insane reactions from those who failed to understand the truth that lay in the ancient rituals. This may have remained his direction in life, using the dark powers to rise high and live the life he dreamed of his whole life, had he not discovered the ring.

Finding the ring was an accident—the purest of chances. Georg was in the home of a fellow officer, having celebrated late into the night the officer's son's entry into the military academy. But after everyone went to bed, he was restless and found himself searching through his host's library for a diversion. It was there he stumbled on a copy of the infamous *Der Hexenhammer*, known to the free world as the *Malleus Maleficarum*, the Hammer of Witches. The book was a true horror, supposedly a manual on the hunting of evil witches, warlocks and wizards in the world. It was, in fact, an excuse to hunt and murder women and anyone the so-called witch-hunters wished to torture to death. Written in the late 15th century, the writers did more for the cause of evil than all the secret cults in Europe. As a follower of the left-handed path, Georg von Bodmann owned several copies of this tome in his collection, amused by the irony of owning a book that called for the killing of his kind.

Flipping through the book, Georg knew instantly that this edition was fairly new and that it had not been touched in decades. The pages exuded a musty scent and a light film of dust rose as he glanced through the paranoid ravings of the authors. Closing the book with a smile, it was then that he felt an object in the crumbling leather spine. Opening the tome wide, Georg shook the book once and the ring fell into his palm, a thick layer of dust covering it.

Cleaning the object with a handkerchief, Georg von Bodmann knew instantly that this find was something quite momentous. The ring was heavier than its size indicated, and made of an odd metal that looked like copper, but was perpetually cold to the touch. It was made in the shape of a scaled serpent, with three coils looping around and forming the band. The serpent's tail was held in its fanged mouth and two baleful yellow gems formed its eyes. Slipping the ring on his finger, he was surprised that it fit perfectly on his hand, and he instantly swore to never remove it.

Ready to explain it away as a family heirloom, Georg was surprised that the piece of jewelry never seemed to attract any attention. This confirmed to him that there was something supernatural about the serpent ring, something hidden beneath the depths of those glittering yellow eyes. And it turned out, he was quite correct.

A short week later, after sacrificing a female beggar he had scooped up in Bonn, Georg watched in fascination as the woman's body began to shrivel before his eyes. It was as if some force was stealing the life energy of his dying victim, reducing her to little more than dust. The eyes of the ring seemed to glow in the darkness and the temperature of the room dropped dramatically. It was as if a polar vortex had opened up in his sacrificial chamber, causing Georg's rapid breaths to appear in small clouds before his amazed eyes. A presence was nearby, waiting and watching his actions. Deciding fast, he turned to his followers and placed them under a spell of control. With no visible emotions, Georg von Bodmann sacrificed one after another on his altar and waited, sensing he had made the correct decision.

In his mind, the first time in the presence of a powerful being from beyond should be a momentous event, filled with grand ceremonies and chanting, candles and important objects, his followers hailing his name as the demon rose from the blackest pits. '

Instead, Georg stood in his small chamber, knee deep in the dust of his followers. The death of his coven was of no importance to him; they had been chosen merely because they were disposable and easily led. None would be missed and his public persona had no connection to them that could be traced. But the very lack of drama was disappointing. Yet, Georg knew that a presence was nearby and he had given it what it demanded.

"Do not be saddened human," a soft, gentle voice stated from the far end of room.

The voice was light, musical and filled with an amused malice that was almost a physical force.

Turning, Georg spotted a tall man—no, not exactly a man—standing near the north edge of the pentagram etched in the floor of the room. He was tall, towering over a foot beyond Georg's six feet, with pale skin that was almost white. He had long platinum blonde hair that fell in thick waves onto his narrow shoulders and wide yellow eyes without pupils. His face was hidden behind a yellow mask that looked as if it was made of metal, but moved on his face with the softness of silk. The man's body was hidden in robes of shimmering white that fell just above his black cloven feet.

"You wish power, Georg von Bodmann—that much I knew before your summonsing. The question is, how much? I can grant it to you, for a price, of course," the pale man said, laughter filling his words.

Georg sighed, knowing the price, and shook his head.

"I won't sell my soul. That's a fool's bargain and everyone knows it ends poorly."

The pale man threw back his head and roared with laughter, the sound echoing throughout the chamber and sounding more sinister than if he had been issuing threats.

"Your soul? Why should I wish such a paltry, shrunken thing? No, I require blood. The blood of humans sent out to die by your orders at the hands of their fellow man. War, chaos and death. That will be my price. The question is, how much power do you want? The lives required grow exponentially by how much you demand."

Georg considered the question, but the answer was easy enough. His deepest dream was to become a ruler, a monarch, like the Kaiser, but more than this, he wanted a return to the ancient days of power, where his word could change the world. That was the true desire of every warlock and servant of the dark path: seeing their every dream come to fruition.

"I want to be an Emperor... the Holy Roman Empire was a great one and could encompass all of the Europe. Could you give that to me?" he whispered, hardly believing his temerity.

But if he could have such an amazing dream come to life, who cared what it cost in the lives of other humans. The price was worth the reward!

The pale man nodded, seemingly impressed.

"A lofty dream, but possible. I have caused kings and queens to rise. The tides of blood change the world in ways your mind cannot begin to grasp. But a few paltry deaths such as the ones you used to summon me are not enough. This will cost millions of lives—a world war, encompassing many countries. That is your path to a crown and a legacy that will not be forgotten throughout the ages."

And, of course, Georg had agreed, later joining the party of politicians and soldiers lobbying for war. As a General-Major in the Imperial Army, he was able to wield impressive influence and seize the moment when, months later, the Great War began.

His subtle hand weakened the General Staff's invasion plans and caused the armies to be stalled in perpetual battle. The death toll was enormous and he even lost two of his sons in the earlier days of the War, but he knew the price would be high. How a minor baron from Hesse would rise to become the master of a new Holy Roman Empire was a source of wonderment to him, but Georg's pale master had not lied so far.

Cutting his finger and rubbing the dripping blood across the ring, he closed his eyes and relaxed his mind. Entering a deep trance state, Georg began to commune with the pale man, the being with a million names and forms, who granted power to those who wished to pay his high prices. It took some time, but finally, a soft laughter filled his mind, signaling that the powerful being was listening.

"Master," Georg thought, knowing words were not needed with this mighty being, "more untrained boys are being sent to the front each day and dying. How much longer before I receive my reward?"

"A short time, my favorite servant," the godling with a thousand forms replied with a giggle. "A few more battles like the last one and you may see your crown soon. Have patience and your wish shall be fulfilled. That is—if you survive the next hour. Awake now, for a great danger is coming to you Defeat it and give it to me, and I will be most pleased with you."

Georg opened his eyes, his mind suddenly fully aware of his surroundings.

He was in his large tent behind the lines, his orderly Vrolok gone for the night. His tent was a distance away from the main forces, rank allowing for a bit or privacy that lower ranks were never afforded in the military. His heightened senses told him that a presence unlike any other was approaching, one that was unlike anything he had experienced in the past—dangerous and powerful, but not another mystic like himself or de Musard, nor a demon like the being with a thousand names who had promised him power. Despite himself, Georg von Bodmann was intrigued and wanted to know what this great danger was, kill it and present it to his master as a gift.

"I know you're out there," Georg called out, opening the flap of his tent and sitting down on his camp chair. "You may as well come inside and tell me who you are and what you want."

The man that stepped from the darkness was obviously inhuman—his size alone would have indicated that to anyone. Standing at least eight feet tall, he moved with the smooth, silent grace of a wild animal as he stepped into the tent and dropped the flap behind him. His chalky white skin seemed to glimmer in the lantern light and his pale yellow eyes studied Georg with an unblinking gaze. His face was a horrific mask framed by thin, black hair that looked more like tendrils on a creeping plant. This creature was a study in horror and he was scrutinizing Georg with an inhuman intensity that made the warlock feel like a bug under a microscope.

"Who are you and why are you here?" Georg repeated, placing his hands on the table.

He was ready to use his powers to deal with this monster and give him to his pale master, who wished to have him for some unknowable reason. He didn't have time to ponder what the demon would do with the creature, but even if he had had the time, he might have been too afraid to contemplate it. One did not question dark, powerful beings; their answers were often too disturbing.

"I am Gouroull," the inhuman creature replied in a low growl. "You are a warlock."

Georg straightened and twisted his face into a sneer, one he had adopted as a young officer when talking to someone of lower rank and social status. The fact that this monster knew his true identity wasn't of much concern; his powers were such that he could control or destroy any enemy. He'd done it many times over the years: his religious, kind father, his highly-intelligent brother, seventeen other officers who might have been competition for a promotion.... the list was long and varied.

"I am no such thing! I should have you arrested!" Georg began, his voice low and harsh as he systematically attacked the creature standing before him now.

Gouroull stopped listening to the warlock, his words nothing more than noise on his mind.

The list West had given him specified that he needed the blood of a user of mystic energies. Gouroull knew that scent all too well, having encountered other practitioners of the occult arts humans over the years, and even having been thwarted by their powers. Individually, a warlock was still a human, just as vulnerable as any other human to disease and violence. But they could summon help in the form of demons or zombies, or use the forces of nature as a weapon. It was dangerous to tangle with them, but they were easy to recognize once one knew the scent of magic that emanated from their bodies.

In this case, it was easy: he had sensed that stench shortly after crossing the lines. Now, he stood in this tent, listening to this warlock rant and rave, all the while his heart pumped the much-needed lifeblood that he, Gouroull, required for the creation of his mate. No longer needing to keep up the pretense of listening, the monster stepped forward.

Georg leaped to his feet and pointed his left ring finger at Frankenstein's creature. The gem eyes of the ring pulsed as he threw all his power at his enemy.

"Back! Get back right now!"

Despite his efforts, Gouroull was pushed back two steps, feeling as if an invisible hand was pressing him towards the tent's flap. Digging his heels into the hard packed earth, the monster began to resist and press forwards.

Sweat appeared on Georg's head. He began to whisper a spell, a powerful one he had learned many years ago from his mentor and relative, Baron de Musard. This would allow him to link minds with his enemy and control his every action. That had been the method he had used to make his brother-in-law step into a propeller blade, his father-in-law to take too many sleeping pills, and so many others. It was a potent and painful spell to use because one felt the pain of one's victim's death, but Georg von Bodmann had grown to enjoy the death throes of his enemies, the pain and loss of dignity at the end. It was a sadistic and masochist feeling, but he had come to relish it.

Gouroull felt the pulse of magic and the harsh touch of the other's mind upon his—a forceful thrust straight into his thoughts and memories. He smiled, his teeth glinting in the lantern's light, and relaxed, allowing this opponent full entry. This would be amusing, quite an experience to undergo; one that had always lead to such interesting results.

Suddenly, Georg von Bodmann reeled back, his hands grasping his head; a low shriek emerged from his throat. He bit his lips, tasting blood, the pain rippling through his body like a searing wave. But that feeling was minor compared to the agony in his mind—the sheer alien inhumanity that he had seen—and was unable to stop seeing!

The creature before him was a monstrosity, a true blight upon the world, capable of destroying all it touched. The violent horror of that being was an abomination upon the soul; it made the warlock feel that his own black soul was nothing but a pale imitation of evil when compared to that of Frankenstein's monster.

Yes, he knew Gouroull's origins and he wept at the abomination that Victor Frankenstein had released upon the Earth.

"You... you... abomination... disease... blight..." he whimpered as he crawled away from the monster.

Gouroull stared down at the fallen warlock, knowing the man's mind had been shattered—now, it was but a broken and useless organ. Death would be a mercy, but even that was something Frankenstein's monster didn't extend to humans, unless they rendered him a service first.

Waiting, he watched as the warlock bit his own tongue, causing blood to leak from his mouth.

Pulling out the vial West had given him to collect the blood of a warlock, Gouroull grabbed von Bodmann by the head and placed the bottle upon his mouth. After it was full, he stoppered it, wiped the outside clean, and looked down at the fallen man.

He would linger, be treated as an invalid for some time, before dying a sad, insane husk of a man. A fitting end. With that, Gouroull left the tent, walking into the night and vanishing from sight.

Hours later, Georg von Bodmann still lay upon the earthen floor of his tent as Yosef Vrolok entered. He had taken the position of orderly, having learned from a noble acquaintance that von Bodmann was a powerful sorcerer. Indeed, Yosef had felt his power the instant they had met... not to mention the ring he always wore on his left hand.

Checking his commanding officer with a clinical detachment, Yosef shrugged. No doubt either a stroke or some kind of psychic backlash. Either way, von Bodmann was a wreck, of no further use. But not so his ring...

With a tug, Yosef pulled the serpent ring off Georg von Bodmann's hand and went looking for the medic. He didn't hurry.

CHAPTER V

The castle was hidden deep in the mountains; it was a difficult and harsh land that few wished to traverse. No matter who ruled this portion of Europe—Romans, Huns, Ostrogoths or Ottomans—they all avoided this region, and the lords that controlled the lands. A few attempts had been made to bring to heel the natives, the last by a lesser general in the service of Emperor Napoleon Bonaparte, but the treacherous climbs, the wolves and the unfriendly inhabitants had resulted in the unit being destroyed before they had even reached sight of this ancient structure.

The people of the region still occasionally discovered the remains of these dead soldiers and bandits and would merely kick them into a hole after taking any weapons or items they might use in their daily lives. A modern invader would be astonished to find the inhabitants of these lands using new rifles as well as swords and spears dating back to the days of Alexander the Great. Truly, a unique and remarkable region.

The current name for the castle was Castle Karnstein—after one of the many bloodlines founded by the ancient vampire who controlled these lands since time immemorial. Nobody, not even his fellow Elders, knew how old the being known as Count Karnstein really was, just that he was one of the Elders of the Undead. He had founded several bloodlines of vampires in Europe, South America and the New World, and was also known by the title "Patriarch," a figure of terror who was the embodiment of nightmares and terror. Many ancient tales of monsters stealing children and consuming them or making them its slaves were based on his treatment of humans throughout the ages; he was the very embodiment of the monsters of the night.

The Count was a man of medium height with dark hair and sensuous, full lips. Like most vampires, he was pale, but unlike them, his features merely resembled those of a dissolute nobleman from a past era. No matter how he dressed—the Patriarch could disguise himself in clothing of any strata of human society—he always looked like a member of the old ruling class, who enjoyed every sensation his position allowed him over others.

It would be easy to scoff or ignore this man, seeing him as nothing more than a wealthy fool who lived from day to day without a thought crossing his mind. But the Patriarch's eyes proved this supposition false, their dark depths absorbing every detail and giving him a cunning, if sinister, air. More than a few impressive individuals had fallen by his hands, having underestimated him to the cost of their lives.

The Patriarch enjoyed life, more so than almost all who walked the Earth, but he did so as one of the most dangerous predators who had ever existed. Today, he chose to use a lesser title, calling himself Count Karnstein, the lord of this castle and these lands.

Guests were coming this night, all fearsome powers in their own right, all vampires with titles of their own. As their host, Count Karnstein knew that taking a legendary name such as Patriarch, could entice those coming into testing his abilities. That was counterproductive to his goals, and the reason for this council. Besides, a name was of no importance to him. He knew that he was ancient and powerful, and everyone coming knew this as well. Count Karnstein merely disliked wasting time;

therefore, he would allow himself to appear less important than many present.

The council itself had taken over a decade to organize, each Lord invited being the master of his or her domain, and therefore suspicious and jealous of the others. But they had all agreed to come, knowing that refusing could result in their loss of some power or position amongst the undead. But every detail had to be discussed and agreed upon—no rushing about it since time was unimportant to their kind. A year was spent on the seating arrangements, all agreeing to no table but a circle of thrones of equal size and manufacture. The placement, down to the very feet between each seat, was another source of discussion, but, in the end, agreements were reached and the council was set to begin.

The gathering was not Count Karnstein's idea; he would have been content to continue to travel the world and spread his seed among the humans. It was *HE* who had requested it and *HIS* requests were little more than commands. The others invited knew the council would occur; they merely had to make a display of stretching the time out by negotiating all of the details. But in the end *HIS* commands would be followed—even Count Karnstein knew as much. It was like fighting the ocean: struggle as you may, that elemental force was greater than anything mankind, alive or undead, could bring to bear.

Sensing this from the start, Count Karnstein had immediately offered his second best hidden castle as neutral ground for the council. Agreement for that had proved easy; the castle was close enough to *HIS* lands, but far enough away that all the others would feel some degree of freedom.

The sound of horns indicated that the first two of the council had arrived and would join him shortly in the main hall. Normally, the castle was full of servants, but today, the Count had sent all but two elderly trumpeters away. The agreement among those coming was that everyone could bring one servant, human, vampire or other. The trumpeters would signal the approach of the guests and would leave, not having entered the castle grounds. Hailing the guests was considered properly respectful, so these lesser servitors had been allowed to their host.

Count Karnstein's servant was his beloved daughter, recently returned from the Beyond, who now called herself Countess Mircalla. As dissolute as her sire in many ways, Mircalla had lived many lives throughout Europe, converting male and female lovers into her slaves and lesser vampires. She enjoyed playing with her victims, especially those secretly attracted to her remarkable beauty, yet openly denying any interest in them. Mircalla had died many deaths, but as a part of the Count's bloodline, he could return her to life with little effort. Hopefully, one day, she would learn to be more circumspect, less public with the conversions of her lovers.

Mircalla glided into the room, dressed in a diaphanous black gown that more than hinted at her voluptuous form. Tall, with silken dark tresses that fell past her shoulders, she possessed a heart-shaped face and light, brown eyes that seemed to dance with amusement and stir the loins of every man and woman she studied. She was a creature of sensual sensations; few were able to refuse her attentions, and all who succumbed to her sexual desires died badly. Highly intelligent but capricious, Mircalla was the only being that Count Karnstein cared for, and he was the only one she would obey.

Running her long fingered hand across his shoulders, Mircalla kissed Count Karnstein's cheek and whispered:

"Which one should I seduce, my father... my love?"

Count Karnstein shook his head slowly, his leonine profile causing him to look more like the wastrel he pretended to be at that moment.

"None. *HE* commanded as much at the outset. Should you violate *HIS* command, I doubt that even I could save you. You will stay at my side at all times until everyone has left our lands. Do you understand?"

Mircalla shuddered at the mention of *HIM* and nodded quickly. She closed her eyes and gathered her strength, posing on Count Karnstein's throne arm and placing an arm across his neck.

"As you command, beloved father. What happens next?"

"We greet each guest and wait. *HE* will come last and then the council will begin," Count Karnstein replied, leaning his head against her ample bosom.

The first to arrive were those considered the least among those gathering, though they were by no means weak or helpless. Those invited to the council were equals in many ways, all undead possessing incredible powers and the backing of other monstrous beings capable of terrible evil. These two, since all the delegates were arriving in pairs at pre-determined times, were merely slightly less powerful than the others and had agreed to be the first to enter.

They walked into the main hall from different directions, north and south, as agreed upon, and gave nods to their host as well as each other.

They were an odd pair, Count Karnstein reflected as unalike as any who would appear this day. And not just physically.

The taller of the two was a blocky man with jet black hair that fell in long points across his high forehead. He had high cheekbones, deep eyes that seemed filled with melancholy, and sharp cheekbones. He was well dressed and wore several expensive pieces of jewelry, an expensive ring, and tie pin. He carried a wooden cane with a silver handle, shaped to look like a snarling wolf's head. His name was Barnabas Collins and he represented the many disorganized members of the American undead. He was a dangerous and powerful vampire, especially for one only slightly older than a century. He was closer in mindset to the old world vampires than most in his new country. An aristocrat in the American tradition, rumor had it that he possessed impressive powers that made him the equal of many who would appear this night.

Count Karnstein nodded at Collins, amused by the American vampire. Collins believed himself to be a good man under a curse, but a quick examination of the man's actions disproved that idea. A practitioner of the dark arts even before he was transformed into a vampire by a witch, the American was known to be a serial user and abandoner of women. Collins would create a perfect woman in his mind and, upon discovering said female did not meet his high standards, would leave or murder her as he fell in love with another. He was dangerous to cross, but Karnstein knew the American would be a loyal ally.

"I want that one," Mircalla purred in his ear, recognizing the appetites of the American and knowing he would be enjoyable for a time.

"Later, dearest, later," Karnstein whispered back.

The American's servant followed him, a tall good-looking man with heavy sideburns and the air of one who found life a sad joke. He had deep eyes and looked dangerous. This was Collins' relative, Quentin, said to be a werewolf, but no change in the man was ever witnessed.

"Not that one," Mircalla added, looking at Collins' servant and shuddering.

There was something very wrong about that man and that repulsed her more than any holy symbol.

Karnstein patted her knee, agreeing with her assessment. Collins had chosen his underling well—the man was indeed dangerous and, in some ways, horrific to their advanced senses. He put everyone off-balance, which gave the Americans power over the entire council. Collins had an impressive mind and after the council was over, they would meet and make plans. His bloodline added to the Karnsteins could become quite impressive.

The second man was shorter, almost bald, and possessed the square form and face of a peasant descended from a line of peasants. He had a large, bony nose, a puffy face, heavy, dark eyebrows and large, gnarled, calloused hands that obviously were used to manual labor. He had some power, but was not even close to that of Karnstein or Collins. This vampire was named Saushkin, and he was representing Russia at the council.

The vampires, witches, werewolves, warlocks and other creatures of Russia possessed a very odd, unique system that allowed them to live together and operate almost in public. Forming two policing units, divided into light and dark, they had created a series of rules that allowed vampires to live normal lives and feed almost openly. It was difficult for any of the ancient undead to understand, and a few attempted to step in and impose their will upon the massive country. That proved to be a mistake, as the elder vampires soon discovered, since the Russian vampires, good magicians, werewolves, witches and other beings operated as an army and destroyed anything that attempted to upset their careful social order. Thus Saushkin represented not merely Russian vampires, but an entire country of supernatural beings prepared to work as a devastatingly powerful army.

The underling at Saushkin's side was impressive in her own right. Taller than the vampire, she was dressed in a heavy white fur coat and mountain climbing clothing that were cut to favor her athletic figure. She had short black hair, deep blue eyes and an air of power that was almost a physical force assaulting anyone looking in her direction. Karnstein knew the type: a witch, powerful, capable of holding her own with even the most powerful of vampires. More impressive was that this one was clearly a member of the light side of the Russian's social order. Saushkin, too, had chosen well. Karnstein and the others knew that a mystic, capable of mighty feats of magic, would shield him and make his vote something to be cultivated rather than dismissed.

Mircalla hissed quietly at the witch, but kept her seat. She had encountered witches and knew that, if turned into vampires, they were even more dangerous than herself. Nothing would happen at the meeting, but Mircalla determined to keep this magic woman safe until she was returned to her odd, backwards country.

The trumpets blared again, signaling the arrival of the next pair to the council. This one was far more dangerous than the American and the Russian, rivaling in power with anyone else at the table. But they were also too focused on their own groups, their personal missions. This made them, in a very real sense, weaker than the others. This was a dichotomy that was fairly common among the elder vampires. The very essence of what made them so frighteningly dangerous, also caused them to be creatures of habit to an extreme degree.

Karnstein knew his faults and obsessions and fought them constantly. These two never bothered to confront their own demons; instead, they embraced them and had made themselves absolute rulers of their own, smaller domains.

The first to arrive into the main hall was a tall, thin, hairless man dressed in a brown leather jacket and black pants. He moved with the languid motions of one capable of extreme speed and agility, both of which were legendary among the vampire community. His face was a skull-like mask, a demonic visage that spread fear amongst both humans and vampires; his narrow eyes were a sickening, inhuman yellow color; his hands were elongated, wrinkled and ended in nails that resembled the talons of a reptile. His name had once been Nest, but he never used it any longer, preferring to be referred to as the Master of the Order of Aurelius, or simply, The Master.

Karnstein could never be amused by ancient cults formed by the undead. Unlike their human counterparts, they were often too ancient to be scoffed at or ignored, possessing lost and often dangerous knowledge. The vampires of the Order of Aurelius were such a group, devoted to the return of the demons known as the Old Ones. Karnstein knew all too well what a calamity the Old Ones returning to Earth would be for all life, including the undead. They would decimate everything in their path, humans, animals, plants, and even vampires, and would remake the world in their own, twisted, demonic image. The few survivors would exist as little more than parasites, insects brought down to the most primitive level. The Order of Aurelius did not realize this was Hell brought to Earth, but deluded themselves into thinking they would exist as the ruling class beneath their inhuman masters.

Why then was Nest invited? Simply put, to not invite him would have been an insult and it was never wise to risk war with such a fanatic. Additionally, Nest was a frighteningly powerful elder, capable of terrible violence when crossed. Rather than risk their larger plans, he was allowed to appear at the council as an equal, though everyone present would be searching for means to destroy him and his cult.

"That one reminds me of Orlok, Father," Mircalla whispered in his ear.

Her voice shook slightly when she named one of the most feared masters of the undead. That was understandable; few had ever dealt with the skull-faced Count without experiencing terror. He was too inhuman, more monstrous than the rest of their kind, and was something of a bogeyman even to the undead.

Karnstein nodded, but didn't agree. While Nest was a horrible, twisted monster, capable of impressive cruelty, he was no Orlok. His harsh behavior towards his underlings was meant to inspire fear, their obedience being his only aim. Orlok, on the other hand, desired no followers, just mindless creatures who would advance his dark dreams. They were two very different beings.

Nest's follower was a beautiful woman, pale skinned, with shoulder-length blonde hair and eyes that danced and were as seductive as Mircalla's own. She was more kittenish than his daughter, playing the part of the innocent schoolgirl to put her victims at ease before she destroyed them or added them to her master's followers. She may have been dangerous, but ultimately, she was no one particularly important compared to many in this conclave. She would be a plague on mankind, but ultimately a lesser one, who would someday die in a rather pathetic manner.

The one who arrived a moment behind Nest was as tall as his predecessor, but far broader, possessing the sculpted muscles of a warrior. He possessed a noble bearing and looked as one born to command, a warlord who would never allow himself to retire. His hair was short and plastered over his long face. His long nose and deep dark eyes gave him the look of a bird of prey, a falcon or eagle ready to swoop down upon an enemy with razor-sharp talons. His name was Viktor and he had been a dangerous general and warlord centuries ago. Transformed into a vampire by the sire of his line, he had taken power away from his elder. A powerful, dangerous member of the Elders, Viktor never truly evolved beyond his feudal upbringing. His coven was based on the ancient rule of might making right, and all his followers obeyed his word because it came from him. His warriors were well-trained and dangerous, fanatics in their own way, but always jockeying for power under his rule.

Karnstein was wary of Viktor, knowing the man was a barbarian who, when pushed, turned to extermination as a response to anyone who countered his will. Formerly employing werewolf slaves, he had lost control of them and his covens were perpetually at war with those dark monsters. Had he been less the barbarian and more the noble, Viktor would have played the vampires and werewolves against each other, controlling both and maintaining his high position. At least, that was how Karnstein would have behaved in the same position. Instead, he behaved like a medieval baron, enraged that anyone would disobey his laws, sounding more like a crazed monk than a vampire elder. Viktor as an odd, violent creature, but also a useful one whose powers and armies could help the vampire cause.

Viktor's underling was an attractive woman with short, dark hair, taller than the other women in the room and far more athletic. She was a killer, a hunter of werewolves and other enemies of her coven. According to gossip, she had lost her whole family in a werewolf attack and was rescued by Viktor, who had raised her as his daughter. A stoic, remorseless creature, she seemed to consider her beauty to be a weakness and behaved like a sexless warrior, incapable of emotions. Viktor encouraged this, but Karnstein believed it was a mistake. The emotions within this female were merely buried beneath the surface, hidden even to her. One day, they would emerge and everyone in their coven, especially Viktor, would be in danger.

It was an hour before the horns blasted again and the next two members of the council arrived. These two came from the most distant locations; both possessed impressive control in their areas of the world. To most present, the lands in Asia were unfathomably distant, despite the progress of ships and trains. Though vampires were ageless, and the Elders possessed minds capable of learning from the changing times, some concepts were difficult to grasp. Asia was to them, and to many Europeans and Americans, a distant mythical land of magic and oddity. To those present, even the ones that traveled through parts of that world, the tales of Baron Munchausen were to be found in the lands of China, India and other locales. And the vampires from that world were as mysterious as the lands they occupied and ruled.

The first to arrive was a short, dark-skinned man wearing a sparkling white turban and a dark-blue jacket with jeweled buttons. His nose was like a slice across his face and his eyes seemed to glow with inner fire. He was from India and, to all present, appeared to be a prince or a king from that distant shore. He held himself with a regal air and his searching eyes seemed to challenge anyone to dispute his right to rule over all. An ancient vampire, more so than many present, his dark beard and carriage made many think of him as a pirate prince of old, one who rampaged through the East and even ventured at times near Europe.

His name was Padma, although he used another title stating that he was a ruler over animals rather than vampires or humans. He was the least powerful member of a coven of vampires, though definitely no weakling in his own right. Padma was a dangerous man, but not a barbarian like Viktor, or a horrific, twisted monster like the Master. He was more noble than Collins or even Karnstein, but in a very ancient manner. He was a relic from a time when rulers were worshipped as gods, and their every whim obeyed without question. He was a living testimony to the old ways, the lost days that many kings and queens secretly wished would return. Concepts like democracy were as alien to him, as his ways were to humanity in this modern era. The others in his coven were of the same mindset, lost in their dreams of "divine right" rule over the world, ignoring that, for all their power, these ancient beliefs were nothing more than the sad dreams of creatures whose antique memories were mementos of the past.

A full step behind Padma was a man a full head taller than the ancient vampire, powerfully built and possessing the yellow eyes of a jungle cat. He was square-shouldered, muscular and possessed feline fangs jutting from his upper and lower jaws. The scent of this man was unusual, not a werewolf, but a shape-shifter of a different and dangerous variety. Karnstein had heard of the weretigers from the East, but had no idea until this creature appeared that they were an actual beast. This one was impressive, but completely controlled by Padma, his master. This demonstrated some degree of weakness by the Indian vampire, that he had to secure complete mastery over anyone he considered a servant. This demonstrated power, created slaves who would do as he ordered, but little else. They would have no imagination or desire to do more than what was required to keep from getting punished by their master.

The next Elder to arrive caused all, even the most jaded vampires, to turn and stare openly in surprise, fear and loathing. The vampire that appeared was a short man with chalk-white skin, long talon-like fingers with jutting green nails, and rows of wickedly sharp teeth. The ancient creature hopped into the room, his arm stiffly extended, moving across the chamber like an insect. This vampire was dressed in long, blue silk robes, a round black cap with a red tassel and white cloth wrappings across his feet. This was a Jiangshi, the legendary hopping vampires of the East, whose very presence sowed terror throughout the lands of the Chinese. They all moved with a strange hopping gait, stealing the life force of their victims, never stopping until they were imprisoned or destroyed by ancient, and often forgotten, methods.

Karnstein and the others knew the truth about these ancient and fear-raising creatures: there was only one Jiangshi on the planet. Though there were hundreds, possibly thousands, of these monstrous beings throughout the world, only one mind occupied these vampires. This creature, known only as the White Emperor, lived through all of these hopping monsters, feeding through each, unseen by humanity and vampires alike. Karnstein and the others likened the White Emperor to a monstrous spider in an enormous web, draining the lives of his victims as a spider would an insect. None even knew if that being was human any longer, but his power was unmistakable and his right to a place at the council unquestioned.

As Karnstein stared at the Jiangshi, he also considered the weakness of these creatures. Slow moving and unable to do anything but feed, these vampires were nothing more than leeches. They could not rule humanity, or even subtly control their food source—they could only venture out and feed. They were the purest vampires in the room, sappers of life and nothing else. The horrific White Emperor filled the other vampires with loathing, representing the truth beneath their facades, the leeches that existed within their very souls. Karnstein and all of the others could look at themselves as powerful, impressive creatures, but they all knew that a simple loss of control would cause them to become nothing more than this hopping monstrosity.

"Say nothing, my love," Karnstein whispered to Mircalla.

He ignored her annoyed pout, but it was safer to remain discreet in the presence of a being such as the White Emperor.

Also he sensed that Padma would be easily insulted, which would be a good weapon to use against that Elder when the council began. To do so before would be a waste, and Karnstein was never willing to use a weapon until it was the proper time. Being a master of politics meant never giving up an advantage, and as an Elder, he was able to be patient and wait for the right moment.

It was several hours before the next two arrived, both at exactly the same moment, stepping into the main chamber at precisely the same second. Neither would allow the other to have the advantage of being ahead or behind the other—their hatred was too great. These two were the uncrowned queens of the undead, each enormously powerful creatures and capricious beings capable of terrible evil. Though there were many elder female vampires, all deferred to these two without question. The few that challenged their power ended up destroyed, usually in such a vicious way as to give the others pause for thought.

Karnstein's eyes fell first upon the woman arriving from the south. He kept his face carefully impassive. He'd met her on several occasions and, despite her incredible beauty, had chosen to keep her at arm's length. She was tall and voluptuous with raven black hair that fell like a dark cloud across her shoulders. She had high cheekbones, deep, dark eyes, silken skin and huge black lashes that caused everyone to stare. She looked like a statue of a Greek Goddess come to life, but not a gentle one such as Aphrodite or the wise warrior Athena. No, this woman possessed the fierce beauty of a goddess worshiped in fear, like Hecate, the Goddess of Witches, or Nox, the Goddess of Night. She was the ice queen that would make men love her, until it killed them and left them little more than empty husks. Her name was

Princess Asa Vajda and she was both a vampire and a witch of horrific power. Her rampages through Moldavia were still spoken of in frightened whispers and to many homes, she was the specter used to terrify children into obedience. Princess Asa Vajda had been arrested and sentenced to death by her brother, an inquisitor, who was one of the few of that time who hunted evil. But like all creatures of the night, she'd been brought back by desperate fools, eager for power. Since that time, Princess Asa Vajda lived secretly, building her power and waiting for the moment she could rule an even greater realm. She came to the council with no attendant, her own power acting as a shield that caused all to keep a healthy distance.

Karnstein was impressed by the Princess, as few others were. She was intelligent, dangerous and capable of evil on a scale that surprised even him. She was a lion who lived among the sheep and fed upon them in a way that made them respect her, as ancient people did to such predators in the days where mankind were still savages. Asa Vajda would be the perfect ally, but one would never be able to show weakness in her presence. It was she that he wished to add to his bloodline, and Karnstein would do his best to ensure this happened someday.

The vampire arriving from the north was also attending unaccompanied, gliding into the room with a smooth, inhuman motion full of sensual movements guaranteed to catch the eye and cause viewer to stare at her with lust. A tiny woman with lithe, sinewy curves, she possessed satiny mocha skin, dark hair, a straight perfect nose and round face that was perfectly sculpted. Her eyes were cat-like and deep brown and the eyebrows above them rose to a pert and unblemished brow. She was dressed in a golden ceremonial breastplate, a large, wide pectoral necklace made of gold with lapis lazuli inlay and an iron crown. Her midsection was bare and across her hips was a wide belt made of silver and gold, holding up tiny wisps of cloth that fell just above the front and back of her knees. This Elder looked like the living embodiment of a queen from ancient Egypt. To see her was to understand how they were considered the embodiment of fertility, using the blood of their subjects as a way of keeping the soil productive.

This woman was Queen Akasha and she claimed to be the most ancient vampire in the world. It was said she had gained her powers in ancient Egypt or one of the fabled lost cities, like Uruk or Nippur. Nobody knew because all information about Akasha were said to have been destroyed by Sargon the Great, who, legend had it, had driven the ancient vampires from his empire.

Karnstein squeezed his daughter's knee, not even wanting to risk her hissing at Akasha. To do so would result in Mircalla's instant death, for the Queen was powerful beyond belief, a warrior capable of reacting instantly at any challenge. She was as dangerous as Asa Vajda, but more demanding. Where Asa Vajda destroyed her followers, Akasha created many and demanded their total loyalty. They were her servants, rather than her slaves, showing that she was wiser than Padma in that, at least. But Karnstein was unimpressed by Akasha, who, though not a relic like Padma, was still unable to decide what she wished to be in this modern age. One day, a goddess, another, a queen, yet another, the fountainhead of a new race. Her constantly changing viewpoint made her easy to flatter and manipulate.

Karnstein knew that, if they fought, she would probably win, but he was more likely to assassinate her and feed on her before she died. Akasha had few equals in battle, but many on the council could arrange her death with ease. Hence she was treated with respect, but also disguised contempt.

The elder vampires waited and then seated themselves in their assigned thrones, waiting and not daring to speak. The seconds stood with their heads bowed; even Mircalla extracted herself from the embrace of her father and stood in her place as the others. Every detail had been discussed and agreed to, years of discussion leading to this important moment, this council *HE* had demanded. Though each of the vampires and their followers were dangerous beings of ancient power, they knew that *HE* was mightier than all of them, and it was best to follow his occasional demands.

Suddenly, a bat flew into the chamber, circling the room twice before suddenly transforming before their eyes into a tall man who glanced down at them all with an imperious look. He was the tallest man in the room, possessing broad shoulders, a narrow waist and large, powerful hands with some hair near the palms. He possessed a wide face, a noble bow and deep-set eyes that seemed to pierce the very soul of every individual he focused on. Dressed in black evening dress with a snow white shirt and a black opera cape with a red silk interior, this Elder seemed to exude nobility, sensuality and the rot of the grave, all at the same time. The man was both a barbarian and a modern man, a lover and a rapist, a warrior and a diplomat, a man of so many opposing parts that it was impossible to sum him up in a few sentences, or even a whole book.

He was, of course, Dracula, King of the Vampires and Prince of Darkness. None knew how he became their lord and master, but he was, and even distant, inhuman beings like the White Emperor acknowledged it.

Each of the Elders present had met him over the years, his face changing at times, but his position always unquestioned. Vampires never used his name, merely referring to Dracula as *HE* or *HIM*, with extreme emphasis. It was a mark of fear and respect—one few beings in history could claim.

"Good evening," Dracula purred, his voice filling the room. "I bid you welcome at this, my council. My thanks to you all for attending."

This was said in an almost ironic tone, since all present knew one did not refuse one of Dracula's demands. To do so would have been to insult the King of Vampires, and such offense always resulted in the final death of the offender. But Dracula used the noble manners he'd learned over the years as a weapon, as dangerous as any power he brought to bear in battle. Everyone present murmured their thanks in as few words as possible and waited as Dracula nodded to Karnstein, who was technically their host.

"There are 249 treaties or agreements between everyone present in this room. Should an incident happen, or best to say when one occurs, an all-encompassing war will begin that could consume us all," Karnstein stated, his words carefully rehearsed.

He and Dracula had planned each statement, knowing this would not offend any of the Elders.

"When we declare war," Dracula intoned, standing and looking down upon all of them, "it shall be to place the humans beneath our heel. Dracula shall not watch his kingdom fall because of foolish agreements made over the course of many lifetimes."

"The White Emperor has never broken a treaty and shall not do so now. We think you waste our time," the Jiangshi whispered, the creature's lips barely moving.

"That is the same for all present," said Karnstein, nodding but once. "Instead, a new treaty shall be reached that will supersede all previous ones."

"Honor shall be satisfied and all shall follow the way of Dracula," the King of Vampires added.

He then sat down on his throne.

"I have a concern," the Master hissed, tenting his long fingers in a slow, languid manner. This was his favorite weapon: speak calmly and gently before he struck with intense and horrible action. "Count Orlok, one of the most powerful of our kind, is not present. He and I are... connected... and his absence here is... insulting."

Dracula chuckled, an inhuman sound that resembled the rasp of an opening coffin rather than a reaction of mirth.

"You think Dracula would exclude his kinsman? I speak for Orlok, who is busy elsewhere on pressing business."

The Master clearly wished to argue the point, but to do so would mean challenging Dracula's word, and that would result in an immediate duel, and likely his final death. He knew that he was close in power to the Vampire King, but not yet his equal. When the Ascension came, Nest would rise far above everyone present and they would all be destroyed.

"Thank you," he stated and nodded his acceptance.

His time would come, until then he would abide and plan.

A short distance away, just outside the castle, Gouroull sniffed the air.

The scent of the walking dead was everywhere—the blood-drinkers with their odd powers and inability to stand in sunlight. They were ultimately a weak breed, useless for Gouroull's purposes and yet, filled with megalomania. The few times he dealt with vampires, they attempted to enslave him and they were forced to battle to the death—their death. But he had a need here and would fulfill his mission. West's list was very detailed, demonstrating that Victor Frankenstein's creation was as much the result of alchemy as science.

A guard with a large brass horn stood by the entry portal, huddling in a small wooden shack, dressed in heavy, woolen clothes, but still shivering in the cold of the mountains. He spotted Gouroull and raised the horn to his mouth, seemingly unsurprised by the giant's monstrous visage. His movements were mechanical, as if he was a clockwork figure and this was his only function. Frankenstein's most dangerous creation knew this man was a herald, standing here to signal the approach of visitors to the lord of the dwelling.

Stepping forward, Gouroull punched the horn, pushing it back inside the mouth of the herald and shattering this teeth and jaw. The man fell with a whimper into his shack, his hands covering his wounded face.

With a hard stomp, Frankenstein's creature flattened the horn and glanced into the shack, spotting some supplies for the occupant as well as a small stove for warmth. Seeing no other horn, Gouroull walked away and leaped up onto the castle's wall, beginning a climb towards the source of the scent he was following.

The fact that there were many vampires present was of no matter to him; the mission for the ingredients necessary for the creation of his mate was paramount.

Leaping across several roofs, Gouroull opened a wooden door and stepped into a long hallway leading to a large room in the distance. He heard several voices, a few sounding human, others sounding both inhuman and harsh upon the ears. Gouroull touched the empty stone vial in the pouch on his hip, ready to be used. He then pushed forward, soon stepping into a large room filled with vampires.

The Elders were not new like most vampires Gouroull had met over the years; they were far more ancient and deadly. He could sense that instantly, though it was of no interest to him, since even the eldest of this kind were vulnerable creatures. Smiling and showing his teeth, Gouroull scanned the room, amused by the shocked looks on the faces of these creatures.

The creature closest to the door, a tall, thin vampire with a skull-like face and yellow eyes similar to Gouroull's, stepped forward and pointed a clawed hand at Frankenstein's monster.

"What, if may I ask, is that?" he said.

A vampire seated nearby and watching with amused interest stated:

"Nothing of my doing, Nest. This is a revenant of some type, but like none I have ever seen. I should step away if I were you, my friend."

The skull-faced vampire shot the other a quick look of annoyance and extended one clawed finger towards Gouroull.

"I think not. I am the Master and I do not yield," he stated, his yellow eyes glowing.

Gouroull stopped before the vampire, still scanning the room for his real target. This "Master" was of no interest to him; ancient of not, he was merely a diseased corpse with delusions of grandeur. He was simply more decayed than the others, although there was one nearby that was barely animated, closer to the zombies he had faced in the past. Frankenstein's creation had an important mission here and these vampires were getting in his way.

Stepping forward, Gouroull found his path blocked by the thin, skull-faced vampire. The creature extended a long bony hand and hissed out something which the Monster ignored. He could feel this vampire was attempting to take control of his mind, a pathetic act the undead seemed to need to do. Gouroull never bothered to control humans; he merely terrified them or killed them. That way, they either complied or they were dead—a good result either way. But vampires seemed to want slaves, both humans and other vampires, to worship them and serve as food.

Reaching out, Gouroull grabbed the hand of the vampire known as the Master and crushed it to powder in one vice-like grip of his own, monstrous hand. The vampire shrieked and lashed out with his free hand, raking his sharp nails against Gouroull's nearly impenetrable gray skin. Frankenstein's creation dropped the elder vampire to the ground, no longer paying any attention to him.

The remaining vampires in the room exploded into fury, many of their movements blurs hard to track by a normal eye. Karnstein quickly ran across the room and pulled Princess Asa Vajda aside, shielding her with his body. At the other end of the room, Mircalla grabbed the American Collins and pulled him away from the enormous revenant who had so easily defeated Nest. Everyone present knew the Master could be a deadly enemy, capable of terrible acts of evil and destruction, but this creature had apparently crushed him without any visible effort. This was therefore a dangerous being and they had to destroy him, or at least keep out of his way until they could cause his destruction.

Karnstein, for his part, was determined to make the best of the situation. Pulling Princess Asa Vajda aside, he smiled as he saw Mircalla do the same with the American Collins. Let the others deal with this inhuman monstrosity, the Karnstein bloodline would continue and grow in strength, he thought. The power of the Princess' witchcraft combined with his bloodline would make them strong enough to rise above the other Elders, even to the level of Dracula himself. And Collin's might would make him an excellent follower of Mircalla, enabling their bloodline to take power in the New World.

"Do not try to do battle with that creature," Karnstein hissed in the lovely ear of Asa Vajda. "You of all of us know better than to fight an enemy you have not studied first."

This bit of flattery was unnecessary, but the Moldavian vampire witch nodded and did not attempt to remove his arms from her waist. She pulled a long wicked dagger from the sleeve of her gown and smiled, showing her sharp fangs.

"Agreed. I am in your debt, Count Karnstein," she purred.

She stepped a little closer to him. For too long had Princess Asa Vajda been forced to live in the shadows, feeding on peasants and searching for her lost love. But she knew Count Karnstein lived more publicly, existing as more than simply an elder vampire who consumed any girl who caught his fancy. Perhaps they could help each other and reach an accommodation?

Gouroull stepped forward, his quarry in sight. The zombie vampire dressed in Chinese finery hopped forward towards Frankenstein's creature, his eyes full of intelligence, his nails extended like spears. Gouroull grabbed the Elder by the wrists and lifted him over his head. With a quick motion, he tossed the Chinese vampire out of a window located on the east side of the room—a toss of about 10 yards. The vampire did not utter a sound as it fell. Gouroull's exceptional hearing allowed him to hear a distant, dull thud as the creature crashed to the ground. It was a long drop and he didn't hear any stirring. Could one kill an undead monstrosity by merely dropping it from a great height? Gouroull didn't care, but it was an interesting question.

Viktor's female underling leaped forward, pulling a pair of blades from her jacket and swinging them at Gouroull with the speed and skill only a trained vampire warrior with many centuries behind them could demonstrate. Her beautiful face was impassive as she spun her weapons with expert skill and slashed out at Frankenstein's creation. Her attacks were impressive, lightning fast, and would have been lethal to human and vampire alike.

But Gouroull was neither human, nor vampire. He knew her knives might be able to pierce his skin, so he had no intention of dealing with her for long. Stepping to the side, he backhanded her across the jaw and sent her flying across the room to crash into an Elder wearing a white turban. The impact sent both of them tumbling to the far end of the room, giving Gouroull enough room to complete his mission.

There was the source of his interest: a tall man, well-dressed and handsome in a dissolute manner. His prominent sideburns seemed to bristle with anger as Gouroull turned his way. He reached into his waistcoat, pulling out a small pistol. He fired the tiny weapon at Gouroull, striking him in the right arm. A small stream of black ichor flowed down the creature's arm, yet he marched forward, as fast, if not faster, than the vampires.

Batting the pistol aside, he grabbed the tall American werewolf and bit down on his neck with his razor-sharp teeth.

The werewolf screamed and went limp, falling to the ground as Gouroull let go of his arms. Frankenstein's creature spat out the meat and blood, tossing it to the ground. He then reached down to the fallen werewolf, who was already healing, and pulled several strands of hair from his head.

Ignoring the vampires, Gouroull walked away from the room, while wrapping the werewolf's hair in the oil-skin pouch West had supplied. That had been what he needed—one of the oddest ingredients on the list. But it seemed that many of Victor Frankenstein's items were needed to create an alchemical formula that would become the lifeblood of his creation. How had his mentor, Pretorius, previously obtained all of these items and discovered that this mixture would create life were questions that Gouroull didn't focus upon, but they were interesting none the less. Had Pretorius obtained help from some creature from beyond? Found the notes of an ancient alchemist? There was no way to know now, but part of his formula involved the hair of a werewolf, and Gouroull had caught the scent of this one as he traveled towards the coast.

Digging the bullet out of his arm, he tossed the lead pellet behind him; then, he vaulted over the castle's battlement, dropping the long distance to the ground. Without missing a step, he began to walk south, heading for the next item on his list.

"You chose to shield that slut over me? I had a treaty with you over 200-years old!" Akasha screamed at Karnstein.

"Who are you calling a slut, harem girl?" Asa Vajda purred back, her voice full of menace. "We all know you were nothing more than the mistress of a barbarian chief, but we allow you your pretensions of royalty."

"You dare? I shall kill you, you and your lover!" Akasha screamed.

Across the room, Padma hurled the barely conscious woman that knocked him down back to her master, Viktor.

"Your warrior was a clumsy fool," he spat. "If she is your best, my coven has no need of your help. Submit!"

"Never!" Viktor whispered, his large bony hands balling into fists. "It shall be war!"

Voices of the undead continued to rise, each turning on their associates and declaring war as Dracula stood above them, impotently attempting to restore order. But none were listening as war was being declared between the Lords of the Undead.

CHAPTER VI

Aiofe Hamilton sighed and sniffed the air. The rats were coming and the battle in their trench would soon begin once again. The previous week, the enemy had advanced and taken the outer trenches; they were now trying to push forward into the first of the five lines of defenses of the Vampire City of Selene.

"I smell rats," Aiofe said, her voice a low growl.

She stretched her back and looked at her friend and fellow servant, Maud Jackson, flicking her tail. "About fifty yards away."

Maud looked at Aiofe, mildly envious that the master had transformed her friend into a cat for these battles. Scratching her bald head, she hefted her huge and heavy hammer and nodded.

"This time, just keep attacking the rats. When the zombies catch up, I can destroy them easily. Last time, you almost got in my way."

Aiofe rolled her eyes, not an easy feat in cat-form.

"How many times must you bring that up? I won't get in your way again. And I did kill that zombie, if you remember correctly!"

"Only because I didn't crush you with my hammer!" Maud replied with a grin.

Though they were the slaves of Lady Boyana Markov, and occasionally contended, they had become friends over the years. Out of the hundreds of others that their mistress controlled, Maud was still surprised her favorite company was a girl she once considered too low-class to acknowledge publicly.

Maud Jackson, before meeting her mistress, was once Lady Maud Jackson, wife of the Earl of Westgate and a prominent member of London's high society. She'd been a beautiful, harsh leader of the set close to the Royals, a dispenser of punishment for *faux-pas* or violations of proper conduct among their elite corner of society. Then Boyana Markov had come, and all her friends and enemies who lived in fear of Maud's judgments now turned their attention to this Bulgarian barbarian. Maud attempted to cut the woman out, but soon found herself isolated and, eventually, turned into a follower of the beautiful, if vulgar, foreign baroness.

For Maud Jackson soon discovered that Boyana Markov was a vampire, a member of the elite society that resided in the lost, hidden city known as Selene. She was not a disgusting, bloodsucking rapist like Mr. Stoker's Dracula, who had so frightened Maud years before. Boyana Markov's people were far older, striking their victims with sharpened tongues and absorbing them into their body. Maud, along with hundreds of others, existed within her mistress and could be released at the vampire's whim, to serve or fight, or whatever their enslaver desired. Though still herself, Maud knew her will was long gone and she didn't think she minded anymore.

Aiofe Hamilton was a far different woman from her comrade and fellow slave. A bar girl in the tavern in Lady Maud's home town, Aiofe was a lively, beautiful red-haired girl who had been a much-prized beauty by her landlord and employer. She was also unofficially known as the mistress of Lady Maude's husband, Frederick, whose preference for paddling and dressing in Aiofe's barmaid clothes was an unspoken joke among the townspeople.

Maud, for her part, ignored Frederick's behavior since he was reasonably discreet, and it kept him out of her house. She pointedly ignored Aiofe until Boyana, who preferred women and only made slaves of those she found attractive, enslaved the lovely barmaid.

Today Aiofe was a cat and Maud was human; tomorrow their mistress might convert them both into parrots or bring them back into the world as hairless slaves serving her whim. Neither minded anymore; they'd been with their dark mistress for over a century, only having returned to Selene when war threatened the city.

Apparently, one of the blood-drinking types of vampire wished to gain admittance to the city and become one of its leaders. This Count Orlok was enormously powerful, a disgusting corpse who would destroy the quiet harmony of Selene's ancient residents. This was unacceptable and Boyana Markov and her slaves held within her body, were all commanded to return and man the trenches to hold off Orlok's army of rats and undead. So far, they had held the lines, barely, with many of Boyana's slaves falling victim to the horrific attacking forces.

The attack came mere seconds later, a skittering, scratching sound filling the air and causing Aiofe's fur to stand on end. The earth seemed to come alive, a flowing wave of brown and gray rolling towards the trenches like a hideous tide. They were Orlok's rats, his most-prized servants, and they arrived as a mass and began attacking the trenches dug by the slaves of Selene's vampires with a courage one would not expect from such lowly creatures. Maud leapt to the attack, her huge hammer destroying dozens of creatures with each strike. Aiofe also dove into the battle, her wicked claws and teeth slicing into the rats and slowing their attack.

Then the sounds of moaning filled the air, drowning out the squeaks and shrieks of the dying, diseased rats. This was a dreadful sound, a wail of despair and indescribable pain and horror that would have driven any normal being mad. These were the zombie slaves of Orlok, murdered men, women and children, who had been brought back from the peace of the grave to serve as shambling soldiers in his war against the vampire lords and ladies of Selene.

Maud stepped in front of Aiofe, striking the heads of the zombies as they approached, laughing with joy at the violence. She had once recoiled at the thought of such horrors, but now, thanks to her mistress, this was what she lived for day and night. Lady Boyana had broken her spirit shortly after they had met, starting with removing all the hair upon her body. Later, she changed the formerly prissy social butterfly into a blood-seeking amazon, a warrior woman who lived for battle and the death and destruction of her mistress's enemies.

Aiofe, for her part, was as transformed as her comrade Maud. Once a happy woman, who had lived for the joy of herself and all who surrounded her, a woman who would lead the tavern in songs and dances and made everyone feel special and important, she was now a calm and controlled killer, who only laughed when her mistress' enemies fell or were forced to become fellow slaves. A cruel, terrible creature, Aiofe was often transformed into a cat, since she did enjoy toying with victims before she murdered them.

This time, the sheer volume of rats and zombies threatened to overwhelm their position. It was as if Orlok had decided to throw everybody he had under his command in a surge, attempting to take the city of Selene through the sheer volume of bodies he could muster.

Maud was soon surrounded by the press and stench of the undead, shuffling, desiccated corpses, the rotted hands seeking to hold her and add her to their numbers. Aiofe was almost buried under the wave of rats, all seeking to tear her into pieces. She lay on her back, her four paws slashing at multiple attackers as her fangs tore at the ever increasing mass of rodent bodies. All seemed lost, but neither were capable of despair—their mistress had removed that emotion from their bodies.

"This is worse than the last time they took the east trenches!" Maud managed to gasp.

Her hammer was barely able to move and strike the skulls of the zombies. She couldn't see Aiofe, but she could hear the scream of the rats her comrade was killing with her wicked claws.

The press of the zombies was relentless, a wave of rotted bodies moving forward, groaning forward and stepping over their fallen brothers and sisters. To any but the enslaved minds of a Selene vampire's doppelgangers, this would be horror incarnate, insanity causing such terror that would snap their minds and bring about their death even faster than the tide of undead.

"We need to pull back!" Aiofe screamed.

She was close to being overwhelmed by the tide of rats who were streaming in, their brown, black and gray furred forms covering her large cat body, each dying as they attempted to destroy the vampire slave.

If the zombie wave was terrifying to the mind of a human, the unrelenting assault of the rats would have brought horror and fear into any living being on the planet Earth. These diseased, twisted monstrosities were the nightmares of all life, death incarnate. They brought about the destruction of empires, destroyed whole regions of life; they were the eaters of the dead, the spreaders of diseases, and all beings feared their rampages.

Just when the assault was about to destroy both slaves of Lady Boyana Markov, the press of zombies and rats seemed to falter and slow. Maud found she was better able to swing her mallet at the zombies and soon had room in which to move. The weapon flew out in larger arcs, decimating greater numbers of the undead. She began to howl in exultation, the slaughter giving her heights of pleasure she rarely experienced since becoming a vampiric slave. This was all she had left—all her other emotions had been blunted by her mistress, turning her, once a reserved lady with hidden reservoirs of deep passion, into an almost robotic simulacrum of her former self.

Nearby, Aiofe also felt the rats beginning to pull back, the tide of the slobbering creatures slowly lessening their weight upon her feline form and enabling her claws and teeth to rend and tear them apart. The remaining rodents didn't relent and kept attacking, their minds being controlled by the vampire who was their master. Their diseased minds were only capable of one thought: attack their master's enemies and consume all living beings in their path. If the zombies were Orlok's soldiers, the rats were his shock troops, terror forces which were relentless, bringing fear to all the world, except the vampires of Selene and their doppelganger slaves. But this night, it was the rats which screamed in the distance, as if a powerful force was crushing the tide of their fury.

Slow, inexorably, both of Lady Boyana Markov's slaves began to see a figure not too far away, a lone man fighting the zombies with rapid, powerful movements. He seemed to be stemming the tide of the rats through the use of the zombies, forcing the terrible rodents to consume their own undead allies. The rats died in droves and the zombies fell in equal numbers.

That not so distant man was a huge creature who seemed capable of destroying both undead and rodent menaces as easily as a vampire would crush a human enemy. Was he another inhuman being assisting the lords and ladies that ruled the Vampire City?

At first, both doppelgangers thought this man might be one of Selene's slaves, serving another vampire lord or lady in their struggle for supremacy among the lesser masters of the city. But soon, they could tell that he was not a fellow slave. The doppelgangers had an in-bred instinct that enabled them to recognize their own, if only to prevent unnecessary conflicts.

Moments later, the battlefield was devoid of undead or rodents, despite the occasional squeak or squeal that could be heard in the distance, a fading sound but still no less horrifying to the ear. Maud and Aiofe stood amidst the piles of the dead, a plain of rotting horror surrounding them in every direction. Artists could have used this scene to depict of one of the famed circles of Hell, or perhaps as the Earth had looked when the Black Death rampaged throughout Europe. However, the two women, one bald, the other in her feline form, remained unmoved, having viewed worse since their enslavement. Instead, they watched their savior approach, impressed by his enormous size.

"He's larger than that German strongman—the one Grigor Iliev enslaved and uses as his bodyguard," said Maud. "He's a true giant and our mistress has nobody of his size amongst her followers. She will love to add him to his collection!"

"Grigor's strongman is Dutch, not German," Aiofe corrected, beginning to clean her wounds in the same languid manner as a cat. "But you're right, he could help the Lady rise above all the others."

"Keep silent! He's coming closer and a talking pussycat is not exactly common in this world!" Maud hushed her friend.

She then lowered her huge hammer to the ground. Despite her bald head, she knew she was still an attractive woman and capable of keeping a man interested in her in the obvious ways.

Their savior was indeed a giant of a man, at least eight feet tall, with pale, chalky skin. His lips were an unpleasant black and the teeth that peeked out from beneath them appeared razor sharp. His hair was long and dark, resembling the mane of a lion. But it was his eyes that were the most frightening. They were deep yellow and seemed to glint with an inhuman malevolence, a demonic intelligence that shook the bald woman and her feline friend.

"My good sir," Maud simpered, smiling up at the newcomer with the grateful smile of a young and innocent girl. "We are ever so grateful for your kindness in saving our lives. Those terrible monsters sought to destroy our home and enslave us. My poor cat and I were so close to death!"

The giant looked down at Maud, his unblinking yellow eyes examining her with cold indifference.

This shocked both Maud and Aiofe, used as they were to all males and most females responding favorably to the former's charms. But this man seemed not only unmoved, but disinterested. Both servants of Lady Boyana Markov experienced a wave of trepidation under that inhuman gaze. It was as if this man was less human than their vampiric mistress, or even that craven undead, Orlok. But his sheer strength bespoke that he was no mere zombie, or revenant, but a being of enormous power.

"Forgive me, my good sir, but I am a poor, weak woman. My name is Maud and this is my pet Aiofe," Maud continued. "Could you please tell me your name—the name of our savior, so I can whisper it to our Lord and Savior in my prayers. Also, my mistress is a wonderful and wise lady, who will wish to reward you richly for saving us..."

Maud allowed her eyes to flash with a hint of lust. This was her favorite means to entice her victims, an act she had learned as a teenage girl and had eventually matured into an ability to seduce the wealthy and the powerful with ease.

Gouroull found the antics of the vampire slave to be rather amusing, if a little ridiculous. She smelled not undead, but not alive either. This woman, and her so-called "pet," were but puppets controlled by invisible strings. He could sense the hidden mind behind these two. They were bizarre beings, even from his experience. The undead he had dealt with before, like Dracula and his cohorts, were creatures he understood; he knew their true power and how they maintained their pseudo-lives. They were weak in his mind, little more than talking corpses whose behavior made them little more than leeches. Even the strongest amongst them fell in battle before him, their great powers availing them nothing against his own strength.

But the vampires of Selene were unique. They, too, possessed a pseudo-life, but their bodies were not rotting away, being kept together by the stealing blood from human victims. They, too, stole lives, but they took their victims into themselves, and used those stolen lives like puppets for their undead masters. This was a confusing method, one which, Gouroull believed, must have been designed by some strange genius. The leech-like vampires had some basis in the natural order he knew; but these?

Gouroull considered this because he had some thoughts for the future. When he secured his mate and they began the creation of their new race, this city of vampires could become their competition. They seemed to need to absorb and enslave as many lives as possible. He could not allow his future children to become these creatures' subjects. Therefore, he would destroy them, as well as obtain certain items from West's list. Orlok alone may have provided him with these items, but now that he had come across Selene's existence, Frankenstein's creation decided to now challenge these vampires and see what they were capable of in battle.

Gouroull nodded once, his yellow eyes focusing on the bald woman:

"Lead," he stated, his voice a low rumble.

Maud grinned and looked to Aiofe with happiness. Their mistress would be pleased at the appearance of this giant. Bringing to her such a powerful creature would surely grant them some more time outside. This was the goal of all slaves—continued life outside their masters. Maud and Aiofe would do anything for their mistress, for she was everything to them, but the void in which they often resided was a fear that all slaves shared—that nothingness in between the moments when they were summoned back to life. Their hope was to spend as much time outside, in the world, serving their mistress as they could.

Maud, with Aiofe scampering nearby, took Gouroull down a path that was enclosed on all sides by enormous black trees. The light vanished almost immediately. The gnarled limbs of the ancient woods stood oppressively over their heads. The air became dustier, heavier and harder to breathe. It was as if they were walking through the deepest of forests, a location untouched by all but the meanest of life. Gouroull remained unmoved, untouched by the feeling of death that hung over the path. This was merely another pathetic attempt by lesser beings to put him, and any other potential victim, ill at lease.

The trip took half an hour, but was one of the few safe paths to the Vampire City. The Elders of Selene, an ancient and mysterious circle seen by few and feared by all, had planned many paths to their city as a mean of defense. In ancient days, their wars with other dark powers had led them to treat all beings as potential enemies—or slaves. The Elders spoke in whispers of enemies now long gone who had warred upon their dark city. With each age that passed, their connections to the outside world had diminished, despite their servants going out into the world to collect more slaves. These became their foot soldiers against the rising menace of the modern world—something that the Elders neither understood, nor wished to explore. They hid in the spires and towering minarets of Selene, their forms growing less human as time crawled forward.

Passing several ancient traps, many of which being so obvious that Gouroull would have easily bypassed them, they finally arrived before a large stone arch. It was a pair of Doric columns with a flat arch, sculpted from a dark stone that looked like black marble. As they approached the columns, the darkness of the stone became even more evident. Light seemed to be absorbed by rather reflected off its surface. It was if it was made from darkness itself. Beyond it was a paved walkway, a cobbled path made from a pale stone that appeared worn by the ages. Nothing was visible beyond that point; even Gouroull could hear no signs of life.

This absence of life, combined with the stillness and the darkness, would have terrified almost anyone else, but to Gouroull, this was nothing special, merely another "dead zone." There were many such areas on Earth and none posed the slightest threat to Frankenstein's creation. Only one place on the planet filled him with something close to fear: a cold region of the Earth where alien life slept. Gouroull knew that he would need an army of his kind to battle these ancient monsters, making his quest for a mate all the more important. He was a survivor and this was his world, one where he himself was the apex predator. Frankenstein's creation would not yield that place to any other being—not without a battle of gigantic proportions.

Maud and Aiofe lead Gouroull through the portal leading to Selene; their presence allowed him to enter the hidden land beyond. The sky above was now a dark curtain that cast shadows on the empty fields. The distance to the city was deceptive; the shadows caused it to look closer at times, far distant at others. The effect was disturbing, especially when the scope of Selene became more apparent with each passing moment.

They entered the city less than an hour later, the path slowly twisting into the labyrinthine depths of the home of the ancient vampires. Selene was a city made entirely of the same dark stone as the earlier portal. Towering spires and minarets reached into the heavens; the dark stone walls loomed in the distance. Each tower was topped with a large onion-shaped dome and no windows were visible in any of the imposing structures.

These were the home of the Elders, the rarely seen masters of this city of vampires. They once resembled the humanity they had enslaved, taking within them whole tribes of savages. Their familiars had been armies, battling and destroying entire civilizations, before they were forced back into Selene by the barbaric hordes of humanity, as well as newer and even more terrible monsters.

Since that time, stories, whispered by the few who knew of Selene's existence, abounded as to what changes had happened to these ancient beings. Some believed they had slowly been transformed into inhuman monsters, revealing the demonic beings within. Others claimed that they were devolving, becoming nothing more than insane animals, feeding on the slaves they absorbed within their forms. Even the lesser inhabitants of Selene were unaware of the truth, receiving commandments from hooded slaves who only spoke in hushed, strangled voices.

Beneath the overpowering spires were smaller dwellings, ranging in size from medium-sized houses to small shacks. Each building was made from the same dark material and, Gouroull realized a moment later, were in the shape of tombs and mausoleums. This was the caste system of Selene: the more prestigious the vampire, the more sizable the crypt. Younger vampires possessed tombs no larger than a shed; older ones were granted mausoleums larger than most manor houses. None were as impressive as the towers of the Elders, but they were still remarkable in their own way. Unlike the blank-walled spires, these tombs possessed intricate designs, gargoyles, devils and monsters, though no angelic or religious symbols were visible.

Selene was as silent as the land surrounding it, a land of the dead whose dwellers walked in silence and spoke in whispers. It was a terrible place, a cemetery whose inhabitants possessed a simulacrum of life. Their doppelganger slaves were only released into the world when the vampires had a need for it. It was said that there was some degree of political maneuverings between the lesser vampires. Their occupation, or perhaps preoccupation, was jockeying for power, attempting to supplant those above their own station and change caste. None, according to legends, were ever invited in the spires of the Elders, something that went oddly unquestioned by those vampires who lived in the shadows of these monstrous towers.

One structure stood apart from the spires and the crypts: a large, square building, completely unadorned. It was smaller than the towers of the Elders, but more imposing than the tombs of the lesser vampires. The Doric columns outside were larger than many of the crypts and there was a cold stillness that seemed to exude from its dark stone. This was the Great Temple, one of the most important places in Selene. Gouroull had learned of its existence from Orlok. The vampires of Selene had a unique mean of healing which they performed at the Temple. When one of the vampires needed assistance, they would present themselves at the Temple and the dark-hooded priests within would then produce a metal key and insert it into a hole into the vampire's chest. They would then turn the key multiple times, revitalizing the creature's life.

Stopping before a medium-sized tomb with the name Markov etched above a pair of large, ornate double doors, Maude smiled at Gouroull. She was attempting to speak seductively while the cat circled behind.

Turning slightly so he could keep an eye on the feline, Gouroull ignored Maude's attempts to seduce him; she was an unliving doppelganger and her actions were of no interest to him. He had another mission and Maude's prattle, as well as Aiofe's attempts to act like a cat, were nothing more than a distraction.

The tomb's large doors opened with a creak, giving the impression of being moved by the sheer will-power of its occupant. Gouroull remained unimpressed; he knew of beings capable of performing such tricks with the power of their mind; they had proved as weak as any human in the end. True beings of power had no need for showy behavior. Their power and strength were enough; nothing more was required. That was Gouroull's way and he lacked respect for anyone who did not operate in that manner.

Lady Boyana Markov stepped out of the crypt, her movements a smooth action similar to that of a prima ballerina. It appeared as if she was gliding across the stone ground, her steps a mere whisper as she approached. But the Bulgarian vampire looked like anything but an artistic figure. Lady Boyana Markov was a squat, bullet-shaped woman with a dumpy body and a large round head. Her face looked like that of an English Bulldog, complete with jowls and prominent teeth. Her hair was a colorless blonde that fell just above her shoulders. Lady Boyana Markov was dressed in a red riding jacket, knee-high boots and jodhpurs, none of which fit her undistinguished, soft body. There was an air of neglect and carelessness about her, as if her many years of existence had become weights that pressed her down and turned her into a pathetic figure.

"Hello, my children," she intoned. Her voice was a low rasp, as if she was unused to speaking aloud. "Have you brought us a new friend? It has been too long since you gifted us with someone worthwhile to join our ranks."

"This wonderful and powerful man helped rescue myself and poor Aiofe from Orlok's evil hordes," Maude said, practically bouncing in place. "He is so strong, my lady—far stronger than that Dutch muscle man your rival employs. I hope we have done well, my lady!"

Lady Boyana Markov walked a slow circle around Frankenstein's creation, examining him the way a buyer would a horse. Her narrow mouth broke into a small smile and she slowly nodded.

"Yes. He will do very well, my daughters. I shall take him and we shall use his power to supplant several of my rivals. Aiofe, I grant you your form again."

With a neglectful wave, Lady Boyana Markov turned her attention back to Gouroull. Behind her, Aiofe suddenly stood where her cat form had previously sat. She was tall, willowy woman, completely naked, with a skin so pale that it almost appeared transparent. She possessed high aristocratic cheekbones, huge brown eyes and tiny teeth visible beneath her broad, sensual lips.

Gouroull watched Lady Boyana Markov with mild interest. Their powers were interesting in some ways, but did not seem especially threatening. Possibly the Eldest of their kind could produce enough bodies to become something of a danger, but he doubted that very much. They were so sedentary, so set in their ways, that they could never contemplate a being such as the one created by Victor Frankenstein. The destruction of their doppelgangers would shock and terrify them, rendering them unable to react. Ancient beings with some degree of power often forgot that their most impressive past was not a guarantee of continued existences. New monsters emerged and some of those, like Gouroull, viewed these ancient creatures as a challenge—or threats to be destroyed.

Lady Boyana Markov stopped circling Frankenstein's creature and opened her mouth wide. A long, red, prehensile tongue shot from her gaping maw, a twin forked muscle that sailed straight for Gouroull's neck with the speed of an attacking adder. This was the method the vampires of Selene used to capture their victims and absorb them into their own beings. For every stolen life, the vampire grew more powerful—as well as more fearful of losing his or her own extended life.

But unlike ordinary humans, Gouroull was no victim. His huge hand flashed out and grabbed the tongue as it was still inches away from his throat. The organ wriggled uselessly in his iron grip, as a light scream emerged from Lady Boyana Markov's mouth. Her two doppelgangers shrieked and leaped upon Gouroull, their inhuman fists striking his body without any visible effect.

Before Maude could reach for her giant hammer, Gouroull struck. Pulling the tongue closer, he bit down on it, severing it from Lady Boyana Markov's body. The vampire screeched in agony, falling to the ground and retracting the remainder of her prehensile organ into her mouth and scrambling away from Frankenstein's creature. Aiofe and Maude stood in shocked horror. Then, they ran to their mistress's side. Gouroull watched them retreat, an amused look on his hideous visage. They were heading towards the giant temple, the source of much of Selene's power.

Pocketing the tongue in a pouch on his hip, Gouroull followed the vampire and her two slaves at a leisurely pace. West required two items from Selene: the first was the tongue of one of its vampires; the second, he would obtain inside the Temple. The little doctor's list was extensive and detailed, but posed no real challenge to one such as Gouroull.

Selene might have proved difficult, since one could only gain entry if invited by one of its inhabitants, but Orlok's attack had made that problem easy. The ancient vampire would be at the gates, waiting for his payment to have facilitated Gouroull's access to Selene. They were neither friends, nor allies; there was no doubt that someday, Gouroull and Orlok would battle each other, but for now, they had a common cause.

Gouroull continued his leisurely pace, reaching the bottom of the Temple's black stone stairs as Lady Boyana Markov and her slaves entered the building. Minutes later, he was inside. It was even darker than the city—a stygian darkness broken only by the meager light of several oddly shaped torches along the walls. Gouroull ignored everything, uncaring about the ways of these vampires. The only area of interest to him was a raised platform located in the center of the room. Lady Boyana Markov was kneeling before it as she was being approached by a tall, spectral being in a dark robe.

Gouroull smiled. Pushing aside the vampire and her slaves, he grabbed the dark priest's arm and plucked the intricate brass key from his fingers. This was the second ingredient Herbert West needed; apparently the metal of the key was unique and essential to the creation of his mate.

With a snarl, Gouroull threw the dark priest back onto Lady Boyana Markov and her slaves, his yellow eyes daring them to attack him. But they just lay there, like broken figures on the floor of the dark temple.

Heading out of the temple, Gouroull left the vampire city of Selene, heading for the gate to meet with Orlok. No doubt, the ancient vampire would now try to proclaim himself master of the Vampire City. But what happened to Selene was of no interest to Frankenstein's creature. His quest would continue regardless.

CHAPTER VII

The village of Mykos was a peaceful hamlet on the Aegean coast. Its inhabitants were an insular, quiet people, mostly fishermen or somehow related to the fishing industry. The town was self-sufficient, rarely needing to contact a doctor or any outside authorities. Their taxes were paid without fail and governments appeared disinclined to risk changing the balance that had kept the town from ever becoming an issue. The law-enforcement officers, tax collectors, and the likes, would visit Mykos for their scheduled rounds without fail. They found little changed there and would leave, wishing all the other villages would be so easy to control.

Outsiders rarely stayed in Mykos longer than a day, finding a disquieting atmosphere beneath the calm appearance of the town. The people were polite to a fault, but disinclined to share anything beyond what one could see from basic observation. There appeared to be no loud parties, no gossiping; the girls never flirted with the local boys or strangers visiting town. Attempts to draw the people into closer contact proved impossible; it was almost as if the whole town was a façade for outside visitors, providing the barest minimum of human contact possible.

Mykos was an odd place, but locals in other towns would merely shrug and remark that its people were no threat since the village had been founded so many years ago. They were content to buy its fish, which was always plentiful and for sale at reasonable prices, and leave the Mykosians to their own lives. If they were secretive, at least it was known that nothing unholy or deranged ever happened in that town. The few people who stayed in Mykos always returned safely and no odd happenings were ever heard of, even in tall tales and local legends.

The closest the town had to an "event" was its spring festival, which outsiders always reported was far duller than those of other nearby towns. The dances were performed with a bored precision and the locals treated the event with the same dull doggedness they used for working their fishing boats. Alcohol and smoking were apparent, but the people seemed to be going through the motions rather than celebrating the beginning of spring. Word was passed around the district of the boredom one felt at the Mykos festival and those wishing to travel would search for more enjoyable locations.

Elina Lasko understood how others felt when visiting Mykos. A lifelong inhabitant, she and her family had resided in the town since time immemorial. Her mother told stories of how King Leonidas had visited briefly and found their ancestors uninterested in either his protection or his threats. The legendary warrior king had left Mykos, confused but content with the gold he had been offered as a gift. There were many such stories throughout their history; her mother, like all the women in town, recited these tales to the children as a part of their upbringing, along with the admonition to keep silent and only repeat the stories to those of the village.

Oddly enough, all the children complied, even Elina who was known to be a bit rebellious. A pretty girl of 16, she possessed the finest mind in the town and often asked questions the others found disquieting. Yet, when the time came to talk to an outsider, a young medical student traveling throughout the countryside for pleasure, she found herself as polite and disinclined to speak as anyone else in Mykos. This surprised Elina, since she

had been determined to speak and flirt with the first outsider boy she found attractive. That way, she could learn
more of the outside world, possibly even leave town and
experience a different type of life. But no, the minute
this occurred, she found herself as muted as the other
women in town.

Walking past her father, who sat on a bench with
three other fishermen staring at the ocean, Elina walked
away from the town square where her mother, sister and
grandmother were finishing the decorations for the celebration. The men never joined in or helped prepare the
feast; as they did every day after fishing, they sat together and spoke of fishing. Nothing else, no other topic of
conversation, seemed to emerge from their lips at any
time of the day, any day of the year. None of them
would argue, joke, disagree or even laugh; they just
spoke of different catches and types of nets until it was
time to leave and return home. There was a sheep-like
passivity among them, as if they were mere shells of
humanity whose only function was to fish and assist in
the production of children. For Mykos always had had a
great many children, with new ones born every year.

In the distance, Elina could see her brother and
cousins swimming with the others, the chosen ones who
were allowed to spend as much time as they chose in the
calm waters of the lagoon near the sea. They were an
odd bunch, who shunned outsiders in favor of their own
company. And it was no wonder, their big unblinking
eyes and hairless scabrous bodies were disturbing to see.
But, as the chosen ones, they were excluded from work
and kept out-of-sight when outsiders visited Mykos.

Elina turned away, wishing she could flee from this
town, but knowing she would never get past the out-
skirts. She had tried many times, but found herself al-

ways turning around and, against her will, returning. But now the inclination was stronger. For tonight, she would be one of the Spring Maidens, one of the eight girls in town presented to the sea as an offering. If she was worthy, Elina would return within a month, pregnant with her first child and given to one of the eight young men. Then her new husband would fish with the other men and she would raise the children, tell the tales of Mykos and help arrange the next year's festival.

The unworthy boys and girls, the ones unable to produce children, would never return, taken by their friends from the underwater city of Yha-Nlhe-te, never to be seen again. It was said that their friends, known to some as the Deep Ones, consumed the unworthy, but most believed their bodies were used to help keep the fishing plentiful. Elina didn't believe that story, having seen the frog-like faces of their friends and knowing there was something sinister about their people. Icos, her brother, was becoming one of the Deep Ones, though he and the rest of the chosen always called themselves *Dagon's Children*. They slowly became less interested in having any contacts with anyone but their own, swimming for long periods of time, day or night, and sleeping in the stone huts closest to the sea. Icos was almost bald; his ears seemed to have shrunk and his skin was now a grotesque greenish brown that was flaking off all the time. She found him repulsive, but others seemed to think he and the other chosen ones were to be envied. Elina merely pitied them and wished for a life more interesting than the one left to her by her ancestors.

A sound off to her right caused Elina to turn and she instantly recognized the tall, powerful form of her mother, Lydia Lasko. She was a true beauty, considered the most beautiful woman in the village. Tall, curvaceous and strong, she had thick jet black hair that fell to her waist and large expressive dark eyes. To Elina, she always resembled the living embodiment of the ancient Greek Goddess Artemis, wild and untamed, strong and unyielding. There was an old statue that resembled her in a cave near the sea, still standing proudly despite the many thousands of years. Perhaps one of their ancestresses had been its model, since she looked like a younger version of her mother.

"Elina!"? Lydia called out, stepping into the light. "Why are you not helping prepare for the festival? There are never enough hands! We have so much to do before our friends arrive!"

"Mother..." Elina started to say, wanting to express her dissatisfaction with her life and future.

Bearing a child of a Deep One, spending all her time producing babies with a man who was barely capable of anything beyond fishing and producing more children, was more like a prison sentence than a life! But Lydia recognized the look and the tone of voice her mother was using. Lydia understood her daughter's fears.

"Elina, my child, I know what you are thinking. I felt the same fear myself when I was your age."

Elina crossed her arms across her chest.

"I doubt that, Mother. You are happy and content with your life! But I find our village dull, I want more!"

"As did I when I was your age," Lydia replied, her voice edged with anger but still quiet. "I thought Mykos was too small. I could be famous, as a dancer or an actress. But then, I went with our friends to their home beneath the waves..."

"Is that what changed you, Mother? I want to see the world. Why would seeing a place under the sea change that?" Elina asked, almost begging, hoping her mother was wrong.

"I saw Yha-Nlhe-te," Lydia intoned, her eyes desperate as she stepped closer to her daughter. "It was so different... Our friends are ancient and their city was not designed by the minds of men. It is wondrous and terrible, ancient and powerful... They are so much more than we, and I learned the truth of our friends."

"What truth?" Elina sighed.

Despite herself, she wanted to know. There had to be a reason why her village had remained unchanged for thousands of years, and her mother was the first one who would answer her questions on that subject.

"That the Deep Ones need us," Lydia explained, her voice almost a whisper. "They can no longer produce young ones, so we help them. In return, they give us good fishing—and gold, if we ask."

"Why should that matter?" Elina demanded, almost shouting. "If they cannot survive, they will die in the end. Why do we need to stay here, unable to do anything else with our lives but fish and make babies?"

"Because they protect us, child!" Lydia exclaimed, grabbing her daughter's arm. "There is a race of monsters called Mi-Go, horrific creatures with wings like bats! Our friends protect us from those monsters who would otherwise enslave us and even steal our bodies! We save all the people of the world by helping the Deep Ones, by serving them as they protect us from those evil creatures!"

"Have you ever seen these Mi-Go's, Mother?" Elina screamed, trying to pull free of her mother's powerful grip. "No! Because it's all lies told you by the Deep Ones, who made us their slaves! Well, I won't do it! I'd rather throw myself off a cliff than let one of those disgusting monsters touch me!"

But Lydia was far too strong for Elina. Her hands held the teen girl in a clasp of iron.

"You will obey! No daughter of Mykos has ever refused our friends in over ten thousand years! No child of mine will be the first. You are going to march down to the sea and embrace the father of your first child!"

Lydia shook Elina and dragged her along, heading not for the town, but the shore where Icos and the other Children of Dagon swam.

"No!" Elina shrieked, fighting her mother with all her strength.

But Lydia was just too powerful, her strength almost inhuman as she pulled her daughter down the path. Elina's struggle was futile and she soon found herself at the shore.

Lydia pinned her daughter's arms behind her back and waited.

"Your true husband will know where you are," she hissed in her daughter's ear. "He will come. You will go with him. You struggle now—that has happened in the past—but once he places his hand on your face, you will do just as he asks."

Elina was about to reply, when a shadow fell over both women. The Children of Dagon suddenly went silent, their huge eyes staring, their too-wide mouths open and unspeaking. Lydia stiffened and released her daughter, shocked by what she beheld.

The man behind them was a giant, eight feet tall with a chalky gray skin. His eyes were an unusual shade of yellow and his thick black hair resembled the pelt of an animal. His black lips peeled back over his skull-like face, like the coiling a snake, revealing sharp, serrated teeth.

The giant watched Elina and Lydia with a detached amusement, neither approaching them nor completely ignoring the two women.

"Who are you? Get away from here!" Icos cried, stepping from the surf. "You are not wanted here!"

The man watched Icos approach, his body as still as a statue, his eyes tracking the naked Child of Dagon as he approached.

Icos was naked, his greenish blue skin flaking as he stepped onto the sand. There was something completely inhuman about him, as if he was more Deep One than human. He pointed at the intruder with a clawed, semi-webbed hand and hissed a series of words that made no sense to any human ear.

Gouroull stood watching the half-human creature as he stepped forward in a lopping gait, continuing to hiss at him in an ancient tongue. He had a stench that was quite memorable: part human, part fish, part something old—and corrupt. His claws were black and sharp, obviously a product of his transformation. Yet he seemed unimportant, so Gouroull just stood and waited.

The other Children of Dagon stepped from the sea, joining in the hissing and pointing, an inhuman chorus focused on Frankenstein's creature. But eventually, they grew silent, surprised by the giant's lack of apparent interest in both their threats and inhuman appearance.

It was Icos who broke the silence, stepping forward and swinging his claws at the outsider's eyes. Gouroull backhanded the fish-human man aside, his enormous arm moving at an inhuman speed, shattering the young man's skull.

Icos crashed into his brethren, who stared in shock at his lifeless body.

"Move aside," a sibilant voice called from behind the Children.

They quickly stepped aside, revealing a creature almost as tall as Gorouull. The newcomer was even further away from humanity than the Children of Dagon. Standing over seven feet tall, he possessed grayish green skin that was covered his wide, ridged scales. His belly and torso were a sickly white. He, too, possessed long, webbed hands that ended in dark talons. But it was his face that was his most frightening feature: shaped like an enormous frog, with huge, unblinking green eyes, it was a monstrous mixture of frog and man. This was one of the Deep Ones, creatures that had ruled parts of the Earth long before mankind.

The Deep One smelled like undiluted corruption, beyond either humanity or fish-kind, an even stranger scent than that of the hybrids standing nearby. There was something utterly alien about him, as if he was not truly of the Earth.

This, in itself, did not frighten Gorouull, who was as alien as this creature. But the fact that the Deep Ones had once ruled the Earth was interesting, since Frankenstein's creature, too, had designs upon the world. Testing this monster would be an important lesson for the future.

"You are not human," the Deep One croaked, flexing his talons. "You should leave."

Gorouull smiled, his teeth even more prominent.

"I have a use for you, Deep One."

The Deep One croaked and hissed, hopping forward and slashing at Gorouull with his talons. But Frankenstein's Monster grabbed his wrists and pushed back.

The Deep One possessed surprising strength. He strained against Gouroull with calm, inhuman force. His neck gills raised and lowered slowly as he pressed against his enemy. But it was Frankenstein's creation that proved the stronger, snapping both of the Deep One's wrists and shoving the creature back into the surf.

The Deep One croaked loudly, a shrieking sound horrific in its inhumanity. It turned and leaped back into the sea, moving far slower than usual due to his injuries.

The Children of Dagon screamed, running towards Gouroull, only to be swept aside quickly by the monster's massive strength.

Then Gouroull walked into the sea, going after the Deep One, disappearing from sight.

Lydia ran towards the fallen form of Icos as the cries of the Deep Ones resounded throughout Mykos. Her own screams of loss could be heard by all, bringing the villagers to the site of the attack. '

The festival was never completed that year and the fishing was dismal; the villagers barely survived the harsh winter. As for Elina, she fled from Mykos that day, never to return or live anywhere near a body of water.

Two days later, Gouroull stepped out of the sea, a medium-sized chunk of stone in his pallid hand. West's list included a piece from a city of the Deep Ones. How Pretorius had obtained such a difficult item, or possessed the knowledge critical to use it, were mysteries that Gouroull would solve one day in the future. But for now, another item had been crossed off West's list.

CHAPTER VIII

Moreau struck the beast-men's back with a whip and snarled:

"Do you remember the house of pain? What is the law?"

The Sayer of the Law began the chant:

"Not to go on all-fours, *that* is the Law. Are we not men?"

The many beast-men gathering before the castle's walls called out in response, their voices high, low, croaking and growls. But none sounded even a little bit human.

"Are we not men?"

The Sayer of the Law continued, his voice even more inhuman than the others. But he was the easiest to understand and by far the smartest of Moreau's hybrid monsters.

"Not to suck up drink, *that* is the Law. Are we not men?"

"Are we not men?" the beast-men all replied again, their eyes still on Moreau's whip and the House of Pain back in the castle.

"Not to eat flesh or fish *that* is the Law. Are we not men?" the Sayer of the Law's voice rose as he chanted.

"Are we not men?" the beast-men growled in response.

The Sayer of the Law looked to his people in challenge:

"Not to claw the bark of trees; *that* is the Law. Are we not men?"

None challenged him, many hung their heads.

"Are we not men?" they asked.

"Not to chase other men, *that* is the Law. Are we not men?" the Sayer of Law asked in finality, crossing his arms across his broad, hairy chest.

"Are we not men?" the beast-men replied, knowing the ritual had come to an end and Moreau would pass judgment.

Moreau's whip was coiled but still in hand.

"Puma-Bear ate fish and clawed a tree. I could bring him to the House of Pain, but I will give him a chance. He will be hunted by a man. This man, Count Zaroff, will hunt Puma-Bear for two days. If Puma-Bear survives, he will be forgiven. If he is captured, he will return to the House of Pain. If he dies, he is not a man, but a beast, and is unworthy of the Law."

"Why does Count-Man hunt us? Men do not hunt men. Are we not men?" the Sayer of the Law demanded, stepping a little closer.

Moreau uncoiled the whip, but did not raise the weapon. The threat of the whip was often enough to keep the beast-men at bay, but today, more might be needed. This was a new element in the creatures' collective lives.

"Count Zaroff is a great hunter. He hunted down beasts in every part of the world, but beasts are too easy for him to kill. He now wants to hunt men—men wise and strong enough to survive. Only a man can survive this great hunter. Man thinks. Beasts have no laws. Do you have the laws?"

"We have the Law," the Sayer of the Law replied, his growling voice low and threatening. "And the Law is not to chase other men, *that* is the Law. Are we not men?"

"Are we not men?" the beasts called back, advancing slightly.

Moreau cracked the whip above the beast-men's heads.

"You are not to chase. You will be chased by a man. If you are fast and wise, you will survive. If you are beasts, you will die. Are you not men?"

"We are men," the Sayer of the Law answered and dropped his hands, signaling an end of the conflict. "If Puma-Bear lives, he is a man. If he dies, he is a beast. If is put in bars, he goes to the House of Pain. That is the Law."

The beast-men, lead by the Sayer of the Law, dispersed, heading back to their village a short distance away. Their growls and howls echoed through the trees and Moreau had no doubt they would be restless that night. But they did accept the hunt by Count Zaroff, which was the one dangerous part of the events of the night.

Heading into the small castle, Marie Moreau coiled her whip and sighed quietly. Introducing new elements into the lives of her beast-men was dangerous. It took weeks of pain and punishment to get them to learn the law, but her father's methods were perfect. The threat of the whip or the House of Pain—her laboratory—taught them that the rules she set forth were absolute. Plus, they had a simplistic view of the universe, so there were methods for adding new things to their current lives.

Marie Moreau was a short woman, only slightly above five feet tall in her heeled boots, with long blond hair that fell across her shoulders and down her back. She had a sharp, hard-edged face and small, blue eyes. Her figure was lithe and tight, almost boyish. Marie was not a beautiful woman, but her ramrod stiff back caused many to view her as a striking woman, one whose no-nonsense air and intelligent brow caused many in the past to walk carefully around her. Abandoned by her father as a child, she was fascinated by the tales of his genius. His notes were sent to her after his unfortunate death, at which time she completed her medical education and determined to prove his genius to the world.

But how to do that best? London, Paris, Rome and Berlin were filled with cretins who believed the Moreau legacy was tainted. Chased out of each and branded a vivisectionist, Marie realized her father had found the best solution. Seducing a Greek official with her body and a small payment, she obtained exclusive ownership of the small volcanic island of Fotia. The island was perfect, uninhabited but close to Crete, possessing a lush forest and room for a large dwelling. She had imported a Austrian castle belonging to a long-dead family named Karnstein, set up her laboratory, and begun her work.

Money was a little hard to come by, the Cretan and Greek captains charged extra to come to Fotia. Then came Zaroff, a man with a noble title and a great deal of money. He replenished Marie's accounts, only asking for the chance to hunt one of her beast-men. As she was always creating more, this was not a terribly difficult request. The beast-men were unfinished creatures, in need of scientifically-created evolution. Her work would improve, she as certain a breakthrough was imminent, and she needed more time and money. It was an acceptable solution.

Zaroff was waiting for her in the main hall. He was a tall, powerfully-built man with a thick full beard and mustache. He was dressed in a black uniform without any adornments and was smoking a large cigar that smelled like burning rope. His dark eyes were ever watchful and he wore a neutral smile upon his face. A thick scar was visible on his head, the result of a dangerous hunt against a Cape Buffalo, according to one of his many tales.

"You were successful, dear lady?" Zaroff asked, exhaling a small stream of smoke into the air.

His manner was unaffected and relaxed, but she could sense the anticipation in his eyes.

"Yes," Marie Moreau replied, hooking her whip into her belt. "The beasts will not interfere with your hunt for two days. If you or your servants go even one minute past two days, they will attack you en masse. And I couldn't stop their assault; threats or beatings wouldn't stop them from tearing the three of you to pieces."

"I am not concerned," Zaroff replied, smiling and visibly relaxing. "If I cannot hunt down your Puma-Bear creature, it deserves its freedom. I believe in the rules of the hunt. My servants will release our prey momentarily. I shall send them a signal, if I may?"

Marie nodded and watched as Zaroff lifted an odd wooden whistle to his lips, blowing a loud and oddly melodious series of notes. He blew the notes a second time and placed the whistle back in his uniform jacket pocket.

"A Tartar hunting call," Zaroff explained as they headed deeper into the castle. "I picked up the skill in my youth. There are still tribes in Siberia who hunt with bows and live entirely off the land, just as their forefathers did for thousands of years. I learned their ways, hunting tigers with only a Tartar bow and a sword. It was a pleasure for a time, but became quite dull. That is the sad truth of hunting animals—even the most dangerous become dull after a short time."

They were met a moment later by Zaroff's servants. They were twins, giant, muscular men with strong bodies and huge jaws. They were named Igor and Ivan and they loved to sing roaring Russian drinking songs day and night.

"My Lord Count, Doctor Madame," Ivan said, clicking his heels. He possessed a strong, melodious voice that was a pleasure to hear. "We have released the odd creature into the woods. The dogs are ready and we can begin at any time."

"Excellent," Zaroff replied, a gleam in his eyes.

The bloodlust of the hunt was growing within him and, in a short time, he would hunt a beast with the mind of a man. A true adversary for the first time!

"Enjoy your hunt, Count," Marie Moreau said, with a brief smile to the Count and his men. "I have no idea when the next violation will occur amongst my beast-men. But your payments are more than welcome, if and when such an incident occurs. Now, if you will excuse me, I must return to my laboratory. My work is at a critical stage."

Marie disliked being forced to indulge in pleasantries, but Zaroff and his men were good guests. Igor proved an excellent chef; Ivan was a singer with operatic level skills, and the Count possessed a host of amusing anecdotes that interested Marie despite herself. Despite her dislike of humanity, these three were welcome to her island... as long as they paid the same high price in gold.

She was about to turn, when the main door to the castle burst open. Grabbing for her whip and pistol, Marie wondered. Had the Sayer of the Law and his followers violated their agreement? It seemed unlikely, but her father had died at the hands of his creations and she would not allow herself to fall victim in the same manner.

But the creature stepping into the light of the hall was nothing like the monstrosities of her island. Standing over eight feet tall with skin paler than marble, this monster was a sight straight out of a nightmare. The twisted slabs of muscle that covered his soaking wet body, as well as the dark, stringy hair that lay plastered on his head and shoulders, added to the terrible image. But it was his inhuman yellow eyes that stared at them that sent chills up Marie Moreau's spine. After years of dealing with horrible hybrids, she had imagined herself immune from fear. But this man, this demon, or whatever he was, certainly was something not meant to live upon this Earth. He was the embodiment of the word abomination, a life that should not exist.

"What do you want? Who are you? What are you?" she asked, her voice rising in panic.

Count Zaroff, a trained hunter of wild beasts since childhood, was unafraid. He had killed polar and kodiak bears larger than this giant. He knew that better than anyone that the right attack would destroy anything. Normally, he would merely have pulled the small pistol he kept in his waistband and executed this grotesque peasant, but that would be a waste of his time. Instead, he waved a hand and ordered:

"Igor, kill this intruder. Then join us on the trail with the canteens and food for the hounds."

"Yes, my Lord." Igor rumbled.

The giant Russian servant pulled out his hunting blade and stepped forward, lunging at the intruder. His knife glinted in the light as he stabbed the newcomer in the stomach, a move he had perfected while serving the Count and dealing with peasants' revolts on the nobleman's lands. Many had sought to challenge the Count over the years, demanding equal treatment under the law and the right to keep some of the food they grew. Igor and Ivan dealt with such fools, killing them with their own hands as examples to others, and with weapons when they didn't wish to waste time beating their victims to death.

But this intruder was Gouroull, the lethal creation of Victor Frankenstein, far more terrible than all of the beast-men of Fotia, a being of frightening power and far less humanity. While Moreau's creatures looked closer to animals than men, they strived to follow the laws and standards of civilization. Gouroull had no such impulses; his mind was alien, terrible, a fiendish intelligence capable of unspeakable acts worse than even the worst mankind could offer.

Gouroull's hand shot out and grabbed Igor's fist, crushing both bones and knife handle instantly. His towering height made the huge Russian look like a child next to Frankenstein's terrible creation. Just as Igor was about to scream, Gouroull bit down on the Russian's throat, ending the man's life instantly.

As Gouroull tossed Igor's lifeless form aside, Ivan was already upon him, his powerful hands grasping the monstrous throat. Frankenstein's creature smiled, his blood-covered face adding a demonic look to his countenance. Despite himself, he was amused by Ivan's attempt to kill him. He clapped his hands against the Russian's ears, shattering his auditory functions completely. Then, with a negligent slap, he shattered Ivan's throat and pushed him aside. Perhaps this human would live, perhaps not. He didn't care either way and all but forgot both Russians.

With a war-like cry of fury, Count Zaroff pulled his pistol from his jacket and fired. The bullet struck Gouroull where his heart should be, but still he moved forward. Zaroff smiled and raised his gun, aiming for the monster's horrific, yellow eyes. Gouroull, his bloodied face looking even more monstrous, leaped forward and snatched the gun from the Russian nobleman's grip. Snapping it in half, he lifted Zaroff off the ground by his neck. Watching the man dangle in his grip, turning purple in the process, Gouroull grinned again and slammed his prey to the floor. Several of Zaroff's bones snapped under the impact.

Stepping over Zaroff's fallen form, Gouroull loomed over the tiny Marie Moreau, looking down on her with his alien eyes. He paused for a moment, knowing that his very presence and actions were terrifying enough, and that anticipation of more violence was as great a weapon as the actual violence itself. Finally he spoke, his voice more inhuman than any Marie had ever hers. It was a sound that would haunt her nightmares for years to come.

"Paracelsus's formula. I want a sample. Now."

Gouroull raised a gigantic blood-stained fist towards Marie Moreau.

She was shocked that this monster knew her father's work so well. Doctor Moreau had found an obscure formula created by the famed philosopher who had changed the world with his views on chemistry and medicine. Combining that with his own work, he had created the beast-men. Nobody knew the truth of Moreau's formula, so she was surprised this monster was aware of it.

Part of her wanted to argue, to delay, but one look into that monstrous face, those yellow eyes, ended such protests in her throat. She reached into the black leather pouch on her waist and handed Gouroull a small vial filled with a yellow liquid. Marie then closed her eyes, preparing to meet a fate similar to that of Count Zaroff and his men—a blow of such stunning power that it would destroy her pathetic frame.

But such an assault never arrived. Opening her eyes, she realized that the demonic being was gone. Kneeling down, she began to check the fallen Count and his men. Zaroff would be in pain but would recover; Igor was dead; Ivan was terribly maimed—she doubted he would ever hear or speak again.

Meanwhile, Gouroull placed the vial in the bag he used for the ingredients from West's list. Walking into the sea, he tossed aside the bullet that had penetrated an inch or so into his skin and headed for his next destination.

The list was almost complete...

CHAPTER IX

Lord Ruthven brushed some imaginary lint from his silken white shirt and settled himself with slow deliberation in the large throne-like chair. According to the antique dealer, it had been originally built for one of the Medici Popes. Which one, Ruthven could not recall, but the story was good enough for the sale.

Lord Ruthven enjoyed the idea of ruling his growing empire while seated in a chair that had once presided over the world's affairs. After all, that was his ultimate goal: power and control of the lesser beings that walked upon the Earth.

And he truly was on the path to power these days. Having recovered from a terrible act of treachery by an Englishman named Lord Wilmore, he had determined to no longer live merely as another undead leech upon society. Ruthven enjoyed moving among the greats of society and seizing the wealth, not to mention the blood and lives, of the unwary—but as that enough? Not anymore. Ruthven knew he needed to be in control, to become the power that others answered to. It took some time, but he eventually discovered the best and simplest path towards his goal: crime. More specifically, the criminal organizations that thrived throughout Europe and earned enormous sums of money from their illegal trade and assassinations.

There were many such groups to choose from, but he discovered one that fit best his needs: secretive, loyal, dangerous and almost forgotten, a former brotherhood in the heart of Italy known as the Camorra and based in Naples. It had once been the cradle of the notorious

Veste Nere, but had long since been abandoned to its own fate by its former masters. Ruthven had seized control of the Camorra through deals and violence, becoming one of the most feared criminal overlords in Southern Italy. That still had not been enough and the English nobleman had set his sights to greater heights. Rome was the next city he wished to fall under the rule of his secretive brotherhood.

It was there that trouble ensued. Not with the local authorities—they were far more concerned with the war. And certainly not with the church—they had no idea he was a vampire able to hold a cross and walk on holy ground. No, the trouble was far more profound and ironic. The difficulty was another Englishman named Sir Francis Varney.

Varney, for Ruthven refused to refer to him by his supposed knighthood, was also a victim of the vampire curse. He, too, had ambitions and an ability to survive nearly any disaster, having done so in some incident involving a volcano—or so he bragged. Varney had allied himself with a savage gang of barbaric bandits from Sicily, equally devoted to obtaining power through threats, intimidation and violence. The Sicilian group, known as the Brotherhood of Silence, also determined to take control of Rome. Small scale warfare ensued and nobody was profiting by the slowly growing battle.

Ruthven despised the Brotherhood; they lacked the artistry and honor of the Camorra. Their tactics were reminiscent of the Visigoths and Huns who had marched on the weakened Rome so many centuries in the past. They had little to no appreciation of the beauty and majesty of the ancient city and her many treasures. To them, Rome was merely a source of money, an asset to liquidate. The way Ruthven saw it, the Brotherhood was closer to fleas sucking on the blood of a rat.

But, despite being lesser beings, even for humans, the Sicilians did possess that insane fury that made them a growing power in criminal circles. That they were barbarians was certain; but even savages can be incredibly dangerous and successful with the proper mind guiding them. And—Ruthven hated admitting even this much—Varney was proving an able and powerful leader. His organization was preventing the Camorra from advancing past their currently established position. Neither side was committed to full warfare, too afraid that both sides would end up losing, which meant that their conflict was purposefully kept to a small scale. Little skirmishes over control of some small neighborhoods, with neither side advancing to any major degree.

Then, Lord Ruthven discovered a method for eliminating the mind behind the Brotherhood's success: a being capable of destroying even the powerful vampires, one with an agenda of its own. The answer was the fruit of the legendary experiments of the late Victor Frankenstein—a terrible creature known as Gollroull. This monster was haunting Europe, attacking various inhuman beings for his own, still obscure, reasons and leaving untold destruction it his wake. Ruthven had monitored Gouroull for some time, realizing at last that the Monster was searching for something specific: the location of a very specific legendary creature.

Happily, Ruthven knew precisely how to assist Frankenstein's creature and sent two of his disciples to make contact with him. They never returned, but, one day, Gouroull suddenly appeared in Lord Ruthven's study.

He looked as frightful as the legends claimed: huge, inhuman and completely alien. Ruthven could barely repress a shudder when he looked into those bestial yellow eyes. His sharp fangs didn't frighten the elder vampire; he could grow just as many should the need arise. But the outlandish and terrifying nature of Frankenstein's creature did fill the undead warlord with some trepidation, a trace of a most unfamiliar feeling: fear.

Suppressing the sensation, Ruthven cleared his throat dramatically; his cold gray eyes locked in on Gouroull's sickly yellow orbs. Showing his own sharp fangs, Ruthven smiled and whispered:

"I am told you seek the risen dead, but not mere mindless undead. Revenants of some power. A true rarity. Is this so?"

"Yes," Gouroull rasped, studying the preening vampire.

He sat like a fat spider in the center of his web, full of his power and greatness, forgetting that he was little better than the insects he consumed. Time would change that feeling.

"I have seen such a one with my own eyes," Ruthven explained, smiling even wider and feeling slightly more confident. "I've had my men check its location, and it is still active, should you wish to proceed. But I will require a small service in exchange such a gift."

"What service?" Gouroull asked, smiling slightly, causing his sharp teeth to glint in the fire light.

"The destruction of the vampire known as Sir Francis Varney," Lord Ruthven replied, leaning forward in his ancient chair. "Bring me proof of his destruction. His head will do. Then I will provide you with a map and exact directions to the place you wish to visit."

He felt like one of the Medici at that moment, ordering the destruction of an enemy while seated in his study.

Gouroull reached into his large pouch and produced an object, large, oval, covered in oilcloth. With a flick of his hand, he tossed it on the table in front of Ruthven. It landed with a heavy *thunk*, rolling to the center before settling on its side.

Ruthven stared at the package, then Gouroull, an unasked question on his lips. Gouroull merely stared back at the vampire, his inhuman eyes providing no clues as to his purpose.

Slowly, his movements tentative, Ruthven reached for and unwrapped the oilcloth parcel. Soft pale skin was immediately visible, followed by dark hair and pointed ears. With a final tug, the face was revealed. It was none other than Sir Francis Varney himself—or more exactly his head. The mouth was covered with a long strip of leather, tied tightly in the back.

"Why is the mouth bound?" Ruthven asked, reaching for the bindings.

"He wouldn't shut up," Gouroull said, just as Varney's eyes opened.

They moved about wildly, his mouth twisting beneath the gag, trying to speak.

Ruthven was about to ask how Varney could speak without a body, but then checked himself. Like himself, Varney was a vampire, a being of legend and unknown powers. It was possible that he and his bodiless enemy could exist forever without a torso. Perhaps they could even grow back all they lost? He didn't know; there was no research on this phenomenon and there never would be if Ruthven had his druthers. He would imprison the head of Varney and watch it carefully over the centuries. This would ensure the future of his plans.

Throwing back his head, Lord Ruthven let forth an inhuman howl, a sound that was part bestial triumph, part sadistic laughter. He spun in a circle, his arms stretched out wide, as he celebrated the defeat of his enemy. His life, though long, was never an easy one. Many times he had been defeated as he was on the verge of a great success. The battle against Varney and his Sicilians had threatened to be just another failure, a painful reminder of the cyclical nature of his existence. But now, the destruction of the Brotherhood would be a simple matter. Varney was their true strength, his monstrous power destroying all who had threatened his savage cohorts. Without his protection, the Brotherhood was little more than a gang of barbarians, easily pushed aside.

With a bow to Gouroull, Ruthven walked over to a desk and leafed through a set of papers. Finding a small blue folder, he removed a single page and approached the giant monster.

"This is a map of a small coastal village in Spain," he explained, handing the map over and showing several different routes to the place in question. "Many centuries ago, a cadre of Knights Templar resided in this area and began to practice black magic. The peasants revolted and hung them all. Some had their eyes burned out; others lost their orbs to the crows. It is something of a theme— they are called the *Muertos Ciego*—the blind dead. This map will lead you to their location precisely. You have my thanks, sir. If you ever require more information, we can make another deal."

Gouroull scrutinized the map for several minutes before slowly folding the paper and placing it in the pouch in his belt. His eyes locked in on Ruthven and he studied the vampire for a moment, before turning away.

"If I may?" Ruthven asked, raising a hand. "How did you know I would wish the head of Varney?"

Gouroull turned and smiled, his teeth glinting.

"Your men told me. Their last words."

"Ah, I thought as much," said Ruthven, nodding. "Such is the way of mortals. They are fragile."

"Not just mortals," Gouroull rasped, as he leaped forward.

He was on Ruthven in less than a heartbeat, his yellow eyes wide with sadistic bloodlust.

The catacombs of Rome were deep, dark and mostly unexplored. Some of the tunnels were thousands of years old, created by people so ancient time itself had forgotten their existence. Gouroull used them to travel about the city. It was a useful secret he might use one day if he needed a place in which to operate.

Sliding aside a large stone, Gouroull found a small tomb. The bones within were little more than dust as no man had walked through this tunnel in centuries. The location was perfect for what he planned to do.

Reaching into the large pouch, he pulled out two objects, placing them both inside the tomb. The heads of Varney and Ruthven, both gagged, stared at him with wild, crazed eyes as he returned the large stone in place, hiding them from view. They would exist like this for centuries. They would likely go mad in days; the rest would merely be pure torture. The thought delighted Gouroull. Now he was off to Spain for the last ingredient needed for the creation of his mate.

CHAPTER X

The town of Berzano was a beautiful location on the Mediterranean coast of Spain. While not a tourist destination, it received regular visitors who were passing through on their way to more popular spots. Occasionally, an academic type would come to investigate the old ruins on the hill, but they were few and far between.

The history of the town was well-known to all in the vicinity and included in several major history books. The ruins were once the keep of the Knights Templar, one of their last holdouts after French king Phillip the Fair had forced the Pope to excommunicate the Order.

Alberto Falaga was just such a tourist, though an uncommon one even by the standards of the town. He was fascinated by the old tales of those long dead knights, the truth of their rituals, and their horrific deaths. Born the second son of a wealthy family of land-owning merchants, Alberto had neither interest nor skill in the areas of business. His father had tried to interest him in the various aspects of their family's empire, but to no avail. Every time he was taken to the warehouses or the office buildings, Alberto would invariably wander off and find some quiet place to read or write. Yelling, pleading and even threats of disinheritance had proved a waste of time.

Finally, it was Alberto's great-aunt, Therese, that had come to grips with the problem. The iron-fisted matriarch of the Falaga clan was unconcerned about Alberto's lack of interest in the business. She thought it best to encourage the young man to pursue other interests. This was a rather curious message from a woman who had once vetoed attempts by Alberto's father to go into a military career, or his brother Diego to start his own automobile firm. When confronted with these truths, the old woman was able to answer with ease.

"Diego and you were merely trying to flee your proper place," Therese explained to her nephews as she spoke to them in her sitting room. "You did not like the notion that you would be forced to work your way up to a seat on the board of directors. You dreamed of adventure—Diego of becoming like Señor Ford! They were children's fantasies, and I stamped them out."

The room was surprisingly small and prim for so grand a woman as Therese Falga-Magro. The few sticks of furniture were neatly arranged and could have easily been purchased for a low price at any bazaar. Only the gold-gilt frame containing the large portrait of her late husband, Carlos, demonstrated any hint of her enormous wealth. Carlos's weak brown eyes seemed to watch Therese in death with the same worshipful and mouse-like fear as it had had in life.

"But Alberto is doing just the same!" Alberto's father stated, holding back the roar of rage he felt inside.

His other two sons were hard-working, unimaginative souls. They would never lead the family; they lacked the inner brilliance necessary for such an elevated position. But Alberto, the boy, was a genius! He could speak full sentences before he was one year old and was classified as a university-level reader at age 10! His foolish interests in history and legends were a waste of time!

"No," Therese' said, shaking her head emphatically. "You are quite wrong. Yes, Alberto has an impressive mind, but not that of a man of business like you, your brother, or my late brother, Gabriel. Put Alberto at the head of our enterprise, and it shall be in ruins within months. His mind looks to higher pursuits."

She held up a withered claw of a hand to prevent any protest.

"Once, I, too, would have despised such a thought," she continued. "But with age comes wisdom. Your son is not suited for our world—yet, he is one of us. We shall help him, use our connections to make him a great man, but in his own world."

Alberto's father sighed heavily, but also knew in his heart that Therese's statements were true. The boy was brilliant, but a dreamer. But then again, great painters were geniuses and many of them were better known than the King himself! It was a hard choice, but he knew better than to try and fight the iron will of the head of the Falaga family.

"What can we do to help Alberto?" he asked finally.

Then, he and his brother listened as Therese set out a path that would make his son a great man in the eyes of the world. After all, a famous son could only help him with all his contacts and his place in the world.

Alberto, unknowingly, accepted his father's change of heart and immediately began a course of study that took him to many famous universities around the world. The University of Salamanca, the Sorbonne, Christ College in Oxford, Harvard, and finally, Miskatonic—all of these schools assisted him in creating his masterwork, a treatise on myths and legends.

The book was a success, thanks in part to his family's influence with the publishers. Now, a member of the University of Barcelona, Alberto was working on a book that would be even more sensational, less academic. The idea had come from a friend in Oxford, who had pointed out the academic influence of men who had worked on popular works, as well as scholarly ones. Alberto agreed with the sentiment and would produce an academic work accessible to the common man—a book of legends of ghosts and monsters in Spain.

The legend of the ghost Templars was an excellent one to begin with for many reasons. They appeared to excite the imagination of scholars and common folk alike. Perhaps that was because the Knights Templar had once been a major power in the world before they were destroyed so quickly? Or perhaps it was due to the many stories about their Order, their secret rites, their lost treasure, and more. Dr. Alberto Falaga was unsure, but the fact that there had been sightings of these eyeless ghosts throughout the years, even into the modern era, excited him. This was the chapter that would ensure that his book would become a worldwide best seller. Then he would return to working on his monograph on the customs on the Day of the Dead.

All the legends of the eyeless ghosts were at a variance from each other; few could agree as to the unholy rituals having been committed by the Knights prior to their execution. Most written and unwritten sources merely referred to these rites as "evil" or "unholy" and stated that the leaders had had their eyes burned out. The remaining knights were strung up and died as crows had picked their eyes. These revolting tales were still believed after 500 years. Therefore, Alberto had come to examine the Templar Keep's ruins and spend an evening or two looking out to the nearby sea, hoping to see a ship full of ghosts.

Opening his notebook, Alberto examined the list of methods he would use to summon the blind Templars from their unpeaceful rest. Blood—he would cut open his hand and sprinkle his blood in the area of their death.

Sex—he had brought a prostitute and they would engage in intercourse there. Even death—he had killed a goat and later cooked and eaten the creature's heart. His last ingredient was strong emotions. This would be a difficult, because strong emotions of any type did not come naturally to Alberto Falaga.

Despite being committed to the study of history and beliefs, Alberto was a man uncomfortable with emotions of any type. His father, mother, brothers and other family members always appeared to be in the throes of some kind of passion. Whether they were screaming at each other over business, politics, or even which spice was best with the chicken meal they were eating, his family were always screaming on some subject or another. Alberto, on the other hand, preferred quiet reasoning, often being forced to wait for them to pause with exhaustion before injecting some logic into the loud debate. This caused the family to view him as "cold" or "emotionless," neither of which was true. If he didn't understand overwhelming emotions, he did feel, and their scorn had hurt him over the years. This was why he had taken a position far away from home, only visiting for special occasions. Distance had made their relationships easier; he was missed then, but he didn't miss their insane emotional responses to all situations.

Seated on a large foundation stone of the ruins, looking out over the waters, Alberto tried to summon up the rage his father felt over politics. Or the near psychotic fury his brother felt every time he was accused of infidelity by his wife. The fact that the accusations were entirely true never seemed to matter; Raphael would scream, foam at the mouth and reach for weapons. Or maybe one of his mother's tantrums when the church's charity sisterhood did not obey her every whim. These all ran through his mind, but try as he might, these strong feelings never appeared. No rages or sorrow, just a general sense of disappointment at his inability to comprehend that aspect of human interaction.

In the end, he reflected, the lack of a final test was unimportant. Alberto was more interested in the legends of such groups rather than the reality. He'd never seen a real ghost, specter, spirit or goblin. The myths and legends were an important aspect of society, one that he was determined to codify. That way, these tales would live on forever, standing the tests of time as had Ancient Egypt. If he could preserve the folklore of humanity, even to a small degree, Alberto knew he would have fulfilled an important duty for the future of civilization.

But part of him did want to complete the tests, so he needed to find a way of getting someone else to experience a strong emotional reaction in this very location. Perhaps if he invited the prostitute back and failed to pay her price? Strong emotions would appear then, but there was a physical risk Alberto didn't like to contemplate... Getting stabbed or beaten to prove there were ghosts in this area didn't appear to be a clever idea. He would sit here for the last time and, in the morning, would finish his notes. Then he would find transport to the port 50 miles away and sail off to his next location, a small town in America called Dunwich. After Dunwich, he heard of several spots in the American South replete with their own stories of monsters and ghosts. That would be sufficient for his Spanish, English and American publishers, all of whom would provide suitably ridiculous and sensational titles for his work. That was the way of the publishing world, an even more difficult business than the many his family owned.

As Alberto stared out onto the water, a wave seemed to be rising in the distance. But he soon realized that what he had taken for a wave was far too small to be a movement of the water. A figure was rising from the seas, a human form, massive in scale. Was this one of the legendary blind Templars, returning to the location of his dreadful execution? Or merely a trick of the light, a phantasm of the mind, caused by sadness and loneliness? Alberto did not know, but he silently moved away from his seat and hid behind a section of gray stone wall, the remains of an outer rampart partially demolished by the maddened villages determined to destroy the unholy rites perpetrated by the Templars. The thought sent a shiver of fear through Alberto. He became excited by the idea of seeing a real ghost walk the Earth before his very eyes!

The figure was indeed that of a man, though enormous in size. The shadows hid him, but, as he approached, more details became apparent. He was far larger than even the tallest man Alberto had ever seen. He remembered the giant from the circus he visited as a child, called the Jersey Giant by the ringmaster; he had been at least seven feet tall. That giant had walked unsteadily, one of his enormous hands clutching a wooden cane that was lengthier than most men. The Jersey Giant appeared to be a sad person in the eyes of the children, but he dutifully put his hand out and let people place theirs against his huge palm. Often two or three hands would be required to equal the size, causing young Alberto to stare with wonder, but also with some sadness for the melancholy of the circus freak.

It was the pallid skin, resembling a type of marble, that caused Alberto to realize that he was not looking at an ordinary man, or even a circus oddity. Giant in size,

137

he could accept; even paler than human was possible; but the combination of the two walking out of the sea to a place where ghosts and revenants supposedly haunted? He knew then that he was seeing a true, otherworldly being in the flesh.

A wave of cold terror filled Alberto as he watched the creature. Despite his enormous size, this monster moved with smooth grace, the type of relaxed play of muscles reserved for only the most dangerous predators. Alberto could see only hints of his face, but one feature sent a wave of cold seat throughout his body.

It was the eyes! They were yellow orbs, larger than a man's, and resembling that of a giant beast. There was a cruel, intense intelligence visible there, as well as an amused contempt. Alberto realized that this fiend could see him clearly, was aware of his fright, and found it quite amusing. But the monster made no move, apparently uninterested in the young academic beyond mirth at the latter's horror.

For his part, Alberto was frozen in place, stupefied by the being before him, unable to flee. He knew there was no he could escape the monster even if he ran away, for that being gave the impression of terrible speed as well as inhuman strength. But moving closer was impossible. Alberto crouched in his poor hiding spot like a rabbit frozen in the gaze of a serpent or a wolf. This fiend could approach him at a slow walk and tear him from limb to limb and Alberto knew he would do no more than squeak like a dying rat.

Yet, the monster appeared disinclined to do so, preferring to turn away and look out over the dark waters. A gray mist began forming, slowly crawling out over the land. The giant appeared unmoving, his stillness granting him an even greater inhumanity than his terrifying appearance. Alberto felt, if possible, a greater fright as this was the first sign of the return of the infamous dead Templars, known to all as the Blind Dead. In every tale he had recorded, the story began with mist filling the area. Then the eyeless monstrosities arrived, sometimes from the waters, other times from the ruins. But the undead always came, with fury in their cold hearts, determined to revenge themselves against the world that had slaughtered them so long ago.

Then, they appeared, tall figures in tattered white robes, their faces skeletal, their eyes empty black pits. They were clad in ruined chained mail and they walked with the unsteady lurch of beings unused to stride upon the Earth. Yet, there was a power about these husks of men, a fear-inducing majesty that caused them to be abominations as great as the giant whom they approached.

Both the creature and the revenants stared at each other, neither moving closer, yet neither fleeing. A low murmur emerged from each—an inhuman sound that caused Alberto to cover his ears for fear of madness. For several minutes, both parties stood, otherworldly beings conferring in a way humanity could never comprehend. Finally, some kind of agreement appeared to have been reached. The leader of the Blind Dead handed over an object to the giant, who took it in his huge hand, examined it and nodded, before turning away. The undead Templars did the same, heading back towards the sea, vanishing mere moments later.

The giant paused a few feet away from Alberto, staring at him with his horrific yellow eyes. He smiled, his teeth suddenly visible beneath his black lips. He lifted the object he held into the light. It was a bone, more properly a finger bone, a white thing even paler than his own skin. The giant deposited it in a large bag, stared again at Alberto, then turned away, vanishing into the night.

Alberto sat frozen for several minutes, aware that his heart was beating as if he had been running for his life. Slowly, his terror diminished and an academic question occurred to him. Had the Blind Dead come because of his emotional reaction to the fiend that had just left? Or had they come because that creature was encroaching upon their sacred place? He didn't know and likely would never find the answer, but one thing was certain: Alberto Falaga would no longer seek the ghosts and hobgoblins of legends. He would proceed to Dunwich and other places, record their lore, but spend all his nights happily locked away in comfortable hotel rooms. Legends were maddening enough—the truth was far too horrific!

Miles away, Gouroull studied Herbert West's list for the umpteenth time. All of the ingredients the little doctor had requested had been procured. Now, he would return and West would bring his mate to life. The time of man was ending; his race would soon rise, and then the world would change in ways only he could comprehend!

CHAPTER XI

There was a new scent in the air, a powerful one that Gouroull had never experienced before in his strange life. If was sweet, corrupt and man-made, a chemical stench unique to world. But the screams of the dying men on the battlefield gave him an immediate answer. The humans were using poison gas on each other. Not content to shoot, burn, or blow each other into pieces, these fiends were now employing toxic fumes to destroy each other.

Gouroull had little love for humanity; they were weak, foolish, short-lived, self-important creatures who believed they were gods, yet behaved like errant children. Their jealousies, greed and petty angers lead them to fight each other and everything else in the universe. Still, Gouroull admired the human race for one thing: they were endlessly inventive in methods of murder. From the first of their kind, using stones and rocks, to this latest development of poison, their creativity in the ways of destroying life was a true art form. A bear or a shark would consume these men and women, but they were not capable of imagining and building devices capable of decimating life for an entire region in mere seconds. That was the true strength of these little things; they were weak, yet creative enough to overcome their position in the natural order.

Gouroull strode through the battleground, unaffected by the clouds of poisonous death. Victor Frankenstein's science had made breathing an unnecessary part of his life. He could walk through the depths of the ocean or inhale gases capable of killing even the most dangerous predators, and emerge unscathed. Gouroull was the apex predator, the most dangerous creature striding the Earth today. This bloody battle zone was little more than a distraction at best.

As he moved with silent speed through the lines of the war, the world came into greater focus. Each step caused Frankenstein's creation to realize that he was surrounded by death. The land, the very Earth that gave life to all beings, was dead or dying in this region of war-torn France. The shells, the poison gas and mankind's footfall had caused these once fertile fields to turn into blood-soaked dust. But that was not the only specter of the Grim Reaper that loomed over this place. There were other smells and sounds, less distinct than the poisons that filled the air. Corruption, terror, decay and sorrow circled above, products of this never-ending battle. To Gouroull these scents were sweeter than a field of flowers, more joyous than the happy laughter of children. He was an alien being, created from horror, strengthened by destruction. Mankind's need to annihilate themselves, as well as the planet they called home, was pure amusement. This was why he would one day replace these noisome ants with his own brood. His soon-to-be-created mate was the method he would use, and one day, his children would be the only beings left upon the Earth.

As he headed closer to his goal, another sound drifted Gouroull's way. His hearing was keen, closer to that of the beasts, and he soon could hear it with greater clarity. It was the sound of crooning, a man's voice singing with some sweetness of tone. In the midst of these explosions and screams of agony, it was very out of place. Despite himself, Gouroull was intrigued and approached, his footfalls unnecessarily stealthy in this field of massacres.

Minutes later, he happened upon the singer. He was a tall, thin man with light blond hair which he had, somehow, managed to slick down. His eyes were wide and blue, and his nose long, in the shape of an eagle's beak. He was dressed in the uniform of a Lieutenant in the British army, but his clothes were tattered and covered with old blood stains. He stood in a large trench, surrounded by dead men, their bodies twisted and torn, their faces rictuses of agony.

"And now," the Lieutenant said to the fallen men, "Old Peter will give you one he picked up in school. I was delightful Yum-Yum in my first year. Sadly, I must play Yum-Yum, Peep-Bo and Pitti-Sing's parts since old Chummy and Bertie ain't here yet. It goes a little something like this... Maestro?"

And so he began to sing, his voice a sad and silly attempt at the vocals of a woman.

"Three little maids from school are we... Pert as a schoolgirl well can be... Filled to the brim with girlish glee... Three little maids from school!"

Gouroull watched the garish dance, the silly chorus and the crazed spectacle as the man moved to a song about lovers from the same play. It was a sad exhibition, one that caused him to stare and watch for some time. This soldier's crazed actions were a form of art, madness in a way even Victor Frankenstein's creation could not imagine. The death and horror had caused the mind of this man, seemingly an intelligent and upstanding member of society, to collapse to a manic state that was more terrifying than if he had been screaming or weeping. The unreality that surrounded this soldier, named Peter, was the purest form of protection; his mind's method of rejecting the inhumanity that surrounded him at every turn.

This sight left a slight trace of fear in Gouroull's breast—an odd sensation for one so dreadful. Had he underestimated humanity? Would their resolve be greater? Would their will to survive despite all odds be a match for his new race's powers of mind and body? It was something to consider; a truth that Gouroull had never confronted in the past.

He would have to plan his actions more carefully, view mankind as a greater threat to his plans.

Seeing that the soldier intended to continue his songs, Gouroull slunk away. He had an appointment to keep with Herbert West.

CHAPTER XII

Gouroull left the front lines behind with reluctance. To him, the horror and death that surrounded the trenches were preferable to a land of peace and gentle life. He was a creature of darkness, born from the twisted visions of a man whose very name was invoked as the embodiment of science gone mad. His mind was unlike those of men in so many ways, an alien thought process that few on Earth could claim to comprehend. And those who did understood Gouroull's motives lived in fear of his actions when in his vicinity...

Soon, the calm away from the battlefield was replaced by a new sensation, a cloud that hung over the land, just as oppressive as the horrors of the war. Gouroull could taste the negative energies that loomed and grew stronger with each step he took. Unlike the terror and corruption of the trenches, this was a different feeling, another kind of feverish horror, different but no less terrible.

It took Gouroull a short time to determine what he was experiencing. There was fear present, but there was also more than fear, a stronger emotion that was almost a presence itself. It was the sensation of despair, one of the most terrible of all dark emotions. It was the purest of food to Gouroull, a force that, when invoked, was as destructive as any bomb or disease that rampaged across the planet. According to his readings, for Gouroull had read many books, despair was one of the great sins according the religion Victor Frankenstein had claimed to follow. This emotion was the true destroyer, more lethal than rage, more powerful than sadness, and more terrible than fear. It was a leech that stole lives, reduced the strongest men to little more than shells. Gouroull reveled in the idea that so much of it could exist in a single location. Each step was ecstasy for him. If horror and fear were his meat and drink, despair was a luxury meal that he consumed with undisguised glee.

Then, he discovered the source, which had been his intended target all along: a hospital behind the war torn lines, a supposed sanctuary for the wounded, broken soldiers who had fought in the Great War. But this was not a place devoted to healing; instead, this was closer to an abattoir where some of the cattle survived, albeit in a fractured state. It was set in what had once been a respectable manor house, a fine dwelling for a noble family. Now, the rooms had been torn down to create a huge ward for the wounded soldiers. Many were missing limbs, even more were so covered in bandages they barely resembled men anymore.

This was the source of the despair; it hung over the building and permeated every inch and the lands surrounding it. It was a burden that oppressed patients, nurses and doctors alike. The medical personnel walked about with hunched shoulders, their eyes dull and their bodies moving like sleepwalkers. It was as if the light of the sun could no longer shine over this building, a truer version of that human construct known as Hell. While ancient philosophers had written about its fiery pits, and the torture conducted therein by monstrous demons, this was a truer vision of a place where the damned were forced to dwell. It was a haven of despair where nothing good existed, a force that destroyed the spirit as well as the body.

One man appeared untouched by all this—a small fussy man, who moved in energetic bursts, dispensing treatment with a clinical detachment that made him appear almost like a clockwork figure imitating life. There was a disconnection from all traces of emotion as he assisted the doctors and nurses with the patients, a cold scientific response to all situations that caused him to be a figure of fear. Many present were larger figures, trained to dispense death in various forms, yet this little man was the most dangerous of all. The powerful force of his personality was a dark beacon, the negative horrors repelled by his inner strength. Only he possessed this power; none of the others in the hospital were drawn to him; instead, they cowed in his presence.

Gorouull waited, watching through the filthy windows. He had no need to interrupt the little doctor, knowing he would soon leave the hospital. This was Herbert West, and healing his fellow man was of little interest to him. West dreamed of defeating death, mastering the inevitable end of life through his bizarre elixir. His time spent among the wounded and dying was merely for form's sake; his true interest was in the small building behind the hospital. There, he would attempt to defy nature and return life to the dead, through methods quite different from those employed by Victor Frankenstein.

Circling behind the hospital, Gorouull stood in the growing darkness and waited for West. He had a larger mission: bringing to life his mate and beginning the creation of his new race. Then, the world would change, but not for the better for humanity. Despair such as that surrounding him now would be paradise itself compared to what he had planned for Frankenstein's weak and despised race.

West appeared, fussily fumbling with a set of keys jangling noisily in his hands. Gorouull stepped from the shadows, looming over the tiny doctor, a spectral presence that caused shrieks of fright in even in the strongest of men. But West merely blinked and stared at the giant, examining Gouroull like a particularly unique specimen. A minute later, he supplied Frankenstein's creation with the ghost of a smile, walked to the door and stepped inside. He locked the door after Gouroull had entered, checking to ensure that all the boarded windows were covered before turning on the lights.

"I wondered if I would ever see you again. Have you procured the ingredients listed by your creator?" West asked, clearing a table of several stacks of papers before bringing out an elderly tome.

"Yes," Gouroull stated.

He began producing each item in their sealed containers. West examined them all with the slow and careful deliberation of a true scientist. Nothing escaped his scrutiny and he appeared to possess infinite patience. No details were too small for the little doctor's investigation. Finally, he nodded several times in an energetic fashion that made him resemble a bird.

"Well done, well done! Exactly as de Musard's copy of Frankenstein's diary stated. So, the first stage has been completed, rather faster than I would have imagined it possible... Follow me."

West gathered up each bottle and headed towards a closed door.

"What do you mean, *the first stage*?" Gouroull asked.

His voice was a low rumble. His yellow eyes narrowed. He did not trust humanity; they were often foolish and stupid. Was West, a flea of a man he could squash with no effort, about to attempt to betray him?

West lead Gouroull into a laboratory filled with ceramic tubes, organs contained in clear solutions and a large glass and metal tank. Gouroull instantly recognized the device as being similar to the one used by Victor Frankenstein over a century ago to create life. It appeared West was no fool, unlike so many humans he had met in the past.

"Stage one is my term for the initial steps Frankenstein undertook in his creation of life," West explained as he arranged each of Gouroull's items in a precise order, adjusting them so their angles were exactly correct. "These ingredients were refined into a compound which, when combined with a sturdy skeletal frame and organs, became the prime element of your creation. The application of an electrical charge caused exponential cell growth—and then life. I will be gathering the necessary organs Frankenstein utilized, as well as the alchemical means he used to revive them. You will supply the final element."

"What element?" Gouroull asked, surprised that he was willing to trust a human once again.

West adjusted one bottle a half inch and glanced over his shoulder.

"The bones of a female—but not just any female. She must be a strong one, a woman of power. A normal woman's bones would disintegrate if subjected to Frankenstein's compound."

"Why?" Gouroull asked, watching West for any signs of dissembling.

"Why what?" asked West, turning to look at Gouroull, his face puzzled. "Oh! I see! Why would a normal woman's bones be useless for our needs? Simple! You are not human—you must realize that much. Your creator only stated that your bones were of a powerful being of days of yore, a being of true power. He attempted to perform his work with common, albeit impressive, corpses, but these experiments failed in the early stages. You will need to find a woman of power, a legendary female. You must find her and return with her bones. Meanwhile, I will be creating the compound of creation, as Frankenstein so theatrically christened it. This will take me at least six months. I will harvest organs and await your return. Once you provide me with the proper skeletal frame, we will be a mere three months away from the creation of your mate."

Detecting no sign of lying, Gouroull nodded.

"Answer a question first."

West stared up at the giant.

"If you wish."

"Why are you assisting me?" asked Gouroull. "I know that your ideas are very different from Victor's."

West smiled and picked up a small glass tube from his bench. A golden liquid inside the container appeared to glow, though that could be a trick of the light.

"This is my work in microcosm. My elixir is meant to return life to the dead. It is a way of changing the chain of life and I will perfect my work in time. This is the chance to make humanity greater..."

"That is also what Victor wished," Gouroull said, wondering where the little man was leading him this time.

West returned the liquid to the table with an angry slap, shaking his head with intense, quick movements.

"No, you are very wrong! You misunderstood your creator completely! He did not wish to cause humanity to rise. He only wanted to elevate himself beyond all—to replace that mythical deity known as God! He was mad, believing that once he had created life from nothingness, he would then replace the old religions and become God! That was insane—a waste of time and a dead end!"

"Then, why do you seek to recreate his work?" asked Gouroull, intrigued despite himself.

West was correct in his assessment; Victor Frankenstein was a megalomaniac. His theories were meant to make himself the greatest man on Earth; his creation was merely a by-product of his genius. However, Victor failed to realize that his creature had no desire to worship him, but simply to create a new race to replace humanity. That was what had caused his ultimate destruction and left Gouroull alone, seeking a mate.

West answered with a grin tinged with madness.

"How else could I learn from one of history's most remarkable geniuses if I did not attempt to recreate his work? It will help refine my experiments and my theories. Science should have no limits. Even if your creator's beliefs were pure madness, I can still use the best of his knowledge and synthesize it into a greater all for mankind's ultimate benefit."

Gouroull nodded once and turned away, recognizing that Herbert West was just as insane as Victor had been. Both were driven by notions that would eventually plunge them into madness. This amused Gouroull, who knew that, one day, Herbert West would become a scourge upon mankind. He would taste despair and his high-minded ideas would be replaced by raw horror and destruction. A wonderful destiny, thought Gouroull.

Heading away from the hospital, his alien mind began tabulating all of the evil legends he had learned over the last century. There were many evil women of great power—and some were even real. He would find the bones of one very soon... Then his new race would rise and humanity would know true terror.

CHAPTER XIII

Gouroull ran away from the hospital faster than any human or beast could have done. He felt some anger about the fact that Victor Frankenstein's process was so complicated, but did understand that it fit the man's psyche. It was not enough to merely bring a body back to life; Victor had had greater ambitions: he wished to design a new race, to be hailed as a God and replace the Creator. Herbert West may be a madman, but he did understand Gouroull's maker better than anyone else.

But that was not the thought that Frankenstein's monster mulled over as the miles passed him by in a flash. He was contemplating the lesser implications of Victor's great work. In a very real sense, Frankenstein's creation was still a slave to the whims of his creator. For how else could the new race be created unless a mate was also brought to life? Gouroull still remembered that fateful night in Scotland, when the body of his mate was about to be lowered into the tank. At the last minute, Victor had changed his mind and destroyed her utterly. The words of his creator still resonated in his ears, killing any kindness that may have existed in is soul.

"*I do break my promise; never will I create another like yourself, equal in deformity and wickedness,*" Victor had screamed, thus beginning their battle to the death—his death.

Gouroull had thought himself rid of all feelings towards his creator as he had looked down upon the man's twisted corpse. A sigh of relief had emerged from his black lips and, after a moment's contemplation, he had moved on with his life, only to discover that his differences from humanity were so profound, that he would never truly belong anywhere. And his desperate need for a mate was only achievable through means not found in nature. It was a dreadful fate, one that had made Gouroull, despite all his power, chase Frankenstein's dream for over a century.

He sometimes felt as if he was a living version of the myth of Sisyphus, pushing his metaphoric boulder uphill every day, and had done so for more years than most humans could contemplate. Traveling all over the world, his quest had resulted in so many failures... It was only his fierce and terrible will that prevented him from falling victim to despair. The only way he could rid himself of this "boulder" that his creator had burdened himself with was to achieve the creation of his mate. Then, and only then, would he be completely free from the specters of the past.

Which lead to an obvious question: why continue this mad quest to propagate a new species created by a madman? He was unique, a singular object in the cosmos. Why did he wish to become like humanity, spreading his blood line? Was it some kind of Darwinian imperative to reproduce, built into the very stuff of life? No, Gouroull knew, probably better than most, that his very design rejected all of nature. That which flowed through his very veins was not blood, and he felt no urge to become a rutting animal.

Then, was it, like some scholars suggested, the product of a deep sadness, based in his disconnection from the race out of which he had emerged? A painful loneliness, a Byronic need for companionship? Did he, within his black heart, possess the soul of a poet, trapped within the form of a monster? That idea was even more ludicrous than the notion that he was forced to reproduce because, like the rest of humanity, he was merely an animal.

The truth was that a mate would provide him with the means to achieve his greater desire for this planet: death. By creating a new race, Gouroull would someday be in competition with the humans. And knowing humanity as he did, that would not be easily endured. Men were constantly at war with each other; imagine how they would feel when a race of monstrous creatures, as intelligent as they but far more lethal, suddenly emerged. Humanity's paranoia would lead them to even more horrific acts of destruction and, someday, in the distant future, death on a scale unimaginable.

Yes, Gouroull was undertaking his quest to see the end of all life on this world. His hatred of life was so deep that there was no mitigation in his horrific fantasies. Frankenstein's creation dreamed of a day when he, alone, would walk the Earth and only dust remained. A lifeless canker of a world would be all that would be left. For him, this would be eternal bliss.

This dream was not fueled by the hatred he felt for the bad treatments he had received from the time of his creation. If anything, they only confirmed his larger view of life and the universe, formed since he had first become aware of other living creatures. Nor was it some pathetic lashing out against the race which had created, and then rejected him. Victor's treatment of Gouroull was exactly how he viewed all of humanity. In the end, it was simply how he felt. Victor's mad artistry, the creation of a soulless life, a being born not of nature but of the highest and lowest sciences, had thrust a demon upon the Earth. Unknowingly, Frankenstein had gathered the most twisted dreams of evil in the single body of giant.

He was pure evil, at least by the definitions of most religions and philosophy.

Gouroull embraced his own evil with glee. Despair, madness, fear and death were all he had to give to the world, and he would spread his gifts to any and all that crossed his path. All other forms of life, from the simplest blade of grass to the most complex organisms, were either to be used, temporarily ignored—or crushed.

He wished for no friends or allies. Underlings would serve his needs until they were of no further use to him; some would merely be ignored, given a brief respite; and to be victims was the ultimate fate of all he chose to battle. That was his life, his sole reason for this quest, no matter how long it took him to complete it.

Gouroull changed direction suddenly, remembering where he could search for the bones of his future mate. It was a lonely location in Northern France, where a terrible demonic woman had once ruled...

CHAPTER XIV

The town of Saint-Alexis was easily forgotten. Larger than a hamlet or a village, it was a thriving town, but one without a great deal to boast about. Located northeast of the city of Caen, set near a small forest, it was typical of the region. Its people were industrious, farm owners in the countryside, and workers employed by several small mills in the city itself. It boasted a thriving main street, a churchyard with gravestones dating back to the Crusades, a picturesque, medium sized church, destroyed and rebuilt several times over the centuries, a well-attended, thriving school for all the children, and a pretty town hall. Nobody important had ever emerged from Saint-Alexis to find his place into the history books. Its biggest problems were petty thievery and the occasional domestic spat. The last murder taking place in Saint-Alexis dated back over twenty years, caused by a drunken fight between a farmer and a traveling musician who had been caught romancing the former's young wife.

Visitors to the town found the people warm and friendly, inviting to strangers and kind. During the various wars of the past, soldiers would often pass through town, and some would even return to take up residence there. Saint-Alexis embodied the type of living that poets hailed as a new golden age. Paintings of idyllic country life could have easily been made using its surroundings.

But beneath the surface of this seemingly peaceful paradise, was a secret. The people were exactly as they seemed: decent, kind, living by Christian rules. Everyone was earnest in their desire to lead an upstanding life, but this was not because of their inherent desire to follow the tenets of religion, or abide by the decency that some philosophers believe lies within the soul of the common man. No, Saint-Alexis was peaceful and law-abiding for the simplest reason of all: fear.

Near the western edge of the well-kept cemetery lay a copse of trees. They were gray-black, ancient, naked, and resembled skeletal fingers thrusting from the dark, dead soil. Next to this line of imposing trees were thick brambles, possessing thorns as thick as a man's thumb. Birds and insects never approached this strange, vegetal island, preferring to remain at some distance at all times. The rare visitors who ventured into the cemetery and asked about the trees and the brambles merely received a shrug and a non-committal answer about the time it took and the difficulty of clearing ancient roots. Only twice had anyone from outside attempted to pierce the natural barrier, and, in both cases, the men were unable to move more than a few feet before suffering grave injuries.

That daunting brush on the edge of the cemetery was the reason for the secret terror that existed in the heart of Saint-Alexis. Every man, woman and child knew the area too well, viewing it as a secret monument to their shame. For within this thicket, which grew stronger with every passing year, lay a simple gravesite and a small, round gravestone.

The grave itself was a simple pile of blackened earth, a dead mound resembling cold ash from a terrible conflagration. The simple stone, untouched by the elements, lay a top of the pile, hastily etched in with inexpert hands.

The inscription read: *Countess Wandessa de Nadasdy - Satan's Favorite Mistress.*

This was the source of the secret infamy of Saint-Alexis, their hidden fear that caused them to act with saintly piety day and night.

Countess Wandessa de Nadasdy was a name forgotten by history books, except possibly for the hidden records preserved by the Holy Inquisition in Rome. Centuries before, during the war between the English and the French, she had come to town, the new wife of a local nobleman, a Hungarian beauty with dark hair and flashing eyes. She became a widow at a young age and appeared disinclined to marry again. Instead, she took a keen interest in her new holdings, part of which included Saint-Alexis. Wandessa quickly overcame all trepidation, proving to be a caring landlord who would even forgive taxes upon the poorest of the town's dwellers. She took several of the prettiest girls as ladies-in-waiting and sponsored a town school to teach all the children how to read and write.

Then she began to host festivals for all in town, often based on old folk tales, with plenty of food, drink and dancing. Countess Wandessa was able to convince even her harshest critics to join her in indulging themselves. Slowly, the festivals became increasingly more common, and their debauchery grew with them. From traditional dances and reasonable drinking, they became Bacchanalian in nature. This lifestyle was easy to maintain, thanks to certain potions provided by the Countess which prevented any suffering from said pleasures. Those who rejected her assistance suffered illnesses, and worse, eventually causing them to eagerly embrace the ways of the lovely Hungarian noblewoman.

Then came the day when she killed a chicken and drank its blood, mixed with strong red wine from Spain. Her ladies-in-waiting sipped as well, followed by many others. This, too, became an accepted part of the festivals—a ritual, one might say—and blood-drinking was henceforth added to the ceremonies. It wasn't long before the orgies began, and even wilder pleasures soon followed. By the time Countess Wandessa and her ladies handed out black robes, which were to be worn during the solemn moments before the pleasures began, the people of Saint-Alexis were all newly baptized in the worship of the Infernal One, the most evil being in the universe, the demon known to all as Satan. Saint-Alexis was now a coven of evil and nobody was surprised when several outsiders from Caern were secretly kidnapped by Wandessa's closest followers and sacrificed in Lucifer's name.

Outwardly, Saint-Alexis had changed very little, by day at least. When the King's tax collectors appeared, they found little of interest in the town, merely another hard working town who was, if possible, more compliant with laws passed by the Crown's noble advisers. But the corruption lay just beneath the surface; by night, the soul-crushing horrors mounted. Some villagers embraced evil with open arms, reveling in the abominable nature of their act; others became little more than walking dead, automatons before the concept existed, except in mythology.

For months, the debauchery continued, with Countess Wandessa no longer appearing during the day with her lovely ladies-in-waiting. They would appear only when the sun vanished, no longer bothering to ride horses as their growing powers made such actions a waste of time. Wandessa herself was, if possible, more beautiful, but no longer participated in any rites, except sacrifices, blood-drinking and initiating pretty girls into her coven. Her strength and speed increased; she once tossed René

159

the miller across the length of the cemetery after he put his hand on her thigh. It was then, and only then, that the denizens of Saint-Alexis began to understand how the dark rites had transformed the once lovely noble woman into something monstrous. Speaking in hushed whispers, all agreed that the Countess's teeth and nails had suddenly lengthened, becoming bestial fangs and talons more suited to a wolf; and her eyes, normally large and brown, had turned deep red, similar to the blood she consumed in golden goblets during each evening's ritual.

But even these demonic examples were ignored by most of the residents of Saint-Alexis. In later days, some came to believe that their willful ignorance of the truth was caused by the Countess's potions, which she dispersed freely after each ritual. Others claimed they were under a black magic spell, carefully woven to sap their will and cause them to become little more than puppets dancing to the Countess's whims. But the truth was far simpler. They ignored Countess Wandessa de Nadasdy's metamorphosis into a creature of darkness and evil because they just didn't care. Wandessa had seduced every adult of Saint-Alexis with a skill that would have impressed the most powerful head of state. Every man and woman in town was under a far worse spell than any created by the minds of a witch or a warlock: a total loss of empathy for their fellow men.

However, they proved to have a breaking point, which occurred at the end of another coven gathering. Wandessa stood on the body of a young man, who had been drained of all life fluids. She looked particularly lovely in the moonlight; even the streaks of drying blood around her mouth added to her inhuman beauty. She raised a dainty hand, causing all of them to cease drinking or exchanging sexual partners. They stared at her, worshipful followers attentive to their dark messiah.

"My children," Wandessa whispered, her voice carrying to every ear with ease. "Walpurgis' night is next week. It is time to follow the commands of the Dark Angel, the Light-bearer, Lucifer Morningstar, King of the Earth. You will each bring your children to the ceremony and we will sacrifice them in his name."

"Mistress?" Albert the baker asked, lifting himself off of Annette, farmer Jean's wife. "Our children? If they are gone... we will have... nothing..."

Wandessa threw back her head and screamed with laughter. It was a terrible sound, the raucous, mocking cry of a crow rather than a human female. Tears of red fell from her eyes and she shrieked with mirth for several minutes. Finally, she calmed and shook her head.

"Oh, silly one. We give only their souls to our master, but they will remain. The spirits of demons will occupy each of them and they will live on. They will rise up and bring about the new age of Xenogenesis, the Age of Satan. Worry not, you will benefit a plenty when the Age of Mankind ends."

With that pronouncement, she and her followers vanished into the night. But the crazed bacchanalia was over and even the most jaded denizen of Saint-Alexis were frozen in shock having heard their mistress's plans. Orgies, blood-drinking, even the sacrifice of strangers and using their skin as a perverted form of transubstantiation were, in their deluded minds, acceptable. But the wholesale murder of their own children? And causing these murdered children to become vessels for demons, intent on destroying the world? Even the citizens of Saint-Alexis were incapable of condoning such a terrible project.

What could they do? They asked themselves. They were all damned, having already fallen into the darkness, embracing the tenants of evil with undisguised joy. Was there any way back from their willful rejection of the light of heaven? The citizens of Saint-Alexis argued long into the night and the following day, their fears slowly being overcome by the horrors of Countess Wandessa's desires. They resolved to reveal all to the Church authorities and willingly accept any punishment. They knew they would most probably die at the stake, but their children would live. The sacrifice was acceptable, if terrifying to every man and woman of Saint-Alexis.

They were about to send a deputation to the Bishop of Caen when a man stepped through the gate of the cemetery. He was tall, muscular and possessed the bearing of a warrior born. They could see that he was well-armed and steely eyed. He silenced them all with a look and ushered them with a single gesture into the abandoned church.

"You damned yourself," he said, his voice rough, but surprisingly cultured. "You kissed the foot of Satan and danced to his tune. The Lord brought me before you at the moment of your repentance. God is forgiving, but mere acceptance of your guilt is not enough."

"What can we do, monsieur?" a woman asked in a voice filled with terror.

The man scanned all of the citizens and seemed to accept the truth of their change of heart.

"You, and every member of your bloodline, must follow the laws of God from this day forward. You must be meek, kind, accepting, and fair. None of you, as long as there is a trace of your sin-ridden blood in your children, must ever be anything but a saint. This is your path of redemption. Do good, but ask nothing beyond that, and you and yours will not suffer the torments of the Pit. Do you consent?"

The citizens of Saint-Alexis accepted and the man left, returning by nightfall with the bodies of Wandessa and her followers. He never learned his name and few had viewed his face, but from then on, citizens of Saint-Alexis always included him in their prayers.

As to Wandessa, she was buried and her coffin was prayed over by everyone in town, remembering that their savior had wished them to demonstrate kindness and forgiveness, even to the vilest, evil being. And to this day, the people of Saint-Alexis still behave with saintly kindness, hoping that the unknown man's demands were the words of Heaven, and that they would not suffer the tortures of the damned.

Wandessa's name became a whispered legend, used to frighten children, but sparingly, for no one in town liked to speak it—an abomination that had almost destroyed the world, thanks to their ancestors. Would their penance ever end? They didn't know, but most believed that a second coming of their savior would be an indication their days of saintly behavior were at an end.

Versions of this tale were whispered among those who lurked in the shadows. Gouroull had learned of it from Pastor Schleger. He had listened with only slight interest, because vampires and witches were only another nuisance that he would destroy in the future. The reason he learned these tales was because learning of the ways of other predators, even pathetic ones who used sex and sacrifices to gain power, would provide him with information he might need to crush them more easily.

Now, it turned out that one of those sad, silly tales was going to assist him in making his scheme come true.

Countess Wandessa's grave was the closest to Herbert West's hospital; therefore, he would start with her, and thus, possibly end his quest quickly. By all accounts, Wandessa had been a powerful, inhuman monster with the face of an angel. Precisely what West had told him was required in the creation of his mate.

West's information did beg the question: what was Gouroull's origin beyond the list of esoteric items Victor Frankenstein had used in his creation. According to the notes West had found, the skeletal structure used in Victor's experiment was not that of a common man. This, in and of itself, was not surprising, given Gouroull's massive size. An ordinary man's bones would have shattered under the perils Frankenstein's creation had undergone. Gouroull had walked the depths of the ocean, fallen from great heights, and been buried deep under the Earth; yet, he lived on, healing rapidly and continuing his war with humanity unabated.

Gouroull had read Victor's journal, now in West's possession, but his creator never once mentioned the origins of his skeleton. Merely that it was larger than normal, far sturdier, and once used by a dangerous legendary creature. This was interesting, but, in the end, Gouroull had dismissed it as irrelevant. He existed and was the first of a new race; that was enough. Perhaps his bones had once belonged to someone greater than man, possibly a fellow hater of life, like a *jotun* or a titan... It mattered not and Gouroull only considered this as important because he needed to find another source of inhuman bones. Frankenstein's monster was the ultimate pragmatist, a realist in all areas.

Saint-Alexis was the town that preserved the immortal remains of Countess Wandessa de Nadasdy.

Gouroull knew this for a fact the minute he entered the region.

There was an underlying fear, a sickly sweet scent of putrescence hidden beneath of veneer of ordinary life. This land, and all within, were damned, their essence having been deeded to the Father of Lies centuries before. Here, every man, woman and child were holding back the Pit by sheer force of will. Gouroull had to grant the long-dead Countess a modicum of respect. Wandessa had seduced an entire town into selling their soul, reducing its citizens to little more than slaves. It was only when she had overreached and attempted to begin the end of all life, using the bodies of the children of the town's denizens, that she had fallen from her pedestal of power.

One more mystery remained, surrounding her destruction. Who was the man who had thrown her down, reducing Satan's Favorite Mistress to another moldering corpse? Nobody seemed to know; all tales of this warrior only told that he was tall and appeared to speak directly from Heaven. No other information remained, not even how he had killed Wandessa and her followers. The question was impossible to answer, but ultimately of little importance. The man was, no doubt, mere dust himself and no threat to Gouroull or his plans.

Discovering the bramble barrier, Gouroull tore the outer layer with uncanny ease. Pushing through the remaining layers, he ignored the tears that appeared in his clothing. His chalk colored skin shattered each thorn and he was able to enter the copse unmolested. The stench of unlife hung above the ashen gray soil, a cloud of negative energy that was the center of the corruption that hung over Saint-Alexis. Though buried and seemingly dead for centuries, Wandessa still despoiled everything in the region. This was no common vampire; Countess Wandessa de Nadasdy was a wound in the world, a source of rot that consumed the soul of all life. A normal man or woman stepping into her tomb would have been paralyzed with terror by the might of the undead witch, laying in her grave awaiting her return to life. They would have fled and lived in fear for the rest of their days—such was the power of Wandessa de Nadasdy.

Gouroull, unlike humans, merely found the arcane might of the female vampire to be amusing. There was power in this woman, but not of a kind capable of affecting him. Was it because of the arcane items used in his creation? There was no way to know, but Wandessa's dark spell had no effect on him.

With little thought, Gouroull tore at the dead soil, toss the earth aside, and unveiled the shrouded skeletal remains of the vampire woman. Wandessa's sharply fanged skull was frozen in a wide rictus and the remains of her midnight black hair were still pasted on its side. But there was life and power in this corpse, a putrid dark energy that radiated from the very bones. Could they be the powerful frame needed to create Gouroull's mate? Gouroull knew he needed to be sure before he took her remains to Herbert West.

Suddenly, a slight gleam in the bare light caught Gouroull's eye. The sparkle came from Wandessa's shrunken chest—a tiny piece of metal visible and shining despite the centuries spent beneath the earth. Gouroull leaned closer and realized that this was a silver crucifix, a symbol of the Christian Messiah thrust into the black heart of the vampire. The holy symbol, though mostly brown from the dirt, was still very shiny despite the many years that should have tarnished the metal. Was this a coincidence, or had a mysterious higher power prevented the rusting of the artifact? In truth, Frankenstein's creature didn't care; he didn't waste a moment's thought on it. He knew there were powers that he could not comprehend, higher truths that men like Victor liked to consider, but, in the end, they were of little use to him in his mission.

"I sense you, lovely man," a voice whispered in Gouroull's mind.

The tone was soft, seductive and openly manipulative.

"You have unearthed me. Please, oh, please, free me from my torment. I can give you so much. What do you want? Eternal life? I can grant that with one kiss of my lips!"

Gouroull did not reply, audibly or mentally. He merely listened, interested in this undead creature. Vampires were a unique breed, powerful in many ways, but the sheer volume of their weaknesses made them very vulnerable. Because of their numbers and powers, he felt they were in competition with him for mastery of the world.

"Eternal life does not entice you? What of love? I could love you in ways you could not imagine!"

Wandessa sent image after image of her naked, sexually aroused body. They were lewd images, animalistic and borderline grotesque. Did humans find such images to be a sexual inducement? Gouroull personally found the visions to be ridiculous, the false writhing a mummer's dance played for fools.

"Please, oh, lovely man! Please free me and I will serve you however you need! Please, won't you free me from this terrible torment?" Wandessa pleaded, her attempts at sexual enticement lost beneath her desperate desire for freedom.

And a hunger that she barely hid beneath her veneer of human emotions, for that was the core of her vampiric nature—a hunger to fill the emptiness that lay at the heart of her being. Vampires, no matter how ancient, no matter how powerful, were empty vessels. They existed by leeching off the life of other beings to feed an empty void that could never be filled. They were essentially parasites, dwelling on this world as ageless, half-dead scrounger of the scraps of life. It was pathetic, immoral existence preying on everything that made life worth living.

Amused by her begging, Gouroull reached down and grabbed the cross. With a light tug, he yanked it from Wandessa's shriveled black heart and held it in his enormous fist. Immediately, the desiccated corpse began to transform, the bloom of life flowing over her frame. Wandessa's body filled out, a curvaceous figure slowly emerging. Her hair thickened and turned raven black as her plump red lips and classically sculpted features emerged before Gouroull's eyes. Wandessa's eyes were cat-like in shape, dark and enticing as she focused on her rescuer. A curved smile emerged from her lips and a set of sharp teeth gleamed in the starlight.

Wandessa opened her mouth to speak, just as Gouroull, a malevolent look in his horrific yellow eyes, thrust the crucifix back into her breast. The power of the motion was such that the vampire witch's heart was pierced immediately and began to diminish. Within seconds, Wandessa was little more than the cadaver Gouroull had ripped from the ground moments earlier.

"Why?" Wandessa shrieked. "Why would you do that?"

Gouroull chuckled and kicked the corpse back into the grave, covering the body with the gray, exhausted

Earth. Within a few seconds, there was no sign anyone had ever disturbed the uneasy resting place of "Satan's Favorite Mistress."

Finally, Gouroull turned away, about to leave. He looked back over his shoulder and answered Wandessa's question with an inhuman snarl, a demonic retort that caused the powerful vampire witch to fall into silence.

"Because I can," he stated.

Then, he left Saint-Alexis to resume his quest.

CHAPTER XV

Greymarsh in Suffolk was a lonely spot, mostly untouched by the modern world and the technical wonders of 20th century England. Radios, telephones, telegraph and automobiles never appeared in this lonely town. It wasn't that the people were actively hostile at the thought of the modern world—they embraced all the new scientific changes—but these conveniences never appeared, somehow stopping twenty miles away, at the nearest large town.

There was a timelessness about Greymarsh, a static lifestyle that never seemed quaint, archaic or decaying. The town itself had existed, in various forms, since the Stone Age. Neolithic tribes had once lived there, traces of their dwellings still visible in the woods just behind Craxted Lodge. The ruins of a Roman outpost were also visible just past the Hog's Eye Pub; and some said the stone blocks near the old fort were the remains of a fortress erected by the Angles, or even earlier tribes. Greymarsh was ancient and mostly forgotten by modern man, which was probably good, given the true history of the region.

The neolithic settlement that had once occupied the spot where the town now stood was the most feared in the whole of Suffolk, if not all of Britain. The men of Greymarsh were a degenerate, barbaric tribe, worshipers of an ancient race only known as the serpent people or the worms. Their very existence was anathema to others; they were the symbol of all that was wrong in the world. It was said that an ancient king had once used the serpents, or their human worshippers, to destroy the Roman occupiers. This king, a warrior of legendary powers, was repulsed by the actions of his inhuman allies that he had led a crusade to destroy the tribe. Others claimed that, on the contrary, he had fled north to rejoin his Pictish ancestors and lived out his remaining days in fear. No records remained since the Roman Empire had retreated and vanished. Then, the darkness of fear and ignorance had extended over the land, unbroken for centuries.

The remaining members of the tribe of the worm had mixed with the invaders that followed: Saxons, Norsemen, Angles, and more... All had been assimilated by the remaining members of the tribe. The secret traditions of worship of their ancient masters were handed down over the centuries. Secret meetings were held, sacrifices were performed, and the line of the high priestesses continued through the ages. The secrecy of the tribe of the worm was wisely and carefully preserved by a tacit, unspoken understanding of shared values by the rare few whose bloodlines stretched back through time.

Their worship, if examined closely, was truly based on religions long since forgotten. There were no traces of the Christian concepts of evil in their ceremonies. The high priestess wore a pair of ram's horns, acting as a hermaphroditic creature, a vessel of power. Her attendants were a man dressed as the Lord of the Wild, Herne the Hunter, and a nude woman, her face hidden beneath wrappings that appeared to be made from local vegetation. The few followers were also naked, their heads bowed, their hands held at waist level, palms facing down. Four times a year, a human sacrifice was offered to the ancient worms, the bodies always carefully disposed of several miles away in a neighboring swamp.

The ancient ways of Greymarsh remained hidden, even after the terrible events of 1652. Somehow word of the activities of the hidden tribe was passed to a witch-finder known as Manning, a rapacious lickpenny of a man who had trained under the infamous Matthew Hopkins, a sadist with a hatred for women, who had taken him on as his apprentice and given him a set of witch-hunting tools.

Manning, who was originally from Greymarsh, but did not belong to the tribe of the worm, was one of the few who penetrated the wall of silence that surrounded the ancient religion. Returning with a team of followers, he soon discovered the identity of the high priestess, Lavinia Morley. The Morley family were the most important landowners in the town, residing in Craxted Lodge. They had been running the cult since the days when their masters actually lived on Earth.

Lavinia's subsequent trial and execution was the stuff of legend, her accusers calling her a witch and a devil worshipper. They could offer no proof, but witch trials were rarely about rooting out evil. Lavinia, for her part, refuted all charges and cursed the Manning family for their lies. She died badly, one of the few women to be burned at the stake in Suffolk; her ashes were collected by other family members.

Since that time, on the day of her death, the residents of Greymarsh held a celebration known as Witch Night. They lit bonfires, danced and behaved poorly for a day. Most would say it was a party to applaud the death of the evil Lavinia, but this was a story concocted by the tribes of the worm. In reality, they had created this holiday so that her name would live on, granting her spirit a source of power from beyond the grave. Death would not be the end for their high priestess; Lavinia would live on forever and herald the return of their ancient masters.

It was this knowledge, garnered years before from Victor's library, that brought Gouroull to Greymarsh. For a man of science, Victor Frankenstein had collected many books on subjects that most in his field would have found ridiculous. The occult, dark poetry, lurid fiction and old legends—Gouroull had read them all, absorbed them all, knowing information was a weapon to be used against his enemies. Now, it was serving his purpose in his quest for the bones of his future mate.

Based on the information he had read, Lavinia Morley was an exceptionally powerful woman. The tales of the witch of Greymarsh were few and far between, but all accounts spoke of a woman with uncommon power. This was one of the necessary factors he required for his mate. This, in and of itself, made a degree of sense. He now realizes that Victor had not made him from sewing him together from ordinary body parts. The few spare notes his creator had left behind said as much. The mad scientist had required that every body part, every organ, be far larger than human.

Stepping across the invisible barrier that existed between Greymarsh and the rest of Suffolk, Gouroull immediately knew that he had come to right place. The change in environment was obvious, a sensation of power that struck him with the force of a wave hitting a rocky shore. This was a different sensation from that of Wandessa. The vampire witch had been a corrupt being, a woman held alive by the strength of her will and the life-blood of her victims. There was a debased quality to Wandessa's strength, a sense of rot that permeated her whole being.

But not so with Lavinia Morley. Oh, she was dead, for the scent of death did permeate the air. It moved about Greymarsh like a soft breeze, covering every inch of the land, unseen and unfelt by all, but the most sensitive. But the power itself was a force, the likes of which Gouroull had never experienced during his many years of life. It was an alien might, an energy from beyond, that was not of this Earth. There was a wrongness to this power, a disconnection from this universe that was almost an anathema.

This was the source of Lavinia Morley's twisted power, and the truth behind the horrors that were at the heart of the tribe of the worm. These degraded, debased beings received their power from beyond. It wasn't the same twisted, dark corruption that had been the source of the magic of the demon; this was something far more sinister. Morley and her tribe worshipped and received their gifts from alien creatures. They were clearly distinct from all life on Earth, beings whose very existence would be poison, should they rise from beyond the veil separating their world from ours.

Gouroull found the thought rather intoxicating: a race whose very presence would destroy life on Earth. But he also felt rage. Such life was his to crush, not some extraterrestrial presence wishing to despoil it for its own purposes. This world had birthed him; he was the cancer that lived in the shadows of its souls. All others with similar goals were intruders, who must suffer the fate of any who crossed his path.

"Hold, Gouroull. You are on my lands. I see into your mind, I know your heart," Lavinia Morley stated as she suddenly appeared before him in the darkness.

She was a tall woman with green skin and an hourglass figure. Her hair was raven dark and her dark eyes watched him with mocking amusement. Her head was partially covered with a headdress of gold, two curling horns sloping from her forehead, over her ears, and ending just short of her pointed jaw. She was beautiful in an alien manner, as inhuman as Gouroull in her own way.

Frankenstein's creature stopped walking, watching her with his malevolent yellow eyes. It would be a truly wonderful jest to seize the bones of the aliens' high priestess and use them to make his mate. But could she then become a risk to his plans? Was her inhuman quality, the source of her might, so ingrained in her very being that she might remain their servant even after her resurrection?

Lavinia's eyes widened; she threw back her head and laughed, her peals of laughter ringing in Gouroull's ears. It was a mocking sound, a cruel taunt of pure evil.

"You wish to steal my bones for your sad little plan? Impossible! I was reduced to ashes by Manning and his followers. What you see before you is my spirit existing on this world. There is naught you can do to me, monster."

To demonstrate, she walked through Gouroull, still laughing.

"Your selfish rage renders you useless to me, creature. We wish similar ends for this world, but I am possessed by a higher purpose. Your quest is a mere childish tantrum, a rage against your very creation. I seek to bring the Old Gods back—they who walked this world before mankind! They shall return and clean the Earth of the infection of life. Then they will rebuild it, creating a new home for their followers."

Lavinia raised her hands in supplication and started to chant, no longer aware of Gouroull. Her words were intoned in a voice of power; she was clearly quoting something ancient and horrific.

"Yog-Sothoth knows the gate. Yog-Sothoth is the gate. Yog-Sothoth is the key and guardian of the gate.

Past, present, future, all are one in Yog-Sothoth. He knows where the Old Ones broke through of old, and where they shall break through again. He knows where they have trod Earth's fields, and where they still tread them, and why no one can behold them as they tread."

She then looked at Gouroull, amusement slipping away and replaced by mocking disgust.

"This is my alpha and omega, my hidden truth. It shall one day be called in every corner of the Earth and all life shall perish. If you wish the end of humanity, lose your rage and join us in our crusade!"

Gouroull stared at the ghostly figured and chuckled in a malicious manner.

"Never. I've sworn war upon all life, even your masters. They, too, will die," he rasped.

He turned away, ignoring her ghostly shrieks. He walked back to the coast, still amused by his new enemy. His quest would continue, alien gods and their deluded worshipers no longer mattered to him—for the present. But someday, they, too, would fall at his hands. Their end would be glorious...

CHAPTER XVI

Albert Cox straightened his uniform as he stared across the balcony to the nearby building. The woman across the way, a tall vision in white silk, entranced him as no other woman had in his lifetime. She was tall with large high breasts barely covered in a white silk sheath. The dress was so tight it appeared to be a second layer of skin, only slightly paler than her natural tone. But it was her hair that caught his eye, a golden shower that fell to her back and seemed to move with a life of its own.

This was a surprise, since he had only come to this party by chance, having met his old school chum, Bertie. Albert stepped out onto the balcony as the other members of the Drones Club attempted to play another of their bizarre games. Last he saw, Tuppy Glossop was attempting to ride Bingo Little across the room as Bertie's butler prevented vases and various knick-knacks from being smashed.

"Hello, do you want me?" the woman asked, smiling his way.

Her teeth were brilliant white as she leaned forward, display an impressive *decolleté*.

"I...um... I..." Albert stammered, unable to process this information.

The woman's beauty hit him like a wave of heat, a powerful, overwhelming emotion. He felt out-of-control, like a stallion witnessing a distant filly while being held back by fences.

"Do you want me?" the woman repeated, her voice a low, husky growl.

Her scent seemed to drift Albert's direction, a musky odor that caused his body to shudder as his loins seemed to grow enflamed. He was suddenly insane with lust, incapable of thinking of anything but her ruby red lips, her golden hair and her enticing golden eyes.

"Yes," Albert breathed.

He moved towards the door of the balcony, but he stopped, seeing his goddess shake her head.

"No, no, no," she said, shaking her head slowly. "You must prove your love to me first. Jump. Jump from your balcony to mine and I will make all your dreams come true."

"Jump?" Albert asked, doubt in his voice.

He wanted this woman, more than he thought possible, but the distance between the two balconies was so great! If he missed, he would plunge down ten or more stories!

The beautiful woman nodded.

"Yes, jump. It's not far, a short little hop to prove that you love me. And think of the pleasures you will feel when I'm in your arms. Come to me, my lover. Jump!"

Albert could not resist her call; her lovely arms were extended in open supplication.

Stepping up on the stone railing, he sneaked a quick look down, feeling a wave of nausea and fear at the great height. But then, he caught sight of her golden eyes, her pearly teeth, her soft pale skin again, and the fear left him, replaced by an overwhelming hunger to possess her, to use her, and despoil her in ways he had never imagined.

With a final lick of his lips, Albert Cox leapt the distance. Her cry of triumph rang in his ears just as he reached for his golden goddess... only to grab thin air!

He missed the other balcony by three feet. His longing transformed into terror and he shrieked as he plummeted to the street below, striking the pavement with a sickly thud.

There was a scream from below and calls of fright from the apartment. Several men stepped onto the balcony. They were wide-eyed with shock and horror, staring down at the crumpled, twisted form of their dead friend.

Lady Sara Durwood stepped into the shadows as Bertie and his friends stepped into the light. She sighed with contentment, feeling their fear, shock, puzzlement and sadness in waves. It was a feast, one that would sustain her for weeks, possibly months. Leaving the apartment, she transformed her hair back into the short, red-gold shape and length she had preferred for the last three hundred years.

Stepping out of the apartment building, she drove off, heading for her home just outside the town of Padbury. This was the traditional seat of her family, the Durwoods, one she occupied in various forms since the death of her parents. For Sara Durwood was a vampire, but not the traditional type known to the world. She was an emotional vampire, who fed on strong emotions. A child of the infamous Karnstein lineage through her mother, she had been shocked to learn, as a young girl, that her parents, her mother and her supposedly dead father, were vampires that stole the youth of their victims. They had been put to death by a hunter and his hunchbacked partner centuries ago. Her brother soon succumbed to a wasting illness, leaving Sara alone in their great estate, with death as her only visitor.

Unwilling to become a pathetic creature, like her mother, or a half-dead monster, like her father, Sara had begun to study the dark tomes kept in family's library.

There, she learned the many paths of the dark witch, the pitfalls of most methods of eternal youth and beauty and the best way to achieve her desires. Becoming an emotional vampire was difficult, but far more satisfying than becoming a blood-stealing undead like so many who wished eternal life. Yes, she was rarely granted any peace, but that was the cost. Sara sought out strong emotions, feeding on the life energies of those involved. And at times, such as this one, she would create a circumstance that was a veritable banquet. It was not the best of life, but hundreds of years later, it was the one she preferred. Her family was long dead, brought down by their own foolish ways, or simply bad luck. Sara, on the other hand, was a survivor.

Entering her home, she felt a presence, a unique sensation. Not alive, not dead, not undead. A creature of unique power and destructive capability. She knew instantly where this being was located. Returning to her car, she headed for the Padbury cemetery, where her ancestors lay. The drive was so familiar she could perform it with her eyes shut. As a girl, she'd run along these lanes; then she'd been driven in a carriage pulled by one of the many footmen employed by her mother. Then, after all her family had been dead and buried, by horseback. It was considered scandalous for a young noble woman to ride a horse unaccompanied, but the Durwood women, all of whom were Sara in various guises, were always forward-thinking and did as they pleased. Even the local vicars merely rolled their eyes and were grateful the Durwoods kept to themselves and were charitable landlords in the best and worst of times.

Sara never had time for such customs, even before she became a vampire. Riding on her own was a pleasure in her youth, and later, as she stopped aging, a means of conveyance. Anyone objecting to her activities were easily dealt with—a little taste of her powers and they were often feeling whatever emotion she felt would serve her best as a meal. Sara knew she was a vain creature, an emotional leech who manipulated mankind with amused contempt. She was better than humanity—that was an obvious fact based on her extended youth and power. But she never underestimated her prey. Humanity had a capacity for violence that would impress even the most malign creature of the night. Weak, short-lived and greedy, humans were sad beings who wasted their potential by focusing on the most trivial aspects of existence. Yet, they were also imaginative, disruptive and incapable of seeing any limits on their desires. Ancient beings, some viewed as gods by primitive societies, fell beneath the hands of these lesser creatures. Sara knew she still existed because she always gave mankind enough respect to prevent them from making her a target of their rampages. Otherwise, like her parents, she could easily fall at the hands of those she viewed as food.

Stopping near the graveyard, she immediately spotted the form of a man, yet not a man, lurking about the tombstones. He was inhumanly tall, with chalk-colored skins and thick dark hair. He moved, despite being impressive in height, with the loose, relaxed gait of a born predator .Sara knew this man, or whatever creature he was, would be inhumanly fast and powerful. That much could be discerned from a glance. And her powers told her this was someone unique, a being unlike any of the supernatural beings she had dealt with during her very long life. Was he the product of a new age, a monster of science? Did the mechanized world spew forth such mysterious new form of life? Sara did not think so; at least, not in the case of this creature. The weight of ages radiated from his enormous form; he was not as ancient as she was, but old nonetheless. There was also a hint of some kind of ancient power, which confused her senses. Very odd, but worth exploring.

Stepping lightly into the graveyard, she leaned against the statue of her long-dead father, Hagen, Lord Durwood. His marble form was still frozen in the act of reaching for his sword, for Hagen had once been the greatest master of the blade in Europe. Brought low by the plague, he'd returned to life, or unlife, through the arcane spells of his wife, Katerina Karnstein-Durwood. The returned being was not truly her father, merely a lesser, rotting, doppelganger, a mere pretender standing in his shoes. He'd fallen shortly after his return, ironically by the sword. The true Hagen Durwood would have sliced the human hunter to pieces in seconds; the vampiric version fell after an extended duel. That was when Sara had learned of vampires and how the graveyard rot permeated the very bones of the undead. She knew she must be wiser than her mother, whose motives were understandable, but her methods foolish.

Watching the invader as he wandered about the tombstones, Sara cleared her throat and smiled as he turned her way. She sensed that to use her powers on him would be a mistake, so she merely studied him, sensing an alien evil behind those dreadful yellow eyes. But she was also curious, so she did not attempt to flee.

"Hello," she said, pulling out a cheroot and lighting it with a small match. "I'm guessing you're looking for the grave of Lady Katerina Durwood. Am I correct?"

"Yes," Gouroull answered, studying the woman who watched him with no a trace of fear.

She was not human, but also did not appear to be an enemy.

Sara nodded, pleased with herself.

"She has no grave marker. The local vicar refused to give her a proper burial. But you'll find her coffin ten feet from where I'm standing. Just there," she pointed with one slim finger. "Why are you looking for her remains?"

"Why do you want to know?" Gouroull asked.

Sara snickered,

"She was my mother. Three times since she was returned to her grave, people have sought her remains. The previous two wished to return her to life so they could be made into vampire. Sad, weak, little men who wished to lash out at the world. Truly pathetic. The first, I merely consumed, reduced him to little more than dust. The second was a nobleman of some wealth but no position... he was a vain, silly, selfish little man, whom I married. I slowly drained him for three years before he died. He's buried in the plot next to the elm tree to your left. You are the third."

"I need her bones. The bones of a powerful woman to make my mate," Gouroull stated.

He stepped over to where this inhuman woman had said the grave was located.

"Hmm," Sara mused.

She didn't particularly care what this monster did with her late mother's bones, Katerina Durwood meant little to her in life. In death, she was merely a reminder of how power could be wasted on the foolish and vainglorious.

"This disturbs you?" Gouroull asked, surprised by the minimal reaction from the vampire woman.

She appeared more interested than concerned and clearly wished to ask him more questions. Usually, he did not bother answering to anyone. When one was the most dangerous being on the planet, the worries of the ants beneath your feet were of no consequences. But, for some reason, this woman, who openly admitted she was not human, was giving him pause. There was no attraction, sexual or otherwise, and she wasn't using her powers to manipulate him. This was a unique circumstance and Gouroull was interested in seeing the direction in which their conversation would proceed.

"Disturb me?" Sara echoed, wondering what this creature meant.

Was she supposed to be frightened by his dreadful, twisted form? Or by the fact that he was even more inhuman than she, an emotional, 300-year-old vampire? Then she realized he was referring to his desire to take her mother's remains and use them in the creation of his mate. The thought caused Sara to throw back her head and squeal with laughter.

"Oh, good sir! Thank you! I haven't laughed that hard in such a long time!" she replied, waving to indicate she wasn't mocking him or his intentions. "To answer you, no, take her, if you wish. We weren't close in life and even less so in death. When she was alive, I found her to be foul-tempered, vain, a tease who loved to entice men to the point that they attempted to woo her. She would then revel in their deaths at the hands of my father. He was the greatest swordsman who ever lived."

Sara waved up at Hagen's headstone before continuing:

"I cared for my father and brother, but both were distant to me. Their deaths made my choice to become a vampire easier. But unlike my mother, I choose to steal human emotions rather than blood. She transformed into a vampire, but, as in all things, her methods were silly and wasteful. Her actions were so open, so obvious, it brought about the attentions of a pair of professional vampire hunters. I am far more circumspect. Which is a rather lengthy way of saying, you taking her bones is unimportant to me. Do as you wish. I doubt I could stop you in any event."

"You don't smell like a vampire," Gouroull said, breathing in her scent.

She possessed a sense of power, an inner reserve that lay sleeping in her soul. He would have thought she was a demon of some type, but she did not smell of brimstone. She as odd, unique, and more than a little dangerous. Gouroull liked that; it meant that he was talking to a viper, hidden in the bosom of humanity. If vampire she was, she was one who subtly sapped mankind of their life-force and brought about their ends in clever ways.

"None of the smell of dirt, blood and rot?"Sara nodded. "True, I obtained my power in a more complicated route. Shall I tell you? Good! I haven't spoken of this in centuries. After my parents died, my brother died of a flux; he was always a weak, pretty boy who was pampered by my mother, even though he secretly sired about ten bastard children with some of the local woman. Perhaps the constant rutting sapped him of his strength? Anyway, I was alone and expected to marry, but I wanted to be free. So I studied my mother's books of dark magic and found a spell that would allow me to ask for what I wished."

"Ask who?" Gouroull inquired.

"Yes, I should say," she smiled. "There is a being, He Who Has a Thousand Names. This… god, demon, or something else, grants the wishes of men, but he is no happy Jinn of ancient tales. The wishes he grants are always meant to spread chaos, pain and destruction. In this circumstance, he was called the Hooded Horror. He was about as tall as you, but very thin, covered in a brown robe. No face was visible, only darkness lay under his the hood. He was very frightening. I say 'he,' since I heard a voice that I thought belonged to a man. So he gave me what I wished: youth, beauty and the like, while laughing at my expense. He knew my life would be long and lonely, but even more so, that I would end up almost as pathetic as my mother, despite my strong self-control. I'm a parasite, a leech feeding on human emotions, and I am always surrounded by pain, often created to keep me young."

Gouroull nodded, realizing that this vampire woman was no threat to his plans. She would probably welcome the destruction of all life, even if it meant her own demise as a secret louse hidden on humanity's skin. He bent down and began to dig, knowing his quest would soon be over, and the real battle would begin.

"I don't mean to stop you, and by all means, do continue if you wish, but may I offer a piece of advice? Do not bother with vampire women for your mate. If some trace of my mother still resides in her dust, you will find her to be as great a burden as she was to my father. To be a vampire is to be selfish. That is at the core of all of us—a desire to go on living because we believe that our own life is more important than anything else in the universe. If you wish a mate, is that what you wish in a partner for eternity? I think—and this is just my opinion, based on having had countless lovers throughout the ages—that you wish more than someone to rut with, and raise children in a happy home. If so, find a woman of strength, not a spoiled, selfish woman who would use you until she becomes a burden. I have had many men and women over the years. And in all cases, I have consumed them, drunk their soul, just because I do not wish to grow old and die."

Sara stepped away from her father's headstone and tossed her cheroot behind her.

"But, if you disagree, by all means take her and do as you will. Perhaps in her third life, my mother will be of some use to someone. But I have my doubts."

She headed back to her car and looked over her shoulder at the giant man who crouched over her mother's unmarked grave.

"Oh, and thank you," she said. "It was good to speak to another with honesty. I shan't expect that it will happen to me again for many years."

With that, she drove away, leaving Gouroull to study the hole he had dug. Was she right? Her advice appeared to be given with honesty and a lack of concern. But she, too, was a vampire, and no more manipulative race ever existed in history. They would lie in ways that would endanger their own life, merely for the pleasure of seeing the results. It was this treachery that caused Gouroull to despise them. They were competitors but it was their twisted ways that caused him to hate them.

A moment later, Gouroull stood upright and walked away from the cemetery. The vampire woman had been right: the bones of a vampire might imbue some of their twisted essence to his mate, a factor that would slow his plans. Let Katerina Durwood remain in her grave, rotting and plotting her eventual return. In the end, vampires weren't worth his time, except as victims. His bride would need the bones of someone powerful and useful, not a parasite with delusions of greatness.

CHAPTER XVII

Bonn was a city suffering, but slowly. It was like a man who was slowly being poisoned by an angry lover. Bit by bit, ever slowly, the strength of its body was wearing away. A shell would be all that remained, in the end. Would the mercy of death come? Perhaps, perhaps not. The universe was a chaotic place, one which sometimes would allow a tormented soul to revive and bloom, even after suffering the tortures of the damned.

Lorelei always thought of cities in that odd manner. To her, they were living entities, some male, some female, and all received the same treatment. Few on this planet would ever understand how many thousands of methods could be used to torture a living body as well as Lorelei. She had brought the swift and slow ends to many souls in her immortal life, and she would continue to do so for ages to come.

For Lorelei was a siren, a being born of the waters who brought about the ends of many lives. Sometimes, she achieved this through her song; other times, through her presence. In the end, few escaped from her clutches. She was a tall woman with a figure that changed, based on her sexual desires. Once, many years ago, she had been a tall warrior maiden with well-shaped muscles, dressed in a metal armor. Another time, she had been a small, dark-haired woman with enormous breasts and a tiny waist. It didn't matter to her how she looked. She would always be a vision of loveliness to all eyes and would move about the cities and towns on the Rhine with deft ease.

Walking into a butcher's shop, she waited until the customers stepped away and went up to the counter. The choices of meat were poor: stringy beef and elderly poultry. The war effort had been diverting more and more of the country's lifeblood to the front; not just men and boys, but the food and drink needed to support a viable society. Rationing had already begun, and Lorelei knew, it would grow worse. This current conflict would be drawn out, a slow grind that would wear down both sides. Every country involved would suffer. The losers would return to a defeated, demoralized home with few resources and an inner discontentment that would last for decades. The winners would gain a brief moment of glory, but eventually find their soldiers were no longer of any use. Many would sicken, in mind or body, while others would find themselves forgotten and ignored. War was a kind of plague, a destructive force that destroyed everything it touched. The loss of life and future lives was a terrible pain, but it was the death of the human soul that was the worst aspect. Men returned home, shattered and soulless, walking dead with eyes reflecting the decimation of their spirit. Others embraced the horrors, becoming little more than avatars of destruction wherever they went. These sought to destroy everything around them, spread the seeds of their torment and make the world a reflection of their darkness.

Lorelei had witnessed these events many times; the dreadfulness of the war-torn land washed over her like a gentle spring breeze. Humans came and died, whether at the hands of each other, disease, or old age. But life endured, and so did the siren of the Rhine. Looking over the poor choices of food, she spotted a not too unhealthy-looking piece of pork. Looking at the woman behind the counter (for all the stores were now run by women), she said in a sing-song voice:

"I will take that piece of pork. You will remember I paid and wish me well as I leave."

The butcher smiled and nodded, pulling out the meat and beginning to wrap it in newspaper with swift, practiced movements.

That was the most basic part of Lorelei's power: the ability to control minds through the use of song. She was careful in its use; performing before the wrong people, she could end up destroyed like her sister, Peisione. Poor Peisione! It had taken her over a thousand years to return to the world, and she'd never been the same. She still existed, her rages causing many ships to vanish without a trace in a sea far from the Rhine. But Lorelei would not suffer the same fate; she used her powers carefully and no longer felt the need to wantonly destroy any who would cross her path.

Leaving the butcher's shop, she visited two more stores, obtaining an ivory comb, to replace the one she had broken that morning, and a small metal knife, because she wished to carve herself a new flute. Each were given freely by the humans, all of whom appeared cheerful despite the specter of war. But there was a shadow beneath the surface, an inner fear that gave the city a stench.

The scent was one predators recognize all too well, that of weakness and fear of death. The shortening supplies, the bad news from the front, the lies of the politicians, all made every man, woman and child feel a secret terror that their world was about to come to an end. Lorelei knew this to be true. Bonn might fall, become an empty shell, like many lost lands on the Rhine. But another city would eventually replace the doomed one; it as a simple fact of nature. Or possibly Bonn would bloom—who knew?

Lorelei had given up trying to predict the future when the barbaric hordes of the region went to do battle against the demon sorcerers of Acheron. Life was easier for an immortal that way; it remained a glorious surprise. Too much routine was death to those born with endless life; it made them go mad—and an insane immortal was a danger, often forcibly put to sleep to prevent unnecessary destruction.

Leaving the city, she walked along the Rhine for a time, finding the spot she wanted and there, sat down. Slowly, she unwrapped the pork, selecting a small piece to eat, chewing and savoring the taste. This would satisfy her for a time, but soon, she would need to seduce more humans into her waters and taste their death by drowning. That was her purpose, the reason she existed. Lorelei did not receive immortality from these deaths; she was a siren, not a common vampire. Her duty was to take these lives for the river itself, to add souls and lives to it. This kept the waters alive, as well as the lands surrounding them.

Lorelei would live on if she resisted providing lives to the Rhine, but the river would diminish. It would falter and weaken, become less over the centuries, and eventually be little more than a stream. She believed that she, too, would become less vital, a shadow of her true self. This had happened in the past. One of the most ancient of their numbers had been the embodiment of the Kansas Sea in North America. But she had neglected her duties and turned into a sad, ancient crone, a spectral presence of fear of what could happen to the negligent.

Sitting and watching the river, Lorelei waited. She was good at this—a skill every immortal mastered early in their existence. Human lives were woefully short; they were such fragile creatures. Behaving like them, attempting to fit all kind of experiences in a life so pathetically short was almost painful to one who measured her existence in ages. You learned the pace of the universe, not that of the tiny creatures inhabiting this planet with life spans that lasted no more than an instant. Lorelei could sit in this spot for years, contemplating matters and watching the Rhine. She would be content to stay there, doing her part for the river, until she knew it was time to move to another location. But not this day—this was not the time for quiet reflection.

Lorelei had a purpose in mind. When the moment was upon her, she lifted the small package of pork and asked:

"Would you like some meat, Gouroull? It's far from the best, but not inedible."

Gouroull was rarely surprised, but this time, he was in genuine shock. This woman, her back to him, had sensed his presence, despite him moving with slow, careful motions. Also, she knew his name! She was alive, not a ghost flitting about the ether able to place herself anywhere at a whim. This was well and truly a surprise for him, and he was unable to think of a proper reply. Instead, he reached out and took the parcel, swallowing the tasteless flesh with several short snaps of his jaw.

These actions gave him a moment to recover from his surprise. He stepped closer, seeing Lorelei for the first time. She was as lovely as the tales told. But Gouroull could sense great, if restrained, power within her perfect form.

"How did you know my name?" he growled, his yellow pupils meeting her deep blue eyes.

The siren's eyes were merely reflective pools, possessing no emotions; they were only blue mirrors that looked at Frankenstein's creation betraying nothing.

Lorelei giggled lightly and shook her golden hair, which shimmered in the growing twilight.

"You know little of the sirens' powers, Gouroull. When you thought my name, as you crossed the Rhine, I learned of your presence, of your intentions, of your thoughts. Any who touch this river and think of me become subject to my power. Some, I lure to their death; others I ignore. In your case, I waited, knowing you would find me after a time."

Gouroull took a step forward, raising his enormous fists into view.

"You can't drown me," he growled.

Lorelei nodded and smiled, her teeth perfectly white and straight, creating a pearl like reflection.

"That is true. I doubt my powers could affect you at all. You are a new being, but I feel a force within you. Very different. I know you sought me, so I sat here waiting for you. Now you have found me. You seek the bones of ancient for your mate, is that so?"

Gouroull indicated she was correct, but her calm disturbed him; few beings, ancient or otherwise, were so at ease in his presence. Only that ghostly vampire woman had been, but she had no substance. Lorelei, on the other hand, was a living, breathing being.

"I'm afraid your search was a waste of time," she stated, rising up and extending her arm towards Gouroull. "Tear off my arm."

Gouroull didn't hesitate. He reached out, grabbed Lorelei's arm by its shoulder and, with a harsh yank, one that would have torn a rhinoceros head off, pulled off the limb.

No blood emerged from her body, or the arm, and the flesh in his hand grew cool to his touch almost instantly. A moment later, the arm he held turned liquid and fell to the ground with a quiet splash.

Lorelei giggled again and stepped forward, her bare foot touching the water that had been her arm. The liquid vanished and, in an instant, her limb was back.

"I am a siren, Gouroull. I possess no bones or flesh. I am a being of water, choosing a form that suits the era in which I reside. I cannot be your mate, for I am a part of the Rhine itself—an immortal, but one with a limited role. Your quest lies elsewhere."

Gouroull nodded and turned to go, but was stopped by her hand touching his arm. He looked back.

"You are probably immortal like myself—and some others. So I would speak to you. I saw your intentions, your desire for the death of all life. It denotes a madness in you. This is an age of machines; you, more than anyone else, belong to it. But many of the long-lived will fight you to protect their power and place on this planet. You will find your road difficult."

"Good," Gouroull replied, his teeth gleaming.

"So be it," nodded Lorelei. But if you would know the truth of your desires, go to the Black Forest. Look for its heart and there, you will find the resting place of the immortals. Perhaps your mate's bones lay in a land where immortals lived, loved and sleep. At the very least, you will meet the Wild Huntsman, a killer even greater than yourself."

With that, she smiled again and stepped into the water, vanishing from sight.

Gouroull turned away from the Rhine, his quest taking him to another place in the world.

CHAPTER XVIII

The Black Forest was alive. That did not simply mean that there was life in these ancient woods—that much was obvious, even from a great distance. The enormous trees, the teeming insect life in the rich, dark soil, and hundreds of animals called it home. But the Forest itself was possessed by an ancient spirit, an invisible presence that seeped into every facet of its life. This was no dancing sprite or talking tree, like in many legends, but a true force of nature itself, an unfeeling, uncaring power that guarded the Forest with the jealousy of a miser.

Humanity was ignorant of such elder supremacies, having lost their connection to the natural world in favor of the artificial civilization. Once mankind had lived in harmony was such entities; now they were unwittingly at war with such ancient beings. Instead of harmony, humans sought to subjugate nature to their whims, transforming primeval living chaos into weak, orderly vestiges of nature.

The secret presence of the Black Forest would never manifest itself, Gouroull knew this much. Such spirits were asleep and barely rousable. Yet, he knew that this land revolted at his very being. Animals and insects melted away as he walked by, and paths appeared to bypass streams of water in favor of dry, lifeless gullies. Had Gouroull been a human, he would have starved to death or died from dehydration weeks ago. As it was, such deprivation meant little to a being created by the mad genius of Victor Frankenstein.

Gouroull had known scarcity of life that few could comprehend. He had, in the past, strode across the great frozen wastes of the north, wandered in boiling deserts wracked by sandstorms, and walked across the depths of the sea. As a being, he was unique, and the natural forces of the Black Forest were only a slight inconvenience.

He had spent weeks seeking the elusive heart of the Forest. All true woods, those that were still primeval wild and untouched by man's hand, possessed a heart. These were not located at the center, as so many believed; they were the souls of the land, a conceptual life force centered in one area, but hard to find. Locating it was extremely difficult, even for those attuned to the Earth powers. But, for a being such as Gouroull, a creature of science, created as a challenge to the natural order, it was nearly impossible.

Yet, he kept searching, and would continue to do so until he had found the secret. He needed no rest and moved faster than a hare through the many tiny trails and animal tracks. Slowly but surely, despite the slumbering spirit's hatred, the Black Forest would yield its secret. Gouroull was a force of nature in his own right, a dynamo of destruction that was civilization's avatar in its war against the natural world. As a being of science, he had no interest or respect for the world. He would despoil the lands, subdue the planet, and destroy anything that stood in his path.

The weeks turned into months, yet Gouroull still roamed the Forest, like an elusive phantom, a terror in the darkness that tore through these ancient lands with a calm, alien determination. His inner malevolence recognized no higher being than himself and his ageless form would weather any attempts to weaken his resolve. The Black Forest was no more threat to him than the sub-zero ice fields of the North Pole. In the end, he would find what he required; time and destiny were on his side.

One day, he discovered the location he had been seeking—the living embodiment of the Black Forest. It was a grove, a small, dark expanse teeming with life, just out of his reach. Its energy pushed him back like an invisible hand. The presence was just beyond his grasp, inches from his clutching hands, watching him with such hostility that most beings on this world would have fled in terror. This was nature itself, unhidden beneath the veneer of gentility so many saw in a forest. The chaotic horror of the land, the unvarnished hatred the spirits of the world felt when confronted by the virus that was humanity. Because, although Gouroull was far more than a human being, he was still symbolic of the rejection by mankind of the natural world.

Gouroull was unmoved by such allegorical warfare. He had defeated the spirit's attempts to force him to give up his pursuit. The slumbering being had now only one recourse: to attack with the multitude of animals at its disposal. But it knew that this would result in massive destruction, a weakening of the very lands it sought to preserve. The death Gouroull would bring to the heart of the Black Forest would create a corruption that would spread and totally despoil the woods. The lands would become a twisted mockery, a horror-filled blight that would torment the world until the end of time. The Black Forest could defeat Gouroull, but the cost was far too great for even a natural body to bear it willingly. Therefore the animals moved aside, avoiding Frankenstein's monster, but staring at him with hostility.

Gouroull moved further into the coppice, his yellow eyes searching intently for the portal to the world connected to ours. This was a new experience for him, stepping into a new realm potentially replete with death. But he thought the siren's advice had been wise; she was an immortal being with little interest in his plan. Her advice was simply a dollop of information, to be used or ignored at will. But a realm of beings whom many had worshipped as gods was of interest to Frankenstein's creation. Possibly he would find the bones he required there; and possibly more answers. Therefore, he sought the gateway with a naked hunger and nearly religious frenzy.

The sheer volume of life, from the tiniest insect to shaggy dark bears that dwarfed Gouroull, made it difficult to study the grove that was the heart of the Black Forest. The true nature of the landscape could only be viewed in brief glimpses in the rare moments when all of the life forms were away. This was the spirit of the forest's subtle and final assault upon the minds of any enemies who might have dared venture into its forbidden depths. This living wave was visually overwhelming, an indication that the power of the woods, while ancient, as still able to strike at even the most basic level. Any trespasser would have been crushed under the enormous volume of life-forms gathered in this one single location, and come to the realization that they were no more than insects themselves compared to these great lands.

But not Gouroull. To him, these creatures were only reminders of his larger plan for the world. The spirit of the Black Woods was his enemy, his lifelong nemesis that he eventually planned to destroy in the course of time. This ancient being represented everything that Gouroull despised about the Earth, the natural forces, the living creatures. They would all be reduced to dust when Frankenstein's monster's task would be completed. This world would become a lifeless husk, a burnt blight in the cosmos, a reminder that life was not worthy of living. That was the true legacy of Victor Frankenstein, the one that would resonate in days to come.

For over an hour, Gouroull wandered the copse, his vision blurred, his steps shadowed, before he found the gateway to the other world. Two small piles of stone stood about ten feet apart, each three feet high. A first glance showed nothing; these were merely piles of rocks in a dark grove in the woods. But a closer look revealed something far more startling. The stone stacks were a complex arrangement, an interlocking weave of exactly placed minerals. Each stone was fitted precisely into the others, above, below and on all its sides. These tiny pyramids were madman's puzzles, a lifelong battle to create order out of the chaos. The two stacks were so exactly against nature, so determinedly a product of the mind of man, that Gouroull was amused. By their very existence, they demonstrated that the Black Forest did not reign supreme in these lands.

Stepping into the gap between the two piles, Gouroull felt a chill wind blow across his face. His tangled anthracite hair moved about his head, a dark curtain framing his twisted features. The wind came from beyond the gate, an icy breeze meant as a final warning to those unwary enough to cross into the lands of the immortals. Frankenstein's creation was even more amused; his black lips peeled back to reveal his teeth. To a human, these impediments might be barriers for both mind and body, but to Gouroull, they were mere inconveniences, annoyances at worst.

Stepping through the gate, his vision blurred, all shapes becoming indistinct and out-of-focus. A moment later, he was standing on a frozen plain, an endless tundra of primordial snow and ice. A harsh wind wiped about the land, dropping its sub-zero temperature to levels that would have made the Arctic feel like a balmy summer beach. Even Gouroull, for all his inhuman physiology, recognized the depths of the cold upon this world. This was the *Fimbulwinter*, the extreme winter that brought about the end of the legendary Aesir.

Victor Frankenstein had, at some point in his life, been fascinated by the legends of the immortals of the north, the Gods of Asgard. The tales of their cycle of birth, rise, death and rebirth filled several shelves of his labyrinthine library. Gouroull had absorbed these tales, taking great interest in the infamous Jotunn, the giants who were the eternal enemies of the beautiful Aesir. The Jotunn were often the object of scorn, theft and lust by the so-called Gods, who were as selfish and foolish as their human counterparts. But to Gouroull, these creatures rising up to destroy their oppressors were a wonderful myth, a prophecy of the days yet to come on his own world.

Slowly, Gouroull adjusted to his surroundings, the details of the tundra becoming more distinct. There were towering columns of ice that curved precariously over his head, and huge mounds that resembled the Neolithic tombs created by mankind to bury their ancient kings. It was then that he realized that these elephantine structures were, in fact, rib bones—the skeletal remains of vast, towering beings unseen by the eyes of humanity.

This wasteland was, in fact, a massive graveyard for creatures that had been the stuff of legends. This was the site of the Battle of the Last Days, Ragnarok, the End Times of the Aesir. To Frankenstein's monster, this was a place of beauty. These lands, according to the myths, had once been filled with the beauty of life and loveliness; now, all that remained was death and ice—perfection from his alien point-of-view.

After a while, Gouroull noticed a lone figure in the distance. It was in the shape of a man, and stood like a frozen sentinel, his massive form covered in a cloak of dark fur that flapped in the wind like a massive, bestial flag. Though unmoving, Gouroull's keen vision showed him plumes of frozen mist appearing from the man's breath. He was alive and watching, bearing the intolerable conditions with a stoic strength that was to be admired. This was an immortal, one of the dreaded Aesir who had once ruled these lands and influenced humanity for centuries. Now, he was the lone survivor, the last warrior of a great people, standing on the cemetery that had been their home.

Gouroull studied the distant Aesir for a time, impressed despite himself. A being who could stand in this frozen plain, this icy death zone, with a calm, unemotional stance was a dangerous being, to say the least. This immortal was a power to be reckoned with, a being born with a strength unheard of. To treat him the way he had approached vampires or other monsters of his world would be a fatal mistake. This one was far beyond such lesser beings, a true immortal of ancient and terrible majesty.

As Gouroull strode across the ice fields, the sheer enormity of the man became more evident. While Frankenstein's creation was one of the largest beings in human history, this man would dwarf those rare creatures even taller than him. He stood at least ten feet in height and, even under his tent-like fur cloak, possessed layers of hard muscle. His head was uncovered; like his beard, it as sprinkled with the snow that swirled about the landscape. As Gouroull had suspected, there was a majestic power about him. He was one who had witnessed the passing of eons and fought every threat with fierce, dangerous, warrior's strength.

Gouroull stopped before the giant, his yellow eyes meeting the warrior's black, unwinking and unmoving. He possessed dark red hair and a thick red beard, as well as kindly eyes, The man's head slowly swiveled, dislodging some snow and he spoke in a booming, bass tone:

"Welcome, immortal. I greet you, but I am unable to provide you with more. I have no food or drink, no fire to light, no warmth or lodging. But I will offer you my protection as befits a guest, should you need it."

"Ragnarok," Gouroull growled, ignoring the words. "This is where it happened?"

The giant nodded once.

"This time, yes. The last time, the battle took place in Jotunheim, and the time before that, in the lands of the dwarf kings."

Gouroull expressed his confusion. Hadn't the point of Ragnarok been that it signified the end of all life and the triumph of destruction? That was the theme of all of the books he had read on the Aesir. Yet, this survivor spoke as if many End of Days had occurred. That didn't make sense.

Seeing Gouroull's confusion, the giant smiled, showing rows of gleaming square teeth.

"Ragnarok is part of a cycle. We rise, we live, and then winter comes. Then the great battle takes place, its outcome different each time. And after a long period of rest, all is renewed again. That is the way."

The giant signaled at the towering rib bones of ice that hung above their heads.

"This time, the Vanir were the enemies," he continued. "They were driven mad, I know not why. They brought back the first of the Jotunn, the most dangerous of them all, Ymir, he who was born of the poison of the lands, the ice giant that consumed all in his path. With Ymir back, all the Jotunn who lived in the ice caves sided with the Vanir. The fire giants of Muspelheim, even the dreaded Surtur, fought beside the Aesir, and the battle was joined again."

Gouroull waited, realizing this one had a tale to tell. Besides, it was interesting to see how incomplete Victor's books had been, in comparison to the reality of Ragnarok. Another proof that humanity was an undeserving species.

"Father Wotan and Surtur fought Ymir side by side, having sworn an oath in blood before the battle. They eventually vanquished the ancient Jotunn, but still perished in the battle," the giant said, nodding at two huge mounds of snow and ice. "I myself fought Fenris and he fell by my hand. The great wolf was near impossible to kill, but in the end, he died. Freyr, Heimdall and Vidar all died beneath the poisonous breath and spear-like fangs of Jormungandr, the Midgard Serpent. Loki, the sly one, tricked his son, the serpent, to swallow his own tail and consume himself. But Loki's mate, the giantess Angrboda, stabbed him in the back. She never forgave him for abandoning her and treating their children like monsters. Ullr and Tyr stood before the gates of Niflheim, the lands of the unworthy dead. None of Hel's dead were allowed to return; they struck down the legions and fell when no more were left. In the end, nothing remained but I, waiting until the time of renewal. Occasionally, I hunt in your world, hoping for my end so that all will begin again. For I can only die at the appointed time, during the Ending, and this time, by not falling with the others, I became doomed to wait. But the renewal will happen, in this age, or perhaps the next."

"What of the women?" Gouroull asked, never forgetting his quest for a mate.

The bones of these Aesir and Jotunn might suit West's demands. Also, he had come here to learn something of the truth of immortality. The siren's advice had been given without malice.

"I killed my own wife before the battle," shrugged the giant, "knowing that it would be a kinder fate for her, had we lost. Frigga died of grief when Father Wotan fell. Freya and the others were either killed by their mates or by their own hands. Death by the sword is the only kindness at the End, so that you do not become a servant of Hel. They are now in Valhalla, awaiting the Return, the next beginning."

"Your women meekly accepted death? All of them?"Gouroull asked, incredulous.

How could a warrior race produce such meek females? Only Angrboda appeared to possess any true spirit.

"It is our way—it has always been and it will always be," replied the giant, nodding. "The women wait as the men do battle. Only the Valkyries are allowed on the field, seeking the honorable dead. That is the function of the women in all the cycles. They bear the children, give counsel and wait in the halls. What else could there be for such beings?"

And that was the lesson the siren had wished him to learn—the intractability of the immortal. These giant beings, these warrior-kings whom humans viewed as gods, were stuck in an endless repeating cycle of their own making. They had no ability to change roles, no matter who stood on each side of the battlefield. In the end, they would murder their females, who would accept their deaths with a meekness that was truly pathetic. And these so-called gods would return to the battlefield and ultimately perish, embracing death rather than attempting to change the universe into one better suited to their needs. In a very real way, they were weaker than the humans Gouroull had come to despise.

The siren's lesson had proved effective. Gouroull would not allow his mate to be so weak and easily swayed. He required someone strong, a survivor with a fierce spirit to stand by his side. One willing to support his quest to end all life on Earth with the same fervor that kept him moving.

Giving the giant a last, pitying glance, Frankenstein's creature turned away. The Aesir warrior resumed his sentinel like stance in the fields of the dead. Gouroull never looked behind, stepping back through the portal and into the Black Forest. The grove was now clear; his path to the east visible. The next step in his quest would lay in that direction.

CHAPTER XIX

On the edge of the deep woods, in a place were few willing to venture, was a small cottage. It was not a hovel, a ramshackle affair thrown together to protect its occupant from the elements; nor was it a luxurious affair, made of candy or with sweeping levels. This was a simple dwelling, a place to live. It was built to last, with two simple, small rooms, wooden floors, and possessed a strong roof, also made of wood. A simple chimney was built into its side, nothing special, just a basic tube of brick that funneled out the smoke from within. It was a simple place, identical to hundreds that dotted the landscape.

Yet, this small home was shunned by anyone passing through the woods. For generations, it had been said, usually only in whispers, that a witch lived in that cottage. Legends of children being turned into mice, men giving up their wives and dying moments later, women growing old in seconds, had been told about the dreaded sorceress who was said to reside in that place. For nobody would give the cottage a name. To some, it was simply called the Witch's Home, but few referred to the place in that manner. Most preferred to pretend it didn't exist and avoided the trails that lead to it at all times. Occasionally, children would sneak out to get a glimpse of the tiny house, but few made it to within viewing distance. A general feeling of fright crept over anyone approaching the cottage, a gnawing sensation of fear that slowly overwhelmed their mind and body, causing them to start at any sounds heard from within the forest's shadows. Sooner or later they would flee, and declare later that they had approached the place, but viewed nothing of interest. Yet, they would carefully avoid it ever after.

Strangely enough, in this one case, all of the tales were true. This was the dwelling of an ancient witch, a woman of true power. And in her many lifetimes, she had despoiled all those who'd crossed her path. Lusty young men who wished for power would beg for her favors while secretly plotting her destruction. Angry wives would demand the deaths of their foolish husbands, and then fall into despair when their desires were made real. And dangerous children were taught the lesson of respecting the property of others after they spent some time as a mouse or a toad. That was the way of true power—those that would come to her, requesting her aid, were often the ones least equipped to deal with the results. That was the lesson of Nyarlathotep, the Dark Messenger from Beyond, the Faceless One, the Haunter of the Dark. Give the fools what they wish and watch as their own base desires drive them to madness and death.

The witch knew she was an evil, malevolent being. She was born this way, had followed this path and, throughout the many ages, never varied her course. She never sought to bring ruin upon the world; like her patron, she would wait, a deadly spider watching as the foolish fly flew into her web. The cravings of the jealous and greedy were her meat; their short-sighted ambitions, her gravy. In the end, their ruin was her joy. But never did she seek these dooms; they were always brought to her door.

The ancient witch had, like her many-faced master, many names. She was called Agamede, Huld, Louhi, Pannochka, Muma Padurii, Atla the witch-woman of

207

Dagon-moor, and so many more names throughout the years. She appeared as an elder hag to some; a lovely yet evil-eyed woman to others. Her form was protean, ever shifting, based on the vision of her victims. Evil was not simply a frightening man with horns and a love of contracts. It altered based on the selfish and terrible thoughts of the human who wished their own desires to supersede all others in the world.

Stepping up to her large caldron, an object she still found useful, she began to chant as she tossed herbs and other unidentifiable items into the boiling depths.

"Double, double toil and trouble; fire burn, and caldron bubble, fillet of a fenny snake, in the caldron boil and bake, eye of newt, and toe of frog, wool of bat, and tongue of dog, adder's fork, and blind-worm's sting, lizard's leg, and owlet's wing, for a charm of powerful trouble, like a hell-broth boil and bubble, double, double toil and trouble, fire burn, and caldron bubble."

The witch stirred a little longer and mused.

"Ah, Shakespeare, you did have a way with words. A little tired at times, yet what a joy."

The words were no incantation, but instead a memory of days when her kind were the great terrors of the world. True witches never feared villagers, knights, or even kings, in those days. By hiding their hearts, they could survive any assault and could repel any attack with the fear of cruel retribution. But no longer. Few true witches were left in the world, and mankind's greatest terrors now lay in their own sciences.

She suspected the growth of weapons of war was due to her master's actions, sowing the seeds of chaos in another manner, but she was not sure. Anyway, there were still enough people in the world who wished to use the ancient paths of evil for their base desires. She, and the few of her kind left, were not entirely forgotten. That was enough to guarantee that their own manifestation of evil would always linger, a shadow of superstition beneath the reason of the modern age.

Pouring her potion into a small jar, the witch sealed it and placed it on a shelf. These were the simplest methods of spreading disaster: a fool who wished a love philter, another who wished a traceless poison. In the end, the taking of these liquid spells was a transaction. The seeker was given a mean to fulfill their wishes and gave a portion of their soul to darkness in exchange. And once darkness had taken hold of a human, it was rare they could expel it. The evil within would slowly corrupt even the kindest soul, justifying actions they might once have viewed with horror.

Pulling out a small three-legged stool she kept under the bed, the witch sat outside and waited. She could speed things along, use a trace of magic to get her visitor to arrive faster, but that was probably a waste in this case. Gouroull was heading through her woods, several of her past names in his very unusual mind. The witch could slow him for a time, even delay him by sidetracking him on different routes that led away from her cottage, but the creature's single-minded relentlessness would somehow break her spells and lead to a face-to-face confrontation. Best to just let him make his own way, and take control of their meeting.

The witch sat back and reflected on the coming encounter. She had dealt with many unusual beings over her extended lifetime, but Gouroull was truly unique. An odd and not unpleasant experience, confronting a completely new, and seemingly malevolent, being. She knew that his power was the result of his creation. Victor Frankenstein's genius was that he had comingled alchemy and modern science, producing a new form of life. Though similar in many ways to humanity, Gouroull was a different life form entirely. Victor had not, as the some versions of his tale claimed, return life to the dead. He had utilized his terrible genius to reshape the flesh of the dead and create a new plague upon the race of his birth. Gouroull was horror personified—the sentient version of a pure elemental force. He would continue on his mission, unswerving, uncaring, destroying anything that stood in his path. He was a most dreadful being—and the witch was delighted by his existence.

"Come out, Gouroull. You have found me. What name did you think I bore? Huld? Louhi? Atla? I am all of those, and more. Come out! Talk to me! Perhaps I can help you find what you seek."

The witch looked into the depths of the woods. The darkness hung over the trees, a blanket that refused to allow the light of the moon or the stars to illuminate their shadows.

Gouroull was not surprised that the hag knew of his coming. Like the siren, some beings seemed attuned to their surroundings. This was a trick he would learn one day—an additional defense against his enemies.

His huge form stepped lightly from the line of bush, his chalky skin appearing even paler in the moonlight. His heavy mane of black hair was so dark it almost blended with the night, and his yellow eyes shone like an evil beacon in the murk. He walked steadily and quickly, and approached the witch, studying her and sensing that this was another being of great power. Contained within her withered frame was alien might, power from beyond. Perhaps that was the truth about t witch magic? They were supplied their power from creatures beyond this world. That would render them as little more than meat puppets for otherworldly beings. Once again, the truth was far less impressive than the reality.

The witch studied Gouroull, her rheumy eyes marking every detail of his form.

"You seek a mate?" she asked finally.

"How did you know?" Gouroull asked, wondering if every being he challenged could read his intentions.

This did not seem likely, but he had to ask.

The witch shook her head.

"Not through my powers, no. I learned of your plan by listening to the stories about you. Your actions have sent shock waves throughout the occult world, Gouroull. Great masters of dark and terrible powers have tumbled beneath you, and you have made terrible enemies. Yet, still you seek to create a mate. It is admirable, if amusing."

"Amusing?" Gouroull growled, not liking the witch's mocking tone.

The witch nodded and smiled, her spare yellow teeth snapping like the maw of a terrible bottom-feeding fish.

"Of course! Any such struggle experienced by anyone upon this world is a delight to me. I am a monster too, Gouroull. I have spread horror, fear and pain everywhere I went. My dark master gave me eternal life and enormous power. In return, I am the swarm of locusts that attack the wheat fields; I am the disease that sweeps through great cities and reduces them to pitiful gravesites; I am the cruel laughter that causes men to kill each other in fits of madness—I am a witch, a sorceress; I am evil come to these lands!"

"I have met witches before," Gouroull replied, unimpressed.

"There are those who call themselves witches who respect the natural order," said the crone, nodding. "There are indeed practitioners of witchcraft who do only good—but that is not who I am. When I made my pact with the Darkness, I agreed to be chaos on Earth. That is my way. Yours is one I do not know, beyond the stories they tell about you. But I believe helping you will help my own mission. Therefore, ask of me anything you wish, and I will give it to you without a price."

Gouroull considered the offer. He was of two minds with respect to dealing with this creature. He could ask, and no doubt would receive, useful information. This one clearly wished to visit evil upon mankind just as much as he did. But he despised her pact with alien entities, who were called gods or demons by the foolish and easily swayed humans. Those presences were so alien that even Gouroull could not understand their aims. They had created their own pawns, like the fish-men he had destroyed in Greece. This meant that they would ultimately end up being rivals, enemies even, for all their talk of chaos and death. They coveted the Earth, but Gouroull had no intention of leaving even a trace of life on this insignificant cosmic mote.

But that battle would take place far in the future. For now, information would be useful, allowing him to complete his mission faster.

"Bones. I need the bones of a powerful female," he said.

The witch nodded and closed her eyes.

"I can see several possible futures, divergent paths of fate weaved by the Outer Gods. The Daemon Sultan and Lurker at the Threshold guide my vision. I am but an insignificant speck to them, but they grant visions to the faithful. You seek the bones of a great woman. Yet, none are worthy. Here are only weaklings; sad, greedy fools. Go south to Africa. There were queens there, powerful women of great majesty and ambition. You will find what you seek there."

The witch opened her eyes and looked up at Gouroull.

"I can see no more; the great Outer Gods expelled me from their presence. Good luck on your quest. I will watch you with great interest."

And then, the witch, her cottage, and the surrounding clearing, all vanished before Gouroull's eyes. He was suddenly standing on the southern end of the great woods he had entered several days back, searching for that creature. Had she been dead, she may have provided the bones he sought. Alive, she had been of use, too. The witch was wise; knowing Gouroull would have torn her to pieces after receiving her prophecy, for just mocking him, she had chosen to disappear. Frankenstein's creature only heard the distant sounds of her mocking laughter—her mirth at having escaped his wrath.

Gouroull turned south and headed towards the coast. But he would return one day and the witch would regret her laughter.

CHAPTER XX

Herbert Fuchs was a haunted man. He was easily startled by loud noises and kept his massive shaggy head down wherever he scurried, resembling a dog who had been whipped too many times by a cruel master. His salt-and-pepper beard was overgrown and scraggly, resembling a garden choked with weeds; his hair was uncombed and gave him the air of a patient slowly losing his sanity. His neighbors rolled their eyes as he passed, believing his obsession with tombs and ancient scrolls had finally driven him mad.

It was well-known at the time, or at least believed, that the study of Egyptology was a subject fit only for foreigners and those of unsound mind. All that poring over ancient scrawls and mummies in the merciless heat of Egypt was enough to drive even the strongest man to insanity. Fuchs had made some impressive finds in the last decade, but with the war on, funding such excursions was now considered a waste of time and money. The kings, queens and heathen gods of the ancient Egyptians would remain hidden beneath the wasted sands of the desert for another score of years. They could wait until after the Hun had been defeated.

Yet, Fuchs never stopped working, avoiding the social life of Cairo in favor of trips to the desert, followed by long periods of study in the local museums. It was a sad sight, but to be expected. Since the British Empire had taken over this part of the world, there were always those who fell in love with the bizarre history of Ancient Egypt. For a time, the finding of exotic items was fashionable amongst those in power. Fund an expedition, find a mummy and some statues, and show it off in museums and at parties for your fellow aristocrats. But like all things, such endeavors had eventually become less interesting. After all, how many dried up mummies could one see? Characters like Fuchs had become little more than a curiosity, a sad, useless relic for those who resided in this God-forsaken land. Even his pretty daughter had taken to stay out of sight these days. Probably a mercy for the poor girl, having to listen to people be ever so sympathetic about her diminishing father.

Still, Fuchs had no time to deal with such silly concerns as his reputation, or whether he had bathed that week. He had a higher purpose, one that would lead to the culmination of his life's work. There was still so much to do, and time was not on his side. The Night of the Great Red God was fast approaching—taking place that very evening in fact—and then, the world would be his for the asking.

Fuchs had so much to complete before that night. Visiting the *souk* of Cairo, he entered a maze-like array of small shops and stalls, seeking precious artifacts and rare herbs. The Scroll of Thoth-Amon contained a long list of ingredients and items, all of which had to be found before the ceremonies could commence.

"Soon, very soon," Fuchs whispered to himself, twisting the ring on his finger.

The ring was an oddity, copper-colored, in the shape of a serpent. The snake's form looped three times around and its tail was held firmly in its fangs. A pair of glittering yellow gems made up the eyes, giving it an eerie, inhuman quality. This was the legendary Serpent Ring of Set, an artifact of mythical value. Supposedly, the High Priest of Father Set had vested his power in this band of metal and used it to torment and, ultimately, destroy all his enemies.

This was deemed to be pure nonsense by all reputable archaeologists; that would have meant that there had been a great civilization even before the days of Upper and Lower Egypt! But Fuchs knew that was exactly what had happened; there had been lost empires that mankind had long since forgotten. And he, Herbert Fuchs, would find evidence of them all, would look down from his lofty academic height at those who had sneered at his theories. And all would be right in the world.

To do that, he first had to complete the great work he had embarked upon after discovering the lost tomb of Princess Tera. She was a name that had been struck from the rolls of royalty after she had murdered her brother, Pharaoh Neferikare, the last king of the seventh dynasty. According to the legends, the Princess had been passed over as Royal Wife by the new king in favor of a Vizier's daughter, one not even of the royal bloodline. Tera, who was also the High Priestess of He Who Ruled the Darkness, Father Set himself, has used the Great Red God's murderous cult to seize the throne and bathe in the blood of her enemies, before the priests of Amun, Horus, Isis and Horus had struck back and killed all of her followers. As a princess royal, Tera could not be executed, but they had embalmed her alive and placed her mummy in a secret tomb, cursed to a slow, lonely end.

That tomb had been discovered by Fuchs, who had learned Tera's history and true power. Once returned to the world, the Queen of Queens would rule all; commoners would work the fields and serve in the armies, nobles would administer the world; there would be no more wars; everyone would follow the ways of Father

Set and submit to his laws; crime would vanish; there would be no more need for money... Earth would become a true paradise.

Some would die, of course, as the price to pay for refusing to worship Father Set, but far fewer than all those who died daily from crime or disease. Choice would no longer be needed; all would be assigned their jobs at birth and live the life they were meant to live. Freedom, such as that praised by the priests who opposed Tera, was a fool's desire. Fuchs now believed this to be true, although he had once been revolted by the notion. But after placing the ring on his finger, an impulsive decision that had come to him quite suddenly, he had realized that this was indeed the only and correct path for the world to follow. It needed a strong and powerful ruler, and her name was Tera, Queen of Queens, High Priestess of the Blood Red God!

At a small stall in the western section of the market, Fuchs found two finger bones from a mummy dead over a thousand years. How he knew that they were that ancient was a puzzlement, but he just knew. Possibly the great ring was lending him some insight into the truth of the world. Fuchs didn't know. But he now seemed able to date any item he examined. Take the bronze knife he had scrutinized the other day. There was a trace of iron within the metal—an impurity. If used for the ritual, that would have spoiled the channeling of the mystic forces and caused the spell to fail. This was why Fuchs was scurrying in and out of so many establishments, some reputable, most not.

Picking up a small brass amulet, he ignored the chatter of the stall owner as he dug through the many phony artifacts for sale. There were objects of some historical value here, a coin from the period of Amenhotep

IV, a knife once used by a Hyksos warrior, a charm from a lesser temple of Amun, and more. Any other time, Fuchs would have wanted all of these pieces, but not today. He had specific needs, items required by the Scroll of Thoth-Amon to be used to raise the future Queen of the Earth from the underworld.

Anubis would not let her go so easily, but the sage who had written the Scroll understood the methods for returning the dead to life. Without the Scroll, there were very few other methods available—the jewel known as the Heart of Ahriman had performed this function once, raising a demon sorcerer of ancient Acheron to life. But those methods were nearly impossible to deploy in the modern world. The Scroll, once used in modern times to bring a disgraced priest back to life, was the best solution available. Fuchs had stabbed the curator who had access to it, replacing the true Scroll in its casket with a similar parchment. Then, his searches had begun.

At the back of the stall, Fuchs found what he instinctively knew was needed. The item was a small sealed box; to most, it would have seemed to be a decorative paperweight. But this was actually an ancient Egyptian puzzle box, created by the lost priesthood of Osiris. These priests, who had some control over the rites of the dead, had created special puzzle boxes of cedar wood meant to protect certain herbs they used in their sacraments. This secret had been lost through the ages, and the majority of these antiquities had been simply tossed into fires, as useless blocks of wood. Nothing could be further from the truth, however, and Fuchs successfully hid his excitement.

After a brief bit of bartering—not to do so would have been suspicious—Fuchs paid for the box and left the shop at a near run. It was not until he reached his basement laboratory that he dared to look upon the wood's surface. Seeing no catch, he closed his eyes and began to feel it with his fingers. Soon, he discovered a slight indentation on one of the sides. From there, it was easy to determine the method of unveiling the box's contents.

Within it was exactly what he had hoped: a tiny pile of leaves from a long-lost plant, known to the ancients as tana leaves. When properly used, with the spell of the Scroll of Thoth-Amon, the dead would be returned to life. This had happened in the past, but never properly. The ancient arts, as practiced by the former owner of the Serpent Ring of Set, were mostly lost. Magic had receded from the world, used only by a spare few. And none of those, at least from what Fuchs had gathered, were as powerful as the High Priest of Father Set had once been.

The final preparations were made with the tana leaves, giving Fuchs several hours to sanctify the blade and the other items needed for the spell. He had known that he would find the tana leaves last, from the whispers from beyond, or possibly the ring. It didn't matter the source of the knowledge, Fuchs was a willing participant. For his entire life, he had been amazed by the legends of the past, preferring Ancient Egypt above all other lost civilizations. Happily, his parents were in favor of an academic career. His discoveries had earned him a place as a don in Cambridge and regular visits to the sites he had uncovered. But this had changed at the beginning of 1914. The war had destroyed his way of life.

The hall clock chimed eleven times, which Fuchs knew was the appointed hour when to begin the ancient rite. Bringing Tera back into the world required power that was believed lost. In addition to the special items required, one had to placate the great Osiris, master of the land of the dead. He was not a jealous deity, but he had rules that even he had to follow. A placeholder was required, one to wait in Tera's stead in the underworld and serve her upon her return. Though she might return and live thousands of years, all eventually ended up back in the land of the dead. Leaving an empty spot in her place was against the laws of the underworld, something impossible in an absolute realm where even masters were subjects to laws created at the dawn of time.

Fortunately for Tera, Fuchs had a daughter, who shared her father's love of research and Ancient Egyptian history. She would take the place of the future Queen of the world, although not willingly. She fought the idea of returning a being of such legendary evil to life, and had attempted to destroy Tera's remains. But Fuchs had thwarted her and, thanks to the ingestion of a concoction of black lotus, she now lay dreaming at her future mistress's feet.

Donning the blood red robes of an acolyte of Father Set, Fuchs purified his hands and lips with vinegar and laid out the many items needed for the ritual. A statue of Father Set made from red clay, a bronze dagger, a brass cup in the shape of a serpent attempting to swallow the world, and many other needed artifacts. They were positioned with precision around the open sarcophagus of Tera, who lay swathed in her linen wrappings. Only her perfect face was visible beneath the bandages that had covered her for the millennium.

Her face, a perfect mixture of regal perfection and cruel anger, had been the source of so much pain. Men like Fuchs were rarely able to resist her fierce demands, falling victim to her rages whenever her whims were not fully satisfied. This ultimately had been her downfall; too many had realized that, if left in command of Egypt, she would have drowned the land in blood. Her plan for the world was too horrific to contemplate, at last for those capable of resisting the allure of her beauty. The High Priestess of Isis had likened Tera's ideas to making humanity descend to the level of insects. The world would become a hive, with Tera as Queen, and all others mindless drones. That was truly worse than death. So that woman, a future Queen and Great Royal Wife, had mounted a rebellion against the evil Tera.

Fuchs did not share that view. In his diseased mind, humans were far too free and chaotic. Tradesmen's sons were rising to the highest positions, and crazed men in the streets ranted about equality. That was anarchy, the abandonment of the old ways. Ancient Egyptians understood their places in the world: the Pharaoh sat above all; the learned and military stood at his left and right; tradesmen and servants were used and treated well, but were not equal to those born to serve the highest in the land. While Tera was not perfect, her views would return order and peace to the world, something which Fuchs prized almost as much as scholarship.

The preparations were now complete. Fuchs unwrapped the Scroll of Thoth-Amon and began to read the ancient words. The language was that of Stygia, a country that had once been located where Egypt now stood, in the time before recorded history. Most scholars believed civilization had begun in Mesopotamia and Egypt, but they could not be further from the truth. There were empires and city-states that had thrived before the ice age had wiped all traces of that world. The Stygians were, according to the rare bits of information that could be discovered, followers of Father Set, and rivals to the empire of demon sorcerers of ancient Acheron. A proud powerful people, they had fallen victims to the barbaric hordes from the North that had sought to destroy all traces of the people who had once slaughtered them, for ceremonies or pleasure.

Tera, in her time as a princess, had learned many of the secrets of these ancient people, and had used them as part of her rituals as Father Set's priestess. This was the source of her power, and her motivation for wanting to change the world in the name of her terrible god.

After he had uttered the final word, Fuchs heard two sounds occurring simultaneously. His daughter exhaled loudly and went still, just as Tera inhaled deeply, still in her coffin. Stepping over the still form of his daughter, he rushed to the side of his dark mistress. Her eye lids fluttered open and she stared out, her eyes vacant.

"You live, my Queen!" Fuchs crowed, helping her slight frame to sit upward. "Beautiful Princess Tera! Beloved of Father Set!".

"I was Tera, I am dead," Tera replied, allowing herself to be lifted out of her coffin.

Fuchs shook his leonine head and sat her down in a throne-like chair made of cedar wood.

"You are indeed Tera; you died but now you live again. I brought you back!"

Tera stared at Fuchs for a moment and said:

"You were the voice from the land of living. You wear my ring—the Serpent Ring of Set!"

Fuchs nodded and took the ring off, placing it in his mistress's hand, watching as she caressed the yellow gems that made up the eyes of the snake before slipping it on her finger.

Abruptly, she stood up, the linen bandages rotting and dropping off her tiny frame in a brown dust cloud. Tera was completely naked, other than a complex pattern of multi-colored tattoos and sigils. She was beautiful, terrible and inhuman, an imperious figure of myth, an ancient deity that brought sexual frenzy and death to her followers. She was also utterly terrifying, a monster who was perfect, but twisted.

Without being told, Fuchs dropped to his knees and pressed his head against the ground. He knew that he was her willing slave, the first convert Tera would make before reshaping the world in her image. If that meant he needed to make his obeisance to her, he was more than willing to do so.

"I am Tera! I live!" Tera proclaimed.

She looked down at the man at her feet. He was a pathetic, inadequate man, but he would serve well. She needed aid in her early days as she brought her followers back into the folds of Father Set. The hidden sects would flock to her banner and, slowly, they would conquer the Earth. This little man would help; he had already willingly surrendered his daughter—the flesh of his flesh. The rest of mankind would be far easier.

"Rise, my servant. You shall be my most favored, so long as you obey."

Tera already knew much about the modern world, having absorbed the knowledge of Fuch's daughter. There were still a few gaps, but it would not be long before she obtained what she required. Then the world would tremble!

"Tell me," Tera said, leaning back in her throne, "the King of your empire has an unmarried elder son? Edward? What an odd name—it is inadequate to fail to pay proper respect to the Gods."

Fuchs was about to answer, when a crashing sound caused him to jump.

"What was that?"

"Your door—it has been destroyed," Tera replied, her voice calm, but licking her lips in anticipation. "Something comes—a being of great power and blood. Male... My next convert!"

It was then that Gouroull stepped inside. He had traced the finding of the lost princess of ancient Egypt to the scholar known as Herbert Fuchs. The location of her hidden tomb was a secret he had uncovered in Scotland, purely by chance. While the voodoo doctor was attempting to create his mate, Gouroull had found some of Victor's notes regarding the bones of women he could use in his work. The list included Tera and the possible location of her tomb, which he could uncover with ease. But this inadequate little man, Fuchs, had discovered her remains first. And it seemed, she was now alive.

"Tall, strong, but twisted... You shall be the first Son of Set, the dagger in the darkness. Your face shall remain hidden beneath a veil of red silk and you shall speak to me in whispers. You will destroy my enemies and know that you are favored by your queen. Now, kneel before me, ugly one!" Tera commanded, pointing to her feet.

Gouroull stared at the woman and shook his head, unmoved despite her power. This was a mighty woman, but he could smell her insanity and bloodlust. This one was no plague upon mankind; she was a spoiled child, a greedy little girl who wanted everyone to love and worship her. He knew in an instant that she was vain, petty and foolish—a creature of whims who would use humanity as her plaything while she bathed in their admiration. Pathetic and silly—two qualities for which Gouroull did not have any use.

"I said—kneel!" Tera snarled, rising up and pointing her ringed finger at Frankenstein's creature.

The yellow eyes of the gem pulsed and a harsh breeze of hot desert air blew hard towards Gouroull.

He snarled and stepped forward, refusing to submit despite an urge to do so. His whole body sought to release itself from conscious thought, to drop and obey Tera's every whim. But his mind, his terrible alien mind, fought back with a primitive fury, a malevolent rage that refused to accept any being as his master. He forced himself to step forward again, rejecting the call for submission that struck him in waves.

"Others have defied me monster, but never again! My slave, kill this ugly thing!" Tera shrieked, pointing at the bronze dagger Fuchs had used in the ceremony.

The archeologist snatched up the knife and, with a high-pitched shriek, ran straight at Gouroull. He knew this one would be the first of many that would fall before his mistress remade the world.

The attack was a serious mistake. While magic was a powerful tool, it was inadequate in overcoming the baser instincts of its victim. To survive, above all else, was Gouroull's most powerful motivation. Seeing the little human running towards him with a blade, one that probably had little chance of penetrating his inhuman skin, broke the spell. Waiting until Fuchs was closer, Gouroull exploded into action. He backhanded the scholar across the face, shattering his neck instantly. Then, he turned towards Tera. Before she could speak again, he was upon her, his sharp teeth snapping down hard on her hand and removing three of her fingers.

Tera screamed—a wail of sheer agony. She instantly felt cold and weak, closer to the underworld that she had so recently vacated. Looking down at her bloody wreck of a limb, her eyes widened.

The Serpent Ring of Set was gone!

"Please!" she begged, looking up at the bloody, giant. "Please! Give me back my ring! I'll give you anything you ask!"

Gouroull spat out the fingers, snatching the coppery ornament as it fell. He examined it for a moment, sensing it possessed a spirit of its own. This ring was connected to someone, or something, long gone and turned to dust, but who still wished to return to this world. The spirit within the metal bands urged him to give the ring back to Tera, preferring the weak-willed spoiled princess to the malevolent monster.

"Please!" Tera begged again, dropping to her knees. "Please!"

Gouroull smiled and threw the ring out of the open window into the Egyptian night. It fell a great distance away and was snatched up before it struck the ground. He turned away, no longer interested in Tera; he had better candidates to consider.

Tera howled and shrieked, feeling the weakness overcome her, the cold rising. Her hands and arms soon withered, turned brown, and the rest of her body began to crumble and fall into dust. After a final, pathetic, cry, she was gone, returned to the underworld forever.

Margaret Fuchs sat up, seeing the wreckage and blood everywhere. Her father was dead and Tera was gone forever. She stood and walked towards the door. The authorities would surely look at this as an attempted robbery of antiquities. That would allow her to sell the precious pieces, return to London, and begin her life anew. After all, wasn't there an unmarried prince?

With a gleam in her eye, Margaret Fuchs began to scream for help...

CHAPTER XXI

Nasta looked up at the rising sun and pulled the horn from his belt. Blowing the instrument three times, he heard the sound echoed throughout the battle line, the sounds of warfare slowly diminishing. The sun was now visible and that meant it was Queen's Day, a celebration from now until sunrise the next morning. Then the battle would restart, and the war would continue unabated until next year. But Queen's Day was a celebration between both kingdoms, Kor and Negari, both of which meant to honor their powerful female rulers.

Nasta was a large man, possessing the huge muscles of a male lion. He was a powerful captain in the Negari forces, fighting with a war mace. During the yearly war games between the two kingdoms, he had defeated every opponent in wrestling, stone lifting and stone throwing. The warriors of Kor and Negari all walked softly around this giant fighting man.

"Would you like some *asa*?" Batalli asked, extending a clay flask towards the giant warrior.

Batalli was a prisoner, captured the month before and given his parole until he was exchanged. He could go anywhere in the city and, as long as he did not attempt to escape, or try hindering the war efforts, he could live in relative luxury, until his people caught an equally important prisoner and trade him for his release.

Batalli was quite different from Nasta; he was a lean man with the tight muscles of a panther. He was a famous captain in the armies of Kor. A skilled swordsman and bowman, Batalli was a master of the games.

The two warriors had faced each other in battle several times, always indecisively. Nasta was massively strong and dangerous when he swung his mace. Many men over the years had fallen before his furious onslaught. Fighting Batalli, on the other hand, was like fighting smoke; he moved with the light feet of a jungle cat and his sword appeared to have a life of its own. They were an even match, and neither relished the idea of defeating the other, knowing that they would lose something inside them when the other one fell. That respect had led them to capture each other several times, preventing that terrible, final battle.

"I will," Nasta answered, thanking his rival with a nod.

Asa was a fermented drink from Kor, a berry that grew near the caves that had once housed the terrible queen of that land.

That queen, known as Hiya, Ayesha, or She-who-must-be-obeyed, was dead and gone, but the Amahagger tribes still honored her memory. Nasta respected that custom; his own queen was dead since plunging off a cliff centuries ago. However, the deaths of such great women did not meant that they would not return one day and take again control of their kingdoms...

The people of Negari knew they were the last descendents of the bloodlines of Atlantis, while the tribes of Kor claimed another lineage, supposedly just as great and powerful. Though many of their ways were different, they were both raised from birth to follow their queens with unflagging devotion. Not to do so would be to admit that their mighty ruler was less than the one from the rival kingdom. In over three hundred years of war, that admission had never been made by either land's warriors.

All who resided in Negari still prayed daily to Nasta's queen, Nakari. They knew she was the last of the blood of Atlantis, an ancient race who had subjugated the tribes of their lands for thousands of years. Nakari's mother, a servant of great beauty, had seduced the last great magician of Atlantis and raised a daughter who was beautiful, terrible and powerful. She ruled for hundreds of years, kept young by potions that were known only to herself, and was feared by all the tribes—save that of Kor.

Nakari and Hiya secretly respected each other and kept their conflict on a small scale, never making use of their great powers. Nakari had perished in battle with a white outsider who had the gray eyes of a wolf and the steely muscles of a born-warrior. Some in Kor whispered that she had died at her own hand, but all knew that it was just as silly an idea as the notion of mighty Ayesha losing her powers and crumbling into dust in the Fire of Life.

"Are there any celebrations in your city on Queen's Day?" Batalli asked.

He had never been prisoner before during the day of the great celebration, so the customs of Negari were unknown to him.

"Yes," replied Nasta. "The great feast will begin and there will be dancing and gift giving. Do you do something else in your kingdom?"

"A great feast and dancing... On such a solemn an occasion? How... odd..." Batalli said, shaking his head.

He found the Negari definitely bizarre, despite producing some impressive warriors. That would explain why they had started these war games so many centuries ago and why they weren't giving up, even when the forces of Kor were so clearly superior in every way.

"Solemn?" Nasta repeated, sounding equally confused. "Queen's Day is a celebration of the majesty of our great and ancient ruler, Nakari, the most beautiful woman in the world. We dance and feast, and sacrifice ten criminals to her before the sun rises again. And when she returns, she will find her people as faithful as ever. How is that solemn?"

Batalli sighed, remembering that, despite his respect for Nasta, his people were barbarians worshipping a false ruler. But one had to be kind and indulgent towards one's inferiors.

Batalli's own tribe had once been just as savage and barbaric, but they had improved since the vanishing of Hiya—She-who-must-be-obeyed. Negari, on the other hand, appeared to still be stuck in their old ways, bathing their dead queen's body in the blood of criminals and slaves, praying that she would one day return and lead them to their dreams of an empire, a kingdom of blood. Only their own missing queen, the great and most lovely Ayesha, had prevented the savage Nakari from attempting to conquer all the tribes of their region. Her powers had been a match for the infamous mistress of the last colony of Atlantis.

"We fast and pray to Hiya as the sun rises in the great temple, near the Fire of Life. Then the women choose their mates for the next year and arrangements are made. We break the fast before the sunrise and say a prayer to Ayesha before resuming our battle with your people," Batalli explained, unable to truly convey the sanctity of the rites of the great Queen of Kor. The ceremonies were life-affirming, making one knew they were in the service of the true mistress of these lands.

Nasta shook his head, unable to comprehend the notion that women may choose their mates. What a backwards system! Kor had no understanding of the way of true strength, might and honor. In Negari, great captains, such as himself, were given the old women as servants. The young women would fight for the honor of becoming bed mates to the great warriors, the losers settling for lesser men and priests. They would produce babies, raise children, and work in the fields or with the animals.

"I fear our differences will never be reconciled, my friend," Batalli said, taking back the flask of *asa* and swallowing a large sip. "That would explain why your queen started the war with Kor so many years ago."

Nasta shook his huge head again.

"No, Kor started the battle with Negari. Come, I will show you our history, personally painted by the hand of Nakari herself!"

He led the smaller warrior through the thickening throng, knowing the dances would start soon. The young warriors often used these occasions to seek new coupling partners. But Nasta had no need for such demonstrations, he was the mightiest captain of the kingdom and had personally fathered twenty-four boys and a host of girls he never acknowledged. He would teach this honorable outsider the truth of what occurred in the past and why Negari was forced to war with the vile men of Kor.

Batalli followed Nasta, amused by the idea that his opposite number believed these sad children's tales. Everyone knew that Nakari had been a savage, evil woman who'd learned ancient and terrible magic in the hope of living forever. It was only the goodness and great power of Hiya that had forced her to stay in her ruined city and torment the slaves she purchased or stole from the outside world.

As to the war, all knew that Ayesha had sent messengers to this sad vestige of a city, only to have them murdered and consumed by the terrible ruler of these lands. War was inevitable—what else could Kor have done, except seek to destroy this kingdom and take all the lands?

Stopping in the outer circle of the ancient temple, Nasta took Batalli to the east wall. There, a series of complex paintings covered the stones, faded with age, yet still clearly visible. The art, to Batalli's eyes, was primitive and uninspiring; the childish scrawls of a weak mind. The figures were drawn as skeletal thin, dark and jewel covered, flanked by pale cow-like men and women from distant lands. There was little attempt at a narrative, or subtlety, but the representations were easy to follow, if one tried even a little.

"These were painted by the hand of beautiful Nakari at the time the war began. There, you see the messenger of Kor presenting gifts to our queen. But his evil servant, an assassin, leaps out and attempts to slay our magnificent ruler. Her most favored councilor, Munto the Leopard-Slayer, was killed protecting Nakari. And there! Nakari seizes the murderer and shatters his spine. The men of Kor then try and join their brethren by attempting to slay our Queen, only to die by her mighty hand! She then demands that Kor apologize, but they refuse and war begins. That is the tale of the war between our people. I do not hold you responsible, Batalli. You are a good and honorable warrior. But until Kor apologizes and submits, Negari has no choice but to continue the war."

Nasta had grown more animated as he told the story. He was usually a stoic, calm man, a warrior in the truest sense. But now, retelling this tale of his people, he was more emotional.

Batalli studied the paintings, seeing the lies in every scrawl. All knew Nakari had threatened the life of Ayesha and the servant, an elder man who had served the mighty queen since birth, had objected. Nakari had executed the old man and, when her council had attempted to intervene, murdered her own followers as well, and then all the diplomats in an orgy of blood. Ayesha, disgusted by the savagery of Negari's ruler, had had no choice but to declare war, and prevent Nakari's insanity from spreading beyond her ruined city. Until Negari was a mere memory, a sad rumor of a lost land, Kor would not cease in their attempts to destroy it and its terrible, foolish, wicked people.

"Thank you for showing me your temple," Batalli said, not knowing any other means of replying.

If he ever captured Nasta again, he could not return the gesture, for impure outsiders were not allowed near the Fire of Life. To do so would mean both of their deaths by slow torture. But it had taught him a great deal about the minds of these barbarians. They would never accept that they were meant to be ruled by Kor; therefore they had to be erased from the world!

Nasta turned back to Batalli, about to invite him to his table for the feast, when, suddenly, a loud crash echoed throughout the temple. It was normally empty on Queen's Day, so none should have been present. Yet, the noise came from within, an area used only during the important ceremonies in honor of the soon-to-be-returning ruler. It could be a servant or a priest misbehaving, possibly drunk. If so, they would be added to the sacrifices as criminals. Their polluted blood would no longer be allowed to weaken the great people of Negari.

"Follow me! You will now see how we, in Negari, deal with criminals!" Nasta snarled.

He ran through the great doors into the inner temple, Batalli at his side. The latter was interested, wondering how the savage Negari dealt with, and even classified, criminals. He had a strong feeling their beliefs on this matter would be radically different from his. In Kor, there were few criminals; the people lived an orderly life. The women chose their husbands, who would fight or work in their jobs until they were aged and would then serve as advisors to the women. It was an effective system, one created after Hiya had vanished and was no longer was present to lead the tribes.

The inner temple was a huge, domed monolith, a titanic structure of stone. It had been erected millennia before by the ancient Atlanteans; they were a tall, proud race who had viewed the inhabitants of these lands as sub-human savages. They worshipped dark, twisted gods and their ceremonial rites often involved the death by torture of their slaves. But, in time, despite their genius at building and their mastery of the mystic arts, the Atlanteans had diminished, until they were eventually overthrown by their slaves. This building was the last of their great works, a creation held together by enormous stone blocks, very precisely placed.

While the rest of the Atlanteans' work in Negari had fallen, due to earthquakes and floods, this temple still stood, although more shakily that anyone realized. It was a crumbling edifice, a tribute to its makers' genius, but it was also a terrible place, a monument to dreadful ceremonies of pain and death. The presence of this relic had contributed to twist the Negari, turning them into a tribe devoted to blood sacrifice in the name of a religion long forgotten by anyone else in the world.

At the far end of the huge chamber rested a stone altar, a leftover from the days when the Atlantean high priests had torn hearts from their screaming victims' chest, all in the name of their dark deity. There was still a somber power within that stone dais, the remnants of many lifetimes of terrible torment of men, women and children. Batalli felt a wave of cold malice emerging from the platform ahead and was immediately repulsed. This temple was... wrong. There was a monstrous evil permeating its very stones, an ancient horror that stained everyone who walked inside its cyclopean depths.

But this dreadful relic of long, and best forgotten days, did not capture the attention of the warrior from Kor. His eyes rested on the stone sarcophagus that lay just beyond the altar. This, too, was an artifact of power—the resting place of one of the ancient priests who had founded this outpost when a great sea split this dark continent. The dead Atlantean, his name now forgotten, had been removed from his tomb and his remains had been tossed into a refuse pile. Then the remains of the great Queen Nekari had been placed within. The priests had scratched out inscriptions hailing her greatness. Even in mighty Kor, all knew that the lid of this stone casket could only be moved by eight powerful warriors, during the annual blood sacrifice to the Queen.

But now, the lid lay on the floor of the temple, shattered beyond recognition. And instead of a host of warriors or slaves near the sarcophagus, there stood a single man. But what a unique figure! He was a giant, taller than Nasta, one of the largest men in both kingdoms. His hands and shoulders were huge; his hair was darker than even that of the men of the distant river tribes; his skin was pale, not the milky perfection of beauty, but rather that of the chalk from the hills beyond Kor, where the path to the desert before the Sulieman Mountains lay. His face was twisted and monstrous, but that was not what caused the two warriors to feel the grip of fear. It was his eyes, when he raised them to meet Batalli and Nasta's, that sent a dark shiver down their spines. They were the dark yellow of a river crocodile or serpent, inhuman in nature. Men, whether ancient Atlanteans or outsiders, were not meant to have such horrific eyes.

It was Nasta who recovered first, pulling his massive mace from his belt and raising it above his head.

"Who are you? Why did you profane the resting place of our Queen?"

The stranger stared at Nasta for a heartbeat, then reached into the sarcophagus with one enormous, scarred hand. A moment later, he pulled a skull from the tomb, white brown with age, and held it up for both men to see. He then placed it in a large bag and reached in again, pulling out another long bone.

"No!" Nasta screamed, raising his mace higher and charging.

Batalli, too, was disgusted by the blasphemous actions of this monstrous outsider. To despoil the dead was one of the greatest sins one could commit, no matter your kingdom. Despite his loathing for Negari, he drew his sword and charged, ready to fight alongside his rival.

The stranger appeared unaffected by the war cries and charges of the two warriors. He placed another bone in his bag before bothering to look at them again. His yellow eyes showed no fear, no anger. It was as if a reptile from the nearby river were watching them both. He possessed the same cold-blooded gaze and unwinking inhumanity.

Then, he exploded into action, snatching the mace from Nasta's hand, snapping several of the man's fingers in the process. His other hand grabbed the Negari warrior by the neck, causing the great champion to dangle from the ground and struggle while emitting the feeble gasps of a toddler. The creature hurled the weapon at Batalli, who ducked to avoid being crushed by the mighty mace.

The stranger, who held Nasta with little to no effort, smiled. Batalli gasped. His teeth were just as horrific as his eyes—the sharp incisors of a savage beast. These terrible incisors snapped out and tore Nasta's throat.

The stranger tossed the twitching warrior aside and stepped back to the sarcophagus, ignoring Batalli. Again, the massive hand reached into the tomb, pulling out a third bone and depositing it inside the large bag.

Disgusted beyond rage, angered by this sacrilegious stranger's disrespect, Batalli screamed again and charged. Unlike Nasta, he was not foolish enough to risk closing too much with the stranger. He would do as he had done his whole life: dart in and out and to the side, striking and slicing with his sword. He would sting this creature, slice him to pieces, and leave the final death blow to be dealt by the savages of Negari. He was about to lunge out and pierce the stranger, when the man straightened to his full height. He smiled, lips and mouth red with blood, and threw a huge piece of the stone casket lid at Batalli.

The famed captain of Kor was surprised and attempted to dodge to the side, but the piece thrown was too huge and too heavy. Batalli was crushed by the impact, and fell to the ground, groaning. His ribs had been shattered, but he might still live and fight another day. Coughing blood, he lay on the floor of the temple, his vision swimming. What felt like an age later, Batalli saw the stranger looking over him, his face no longer bloodied, his eyes still watching. A small, dreadful smile crossed the creature's face and slowly he reached down.

He grabbed the Kor warrior's neck with a hand that felt as cold and hard as marble. The hand twisted and Batalli saw no more—his neck shattered.

Gouroull surveyed the wreckage for a moment. He had no interest in the silly ceremonies or history of these people. He had just found the bones of his future mate. Nakari was a powerful, terrible woman with the appetites of a jungle beast and a desire to enslave all. It would be easy to convince one such as she to take up his quest and destroy all life on Earth.

But that was the future... For now, he needed to return to Herbert West and watch as the final preparations would be made to bring forth the dawning of the new race: the Spawns of Frankenstein's Monster!

Musi, the wife of the doddering high priest, heard the commotion in the temple and waited until all the sounds died out. She walked in the great chamber and surveyed the destruction. Her first thought was horror and fear, but then a malicious light came into her eyes. Though young and beautiful, she was wiser than any of the men who ruled her city. And this was her chance!

Screaming and shrieking, she awaited the warriors and their women as they poured into the temple, their celebrations ended. Musi stood next to the altar and straightened up to her full height, pointing a long finger at the throng. She waited several heartbeats as they slowly hushed, shocked by the open coffin and the bloody, torn corpses of Nasta and Batalli, the mightiest warriors of the two kingdoms.

"Nakari has risen and fed upon Nasta and Batalli!" Musi shouted. "I am now her high priestess, ruler in her name! Kneel, kneel and pray to mighty Nakari! A new age begins in Negari! Kneel!"

Musi's words echoed throughout the chamber. She had plans for this kingdom, a new beginning under Queen Musi!

The men and women of Negari dropped to their knees and began to pray, as their high priestess had commanded them to do...

CHAPTER XXII

Gouroull stepped back onto the shores of Europe, having been away from these war-torn lands for some time. The Great War between the humans appeared to be nearing its end, but he suspected that it would be only a brief pause. There would surely be another war soon, even bloodier. That was the nature of mankind; they relished war at all times, and only pretended to hid beneath the veneer of civilization. To Gouroull, this self-deception that was at the core of their being. It was another tool to use against them when the day came. Ultimately, his race would replace mankind and leave this world an exhausted, wasted graveyard.

He was mere days away from Herbert West, the fussy little doctor with the nimble mind. There was a madness in West, a crazed spirit similar to that of Victor Frankenstein. But West was even more delusional than Victor, and would come to a far worse end. But until that time, Gouroull would use the man's agile intellect to create his mate.

"Hold, Gouroull. I would speak with you," a voice said from the darkness.

He recognized it as that of the witch, the weaver of spells, who had insulted him a time ago.

She stood ahead, on a rise near a smoldering camp fire. Her craggy face was even more haggard; her sparse white hair and glittering eyes were visible, even at that distance. She was smiling, her yellow teeth looking more rotten since they had last met. A low cackle emerged from her lips, mocking and evil; she seemed amused by his surprise.

Gouroull snarled and rushed forward. He stepped across the embers of her fire in the blink of eye. His huge hands reached out—but snatched only empty air. The witch was gone, fading away like smoke from a dying fire. A loud, evil shriek of mocking laughter emerged to his left and he whirled in place, surprised again to find the ancient creature standing mere steps away.

"Do you think I would be so foolish as to speak with you face to face?" the witch said, an amused cackle in her voice. "This is a spell, a powerful sending I have not used in an age. I come to you in the name of my master, The Faceless God, The Howler in the Darkness. He has a message for you."

"Speak," Gouroull grumbled, angered at this elder thing eluding him once more.

The witch nodded and smiled, her tone changing from derision to the proclamation of a holy man reciting words memorized and spoken before a prayer.

"The Faceless God offers you a mate, one to fit your every need. She will bear your young and they will serve you. But you must do so in His name, His vision, not yours. What say you?"

"No," Gouroull replied, not even bothering to consider the offer.

The witch's face was impassive and her spectral form suddenly appeared before Gouroull again.

"Think not hastily, monster. You will have everything you wish, with only a small adjustment. You may bring chaos and fear down upon the Earth; my master welcomes such behavior in his servants. Death and destruction are his gift to all. But eventually, he wishes to bring in other life forms—more to his liking. This world will be changed to fit his whims—a far more horrific fate than the destruction you wish to rain upon the Earth. It is a greater mission. Your blood, your children and their children, shall flourish, replace the humans and become the new form of higher life. All you have to do is agree to serve the Dark One. It is a deal few can boast; a promise by an Outer God to raise an entire new species to greatness. What say you now, Gouroull?"

"No," Gouroull answered again.

He resumed his walk, but the witch once again appeared in front of him. This time, he just walked through her, winking out her illusory form by mere contact.

The witch reappeared at his side, just out of reach, keeping a step ahead of Frankenstein's creature. She seemed confused and an edge of fury entered her eyes and her voice.

"How can you refuse such an offer? A slight adjustment to your plans and you will receive everything you could dream of, and more! Why, why would you not even consider it? This is an opportunity many would beg to be granted!"

Gouroull stopped moving, turning slowly to face the ancient hag. His yellow eyes met her black ones and he said:

"Who am I speaking to?"

The witch stopped and looked puzzled.

"You met me before, in the woods. I am the witch!"

Gouroull stared unblinkingly.

"Do I speak to the puppet, or the puppet master?"

The witch straightened, her face growing tighter. She suddenly appeared stronger, more in control and less human. There was a new air of power and will in her form and she radiated pure malevolence.

"You speak to the master now, Gouroull. Speak as you will, the Dark One is listening."

Gouroull did not move for several minutes, the seconds slowly stretching away. Only the distant sounds of insects and birds could be heard, echoes of lesser life in the world.

"Your servants are slaves. Your puppets. I serve no man or God. Only myself."

The dark being who inhabited the form of the witch nodded slowly.

"What if I promise you that I will give you the gifts I promised, and then never speak to you again?"

Gouroull smiled, his razor-sharp teeth shining with an evil, terrible light.

"You lie. You will tell any tale."

The witch looked angry, her face twisting into a mask of fury.

"You know not what you reject. Know this, monster, reject my kind offer and you will regret your hasty choice. My servants will all become your enemies; my powers will hinder your every step. Your life will be one of failure, torment and horror. Ashes will be the only taste left in your mouth, and you will never see a moment's peace. You will learn you are nothing, but an insignificant insect in this universe, a weak and feeble speck of dust in the cosmic awl. And you will die a slow and painful end, having achieved nothing, forgotten by all. If you declare war on your betters, then you will die an ignominious death. Is that your wish?"

Gouroull's dreadful smile only widened.

"War with you and your ilk? Yes," he replied and continued to walk away, heading towards Herbert West's lab and the start of a new age—the age of monsters!

The witch stood frozen, watching Frankenstein's monster stride away.

The terrible, evil god that inhabited her form chuckled, then screeched with monstrous laughter.

Gouroull was perfect—a wonderful cosmic joke upon the universe. This would be a delight. Because everyone knew that the Outer Gods had never truly lost a battle. They were pure cosmic forces and, in the end, all beings fell within their plans, one way or another. Even Gouroull was a puppet on a larger stage, though an amusing one, more so than most. This would be an enjoyable age!

CHAPTER XXIII

The Great War was coming to a close; the end was near and all knew that the forces of the Kaiser were close to collapse. The British, French and American forces were pressing forward, and it was believed that the rulers of the Central powers would soon begin pressing for peace.

Many were referring to this war as "The War to End All Wars," but Gouroull found that fanciful title to be amusing at best, naïve at worst. Mankind would find another excuse for returning to slaughtering each other soon enough; war was a facet of their very existence. It was as important to their twisted souls as meat and drink, and, despite holding themselves up as paragons of virtue, they were far less than even the lowest life forms.

The trip through the war lines was simplicity itself. Gouroull moved with the speed of a hare, but with incredible stealth despite his size. Slipping past the demoralized Germans and Austrians, and the jubilant British and Americans, wasn't difficult. They were seeking enemy soldiers and his shadowy swift movements were often believed to be a mere trick of the light or a false image.

He had no reason to engage the soldiers this time; his final mission for Herbert West was completed. Then would come the slow and painful wait as the final steps of the legendary Victor Frankenstein's mad science was brought to life in this world a second time. There would be two of Gouroull's kind in the world, and the very Heavens would quake in fear.

Herbert West, for his part, was delighted upon seeing the bones of Nekari.

"Good, good! Excellent even! Your creator had placed her name, and that of her counterpart, Ayesha, I believe, as high choices for your mate. The bones are in adequate condition, but first, I must process their repairs and strengthen the structure. It will take me approximately three months before the final steps, and then I will begin the electrical charge necessary for reanimation. Leave me for now."

Gouroull left, amused that the fussy little scientist was ordering him as if he was one of the nurses in the nearby hospital. But West did not possess fear of the living or the dead. He was insane in his own way, a worshipper of science and science alone. Fear, in his mind, was a mere chemical process, one to be ignored or overcome by drugs or force of will. Gouroull, for all his terrible aspect, was merely another subject for his mad experiments.

Gouroull did not go far away from West's secret laboratory; he lurked in the murk that existed in even the brightest of days. Frankenstein's monster observed the little doctor as he painstakingly followed every step from Victor's note books. Gouroull's creator had been a meticulous man, for all his lunacy, an artist with the scalpel and the test tube.

Slowly, with the patience that only a scientist could possess, West followed each step and the bones and disparate organs were slowly transformed into the frame of a woman. She would be as tall as Gouroull, with a powerful, yet unmistakably female frame, and the same chalk colored skin. This would be his mate, Eve to his Adam, the co-progenitor of their new race.

Then came the day when West began to fill the generators with fluid, checking them with the same detailed attention as he had applied to the construction of Gouroull's future mate. Satisfied after a few minor adjustments, he began to connect a series of wires to the still unliving female body. Again, the little doctor left nothing to chance and checked every necessary step twice.

"Gouroull?" West asked, stepping into the doorway of his laboratory. "Are you ready?"

"Yes," Gouroull replied, stepping into the light of the full moon.

He rarely felt any form of emotion, but, this time, there was a small thrill of anticipation within his giant breast. Several times, he had been was brought to the brink of greeting his mate, only to have that opportunity destroyed by others. But not this time! Herbert West was now only minutes away from completing her creation.

West smiled, his insanity becoming even more apparent. He knew that he was on the brink of watching the work of the legendary Victor Frankenstein come to fruition again.

"I am about to begin the final stage," he said. "Three jolts of power—the same approximate amount your creator utilized. After the third flash, *she* should begin to revive. Until that time, do not approach the body. Your creator maintained that the close proximity of another person would be detrimental to his process. I think it's nonsense myself, but we will honor the great man's wishes by slavishly following all of his procedures--even if some could be improved by modern methods."

Gouroull assented and West returned to the lab, the metal door closing firmly with an audible snap.

A moment later, the smell of ozone filled the air and a bright flash of light illuminated the windows of the small laboratory, followed by the cracking sound of thunder. It was as if a miniature storm was raging within the building. That was the sound of birth, to Gouroull's mind—the first noises his living ears had ever heard in this world.

"Good evening, monster," a smooth voice said in the darkness.

A tall man with dark hair stepped from the shadows. He was wrapped in an opera cloak as well as the formal dress one would wear for a gala night. He was handsome, regal and possessed a long black mustache, a pointed beard, and a cruel mouth with pointed teeth. His hands were large, with talon-like fingernails and hair on his palms.

"Dracula," Gouroull breathed, knowing this was the true vampire-king, not one of his servants such as he had fought in China and Europe. This was the son of the dragon, the ancient scourge, the Prince of Darkness—the King of Vampires!

Dracula bowed.

"I am honored you recognize my true self. You have been something of an inconvenience to me. Your actions in China hampered my plans there,[11] and your recent assault upon the vampire council place me personally in danger. The situation is impossible and I will stand for your actions no longer."

Gouroull smiled and raised his hands. A battle with the master of vampires on the day of his mate's creation

---

[11] See "The Blood of Frankenstein" in *Tales of the Shadowmen* 10.

seemed to symbolize perfectly the death of the old ways and the beginning of a new age of horror.

Dracula threw back his head and released a bark of laughter, becoming as still as a statue.

"Dracula does not brawl with the likes of you, monster. Dracula holds the fate of nations in his hands. No, I brought you someone who seeks your end."

From the darkness behind the King of Vampires stepped a man, almost as tall as Gouroull, but possessing far broader shoulders and hands. Despite the large slouch hat and heavy coat, Gouroull instantly recognized the creature.

"Creeper," Gouroull breathed and snarled.

"Gouroull," the Creeper replied, his gargantuan fists raising into view.

No more was said. The two fiends charged forward, their titanic strengths meeting in a heartbeat, the battle beginning. Their last confrontation had been interrupted and both wished to know who was the greater, who would be left alive at the end of their clash.

Dracula watched as the two colossal figures strained against each other. These two were a close match, but in the end, the vampire lord cared little for the outcome. Striding past the combatants, he stepped into the laboratory after a second flash and another thunderclap erupted.

West's screams of protests could be heard for a moment, before Dracula's languid reply, and the little doctor's tiny frame was tossed out of one of the covered windows. Dracula stepped outside a few seconds later and the roar of flame could be heard, filling the air.

"No!" West shrieked as Dracula vanished, transformed into mist before his eyes. And then, less than a breath after he screamed, the building exploded in a burst of flame and noise, hurtling Herbert West, Gouroull and Creeper far into the night.

Gouroull was the first to rise, seeking the Creeper, but the huge man-monster was no longer in sight. Then he spotted the destroyed building, the lab burning, the light turning the night into a false daylight. His mate had been destroyed, he realized that instantly. Dracula had his revenge. His yellow eyes sought West and found the little man rising, dirty and bruised, but otherwise uninjured.

West began to giggle and shake his head.

"That was the wrong process. A proper elixir is the true path, not these ancient and archaic methods. Return the living to life, make them walk again. Death will be defeated. The first step is finding a new lab and chemicals. Then, securing bodies and testing the compounds on the subjects..."

Gouroull looked away, realizing that West's mind was now fully and entirely obsessed by the madness in his soul. He no longer sought any pretense of humanity for his work. He was a monster in his own right and would bring his own brand insanity to the world. And he was no longer any use to Gouroull.

Gouroull faded into the darkness, heading away from the fire and the voices of soldiers coming to fight the blaze. His quest would continue; he would create his mate, and then the living would know the true meaning of fear. The spawn of Frankenstein would become their waking nightmares. It was his dream, one he embraced with a malicious, evil glee. For he was not afraid of the horror that existed in his black soul. He was Gouroull, Frankenstein's Monster, the enemy of all life.

Afterword

A book is the sum of many moving parts. I heard that somewhere, and it's one of those sayings that stuck with me, something so simple and almost stupid, yet wise at the same time. Like, "What is the sound of one hand clapping?" When I was younger, I probably would have slapped the asker across the mouth as an answer (joke, I hope); now I'm not so sure.

This book was the sum of a lifetime of horror, literary and visual, coming through my diseased mentality. It wouldn't be right to not attribute where many thoughts came from, I've learned that much from reading the amazing Kim Newman, as well as one of my good friends, Rick Lai, although both of them are infinitely better and more knowledgeable than I am on this subject. I'm not going to explain the history of this version of the Frankenstein Monster a.k.a. Gouroull. My incredible editor/mentor Jean-Marc Lofficier did that earlier for you with greater precision than I could ever hope to wield. As for the rest, here goes with the many locations I attempted to visit in *The Quest of Frankenstein*.

Chapter 1: The Creeper is a personal favorite, a human monstrosity played by Rondo Hatton. Hatton was a victim of a disease known as acromegaly, a disorder of the pituitary gland that caused his features to grow larger. He used these unusual looks in Hollywood where he played one of the first unkillable serial killers, the "Hoxton Creeper," a giant crook who shattered his victim's spines. You can see him playing this part in *The Pearl of Death*, starring Basil Rathbone as Sherlock Holmes,

House of Horrors and *The Brute Man*. Rondo's image is used to this day as the Rondo Hatton Classic Horror Awards statue.

Chapter 2: Herbert West was created by the legendary horror writer, H.P. Lovecraft, in a series of short stories usually called *Herbert West-Reanimator*. This character grows more twisted with each story, as was the case of many of Lovecraft's characters and is a true pulp horror goodness. Most people know the name from the films of the same name starring Jeffery Combs as well as tales written by my friend, Peter Rawlik.

Chapter 3: The ghoul is an original character, based on the myths of that horrific type of monster. I've always found ghouls to be terrifying monsters, but they're often either mindless or barbaric. The idea of a well-spoken one was something I'd always wished to write.

Chapter 4: The "pale man" is a version of H.P. Lovecraft's evil cosmic tempter, Nyarlathotep. This creature is a personal favorite of mine, an alien demon who, unlike his Outer God counterparts, enjoys messing with humanity and creating chaos. The warlock is original and also symbolically shows how some approached the lives of others during the war. De Musard was a character by Philip José Farmer, one of the greatest writers of science fiction, horror and fantasy of all times.

Chapter 5: The vampire congress was fun to write as I was able to indulge my past love for such films. That love has been weakened greatly by the recent plethora of "nice" vampires, but there are enough bloodsuckers I can enjoy otherwise. Count Karnstein and his daughter are inspired by the original vampire novel *Carmilla* by J. Sheridan Le Fanu. This story predated Bram Stoker's *Dracula* and was very influential in fiction. If you find a taste of the Hammer version of these characters, I will readily that admit I did have Ingrid Pitt in mind when writing Mircalla.

The American vampire is Barnabas Collins from Dan Curtis' original television series *Dark Shadows*, a personally favorite of mine. His werewolf friend is Quentin Collins, from the same show. The amazing thing about *Dark Shadows* was that the "heroes" were often almost just as twisted and evil as their enemies.

Saushkin and the Russian witch are tributes to the Russian book series, *The World of the Watches*, one of the greatest urban fantasy series currently in print. The author, Sergei Lukyanenko, is a master of his craft, having created a world unique and filled with wonders.

The Master was the first villain of the television series, *Buffy, The Vampire Slayer*. He was played with delicious low-keyed evil by Mark Metcalf and was a true work of art by writer/producer Joss Whedon. His underling, Darla, was another character depicting a vampire in the modern world. Julie Benz's first appearance in that series was masterful, setting a tone for greatness as well as fun.

Viktor and Selene are the antagonist and protagonist of the *Underworld* series of films, written by Kevin Grevioux. Kevin himself played a part in it, that of the huge and deadly werewolf Raze. He is a true fan of comics, horror and other fun pursuits. I particularly enjoyed the first few film; the action mixed with the gothic horror was a great diversion.

Padma and his shape-shifter were characters from Laurell K. Hamilton's *Vampire Council*, a best-selling series of urban fantasy novels. The Chinese vampire was because yours truly spent many years watching the *Mr. Vampire* films and other knockoffs from Asia. I threw in my own twist on the legend of the "hopping vampires" because, like all writers, I see legends as something to be interpreted through my own, off-kilter imagination.

Princess Asa Vajda was a pleasure to include in this mix. She is a terrifying monster created by Mario Bava, and played by the queen of horror, Barbara Steele, for the movie *Black Sunday*, in my mind, one of the greatest of all modern horror films.

Akasha is a character I know second-hand, having not read any of the Anne Rice novels in which she appeared, but I do remember the photos of the late singer Aaliyah playing her part in the film (which I have not seen). She looked beautiful and deadly, a true vampire queen.

Dracula himself is one of the many versions that appeared of the character over the years. The legendary king of the vampires is truly a protean creature, showing up in so many guises, amazingly all evil, except for a few.

Chapter 6: Selene, the city of vampires, was created by a true giant of French literature, Paul Féval. His book *Vampire City* [12] created a new breed of monster and featured author Ann Radcliffe battling the evil vampire lord Otto Goetzi.

Chapter 7: H.P. Lovecraft created the Deep Ones in *The Shadow over Innsmouth*, probably one of his most impressive tales. They're another favorite of mine, fish

---

[12] Black Coat Press, ISBN 978-0-9740711-6-9.

men that can breed with humans…very creepy stuff by a horror grandmaster.

Chapter 8: Marie Moreau is the daughter of the twisted Doctor Moreau, star of H.G. Wells' *The Island of Doctor Moreau*. The 1932 film version is a personal favorite of mine. Zaroff is the twisted hunter from the short story, *The Most Dangerous Game* by Richard Connell. He is a wonderful villain and the tale itself is a realistic yarn full of action, adventure, and human-based horror.

Chapter 9: Lord Ruthven is another legendary vampire, created by John William Polidori, who was present at the house where Mary Shelley, Lord Byron, Percy Shelley and Claire Clairmont told ghost stories to each other and decided to create their own tales of terror. The result was Mary Shelley's masterpiece *Frankenstein* and Polidori's *The Vampyre*.[13] Lord Ruthven became a powerful influence on modern vampire fiction and has appeared many times since his first story.

Sir Francis Varney was a Victorian vampire from the Penny Dreadfuls by James Malcolm Rymer. The character is legendary, but I found getting through the story somewhat difficult at times. Still, he is a major character from the past.

Chapter 10: The Blind Dead, also known as the Blind Templars, terrified me as a kid. A series of Spanish horror films, they were created by Armando de Ossorio, a genius of Euro-horror. The first film, *Tombs*

---

[13] Black Coat Press, ISBN 978-1-932983-10-4.

of the Blind Dead, had me sleeping with the nightlight on for a few nights after first viewing it at age 11.

Chapter 11: The sad, mad soldier is meant to show what real horror is in our mundane world. The human misery of war is more frightening than anything crafted in legends or my own imagination. I used Dorothy L. Sayers' Lord Peter, a character known to have suffered shell-shock in WWI, to demonstrate the devastation that can happen to the human spirit.

Chapter 12: Herbert West again, though the philosophical discussion is one I'm happy that I was able to write.

Chapter 13: Quoting Mary Shelley's Victor von Frankenstein was a joy—something that hadn't been planned, but just happened. What a terrible, terrifying monster he was—a universe-changing character in fiction.

Chapter 14: Again, we return to Spanish horror, this time with Paul Naschy's Waldemar Daninsky series. In the film *The Night of Walpurgis*, we meet the lovely, evil Wandessa de Nadasdy. She was played by Patty Shepard and was one of the first vampire women I found attractive—a guilty pleasure to say the least.

Chapter 15: Lavinia Morley is a character that could have been a horror legend. She was played by the amazing Barbara Steele in the film *Curse of the Crimson Altar*; unfortunately, it was poorly written and directed, closer to an episode of *Scooby-Doo* than a true horror movie. There enough positives to make me enjoy it (such as the appearances of Christopher Lee and Boris Karloff!) but it was still a near miss, with a few memorable moments.

Chapter 16: Lady Sara Durwood was a minor character in the last of the Hammer vampire films, *Captain Kronos-Vampire Hunter*. The film is more swashbuckler than horror movie, but is a real joy to watch. After my first viewing, I wondered what had happened to Sara Durwood after the devastation of her life. I never really toyed with the idea of a story featuring her, until years later when I heard the words "emotional vampire" used by a non-horror fan. The term was meant to convey a man or a woman who live in a state of perpetual emotional upheaval, usually of their own making. Combining that narcissistic process with access to occult lore, I realized that it was where I wanted to send Sara Durwood.

Chapter 17: Lorelei the siren is a legendary figure of mythology. A real pleasure to write her.

Chapter 18: The Hunter of the Black Forest is the last of the Aesir, the Norse Gods. A sad figure from a sad cycle.

Chapter 19: The witch is an amalgam of many witches of legends and literature: Baba Yaga, Louhi, Pannochka, and more. She was fun to write, a creature even more evil than Gouroull!

Chapter 20: Princess Tera is the monster mummy from Hammer's *Blood From the Mummy's Tomb*. I had some fun adding a little of the Robert E. Howard history of the world to this tale, while creating a spoiled psychotic mummy—the only one likely to follow such a crazy plan. The Serpent Ring of Set is a legendary object from Howard's work, appearing in ancient as well as modern times.

Chapter 21: Nakari of Negari was a foe of Robert E. Howard's Solomon Kane in *The Moon of Skulls*. A beautiful, evil queen, she was one whom he killed far too soon. Ayesha and Kor are from the legendary novel *She* by H. Rider Haggard, whose work is still influential to this day.

Chapter 22: The one speaking through the witch is, of course, Nyarlathotep, the many-named cosmic chaos god. I added a name or two of my own creation when speaking of him earlier and in this chapter.

Chapter 23: Both the Creeper and Herbert West return, along with a version of Dracula closer to Stoker's creation. I'll never forget the chill of fear I felt the first time I read that Dracula had hair on his palms. For some reason, that frightened me far more than his sharp teeth.

There you have it! Special thanks to Jean-Marc Lofficier, Gail Schildiner, Ruth and Julian Schildiner, Shihan James Amorosi, Win Scott Eckert, Rick Lai, Chuck Loridans, the Wold Newton Meteoric Society, Howard Hopkins, Ron Fortier, Rob Davis, Tommy Hancock, Joe Gentile, Andrew Schildiner and Jay Piscopo.

Frank Schildiner

SF & FANTASY

Adolphe Alhaiza. *Cybele*
Alphonse Allais. *The Adventures of Captain Cap*
Henri Allorge. *The Great Cataclysm*
Guy d'Armen. *Doc Ardan: The City of Gold and Lepers*
G.-J. Arnaud. *The Ice Company*
Charles Asselineau. *The Double Life*
Henri Austruy. *The Eupantophone; The Olotelepan; The Petitpaon Era*
Barillet-Lagargousse. *The Final War*
Cyprien Bérard. *The Vampire Lord Ruthwen*
S. Henry Berthoud. *Martyrs of Science*
Aloysius Bertrand. *Gaspard de la Nuit*
Richard Bessière. *The Gardens of the Apocalypse; The Masters of Silence*
Albert Bleunard. *Ever Smaller*
Félix Bodin. *The Novel of the Future*
Louis Boussenard. *Monsieur Synthesis*
Alphonse Brown. *City of Glass; The Conquest of the Air*
Émile Calvet. *In a Thousand Years*
André Caroff. *The Terror of Madame Atomos; Miss Atomos; The Return of Madame Atomos; The Mistake of Madame Atomos; The Monsters of Madame Atomos; The Revenge of Madame Atomos; The Resurrection of Madame Atomos; The Mark of Madame Atomos; The Spheres of Madame Atomos; The Wrath of Madame Atomos* (w/M. & Sylvie Stéphan)
Félicien Champsaur. *The Human Arrow; Ouha, King of the Apes; Pharaoh's Wife; Homo-Deus; Nora, The Ape-Woman*
Didier de Chousy. *Ignis*
Jules Clarétie. *Obsession*
Michel Corday. *The Eternal Flame*
André Couvreur. *The Necessary Evil*; *Caresco, Superman; The Exploits of Professor Tornada* (3 vols.)
Camille Debans. *The Misfortunes of John Bull*
Captain Danrit. *Undersea Odyssey*
C. I. Defontenay. *Star (Psi Cassiopeia)*
Charles Derennes. *The People of the Pole*
Chevalier de Béthune. *The World of Mercury*
Georges Dodds (anthologist). *The Missing Link*

Charles Dodeman. *The Silent Bomb*
Harry Dickson. *The Heir of Dracula; Harry Dickson vs. The Spider*
Jules Dornay. *Lord Ruthven Begins*
Alfred Driou. *The Adventures of a Parisian Aeronaut*
Sâr Dubnotal *vs. Jack the Ripper*
Odette Dulac. *The War of the Sexes*
Alexandre Dumas. *The Return of Lord Ruthven*
Renée Dunan. *Baal; The Ultimate Pleasure*
J.-C. Dunyach. *The Night Orchid; The Thieves of Silence*
Henri Duvernois. *The Man Who Found Himself*
Achille Eyraud. *Voyage to Venus*
Henri Falk. *The Age of Lead*
Paul Féval. *Anne of the Isles; Knightshade; Revenants; Vampire City; The Vampire Countess; The Wandering Jew's Daughter*
Paul Féval, *fils. Felifax, the Tiger-Man*
Charles de Fieux. *Lamékis*
Louis Forest. *Someone is Stealing Children in Paris*
Arnould Galopin. *Doctor Omega; Doctor Omega and the Shadowmen* (anthology)
Judith Gautier. *Isoline and the Serpent-Flower*
H. Gayar. *The Marvelous Adventures of Serge Myrandhal on Mars*
G.L. Gick. *Harry Dickson and the Werewolf of Rutherford Grange*
Delphine de Girardin. *Balzac's Cane*
Léon Gozlan. *The Vampire of the Val-de-Grâce*
Jules Gros. *The Fossil Man*
Edmond Haraucourt. *Illusions of Immortality; Daah, the First Human*
Nathalie Henneberg. *The Green Gods*
Eugène Hennebert. *The Enchanted City*
V. Hugo, P. Foucher & P. Meurice. *The Hunchback of Notre-Dame*
Romain d'Huissier. *Hexagon: Dark Matter*
Jules Janin. *The Magnetized Corpse*
Michel Jeury. *Chronolysis*
Gustave Kahn. *The Tale of Gold and Silence*
Gérard Klein. *The Mote in Time's Eye*
Fernand Kolney. *Love in 5000 Years*
Paul Lacroix. *Danse Macabre*
Louis-Guillaume de La Follie. *The Unpretentious Philosopher*
Jean de La Hire. *Enter the Nyctalope; The Nyctalope on Mars; The Nyctalope vs. Lucifer; The Nyctalope Steps In; Night of the Nyctalope; Return of the Nyctalope; The Fiery Wheel*
Etienne-Léon de Lamothe-Langon. *The Virgin Vampire*

André Laurie. *Spiridon*
Gabriel de Lautrec. *The Vengeance of the Oval Portrait*
Alain le Drimeur. *The Future City*
Georges Le Faure & Henri de Graffigny. *The Extraordinary Adventures of a Russian Scientist Across the Solar System* (2 vols.)
Gustave Le Rouge. *The Mysterious Doctor Cornelius* (3 vols.); *The Vampires of Mars; The Dominion of the World* (w/Gustave Guitton) (4 vols.)
Jules Lermina. *Mysteryville; Panic in Paris; To-Ho and the Gold Destroyers; The Secret of Zippelius; The Battle of Strasbourg*
André Lichtenberger. *The Centaurs; The Children of the Crab*
Listonai. *The Philosophical Voyager*
Jean-Marc & Randy Lofficier. *Edgar Allan Poe on Mars; The Katrina Protocol; Pacifica; Robonocchio; Return of the Nyctalope;* (anthologists) *Tales of the Shadowmen 1-11; The Vampire Almanac* (2 vols.)
Xavier Mauméjean. *The League of Heroes*
Joseph Méry. *The Tower of Destiny*
Hippolyte Mettais. *The Year 5865; Paris Before the Deluge*
Louise Michel. *The Human Microbes; The New World*
Tony Moilin. *Paris in the Year 2000*
José Moselli. *Illa's End*
John-Antoine Nau. *Enemy Force*
Marie Nizet. *Captain Vampire*
C. Nodier, A. Beraud & Toussaint-Merle. *Frankenstein*
Henri de Parville. *An Inhabitant of the Planet Mars*
Gaston de Pawlowski. *Journey to the Land of the 4th Dimension*
Georges Pellerin. *The World in 2000 Years*
Ernest Pérochon. *The Frenetic People*
Pierre Pelot. *The Child Who Walked on the Sky*
J. Polidori, C. Nodier, E. Scribe. *Lord Ruthven the Vampire*
P.-A. Ponson du Terrail. *The Vampire and the Devil's Son; The Immortal Woman*
Georges Price. *The Missing Men of the Sirius*
Edgar Quinet. *Ahasuerus; The Enchanter Merlin*
Henri de Régnier. *A Surfeit of Mirrors*
Maurice Renard. *The Blue Peril; Doctor Lerne; The Doctored Man; A Man Among the Microbes; The Master of Light*
Jean Richepin. *The Wing; The Crazy Corner*
Albert Robida. *The Adventures of Saturnin Farandoul; The Clock of the Centuries; Chalet in the Sky; The Electric Life*

J.-H. Rosny Aîné. *Helgvor of the Blue River; The Givreuse Enigma; The Mysterious Force; The Navigators of Space; Vamireh; The World of the Variants; The Young Vampire*
Marcel Rouff. *Journey to the Inverted World*
Léonie Rouzade. *The World Turned Upside Down*
Han Ryner. *The Superhumans; The Human Ant*
Pierre de Selenes: *An Unknown World*
Angelo de Sorr. *The Vampires of London*
Brian Stableford. *The New Faust at the Tragicomique;The Empire of the Necromancers (The Shadow of Frankenstein; Frankenstein and the Vampire Countess; Frankenstein in London); Sherlock Holmes & The Vampires of Eternity; The Stones of Camelot; The Wayward Muse.* (anthologist) *News from the Moon; The Germans on Venus; The Supreme Progress; The World Above the World; Nemoville; Investigations of the Future; The Conqueror of Death; The Revolt of the Machines; The Man With the Blue Face*
Jacques Spitz. *The Eye of Purgatory*
Kurt Steiner. *Ortog*
Eugène Thébault. *Radio-Terror*
C.-F. Tiphaigne de La Roche. *Amilec*
Simon Tyssot de Patot. *The Strange Voyages of Jacques Massé and Pierre de Mésange*
Louis Ulbach. *Prince Bonifacio*
Théo Varlet. *The Golden Rock. The Xenobiotic Invasion; The Castaways of Eros; Timeslip Troopers* (w/André Blandin); *The Martian Epic* (w/Octave Joncquel)
Pierre Véron. *The Merchants of Health*
Paul Vibert. *The Mysterious Fluid*
Villiers de l'Isle-Adam. *The Scaffold; The Vampire Soul*
Gaston de Wailly. *The Murderer of the World*
Philippe Ward. *Artahe ; The Song of Montségur* (w/Sylvie Miller) *Manhattan Ghost* (w/Mickael Laguerre)

MYSTERIES & THRILLERS

M. Allain & P. Souvestre. *The Daughter of Fantômas*
A. Anicet-Bourgeois, Lucien Dabril. *Rocambole*
A. Bernède. *Belphegor*; *Judex* (w/Louis Feuillade); *The Return of Judex* (w/Louis Feuillade); *The Shadow of Judex*
A. Bisson & G. Livet. *Nick Carter vs. Fantômas*

V. Darlay & H. de Gorsse. *Arsène Lupin vs. Sherlock Holmes: The Stage Play*

Séamas Duffy. *Sherlock Holmes in Paris*

Paul Féval. *Gentlemen of the Night; John Devil; The Black Coats ('Salem Street; The Invisible Weapon; The Parisian Jungle; The Companions of the Treasure; Heart of Steel; The Cadet Gang; The Sword-Swallower)*

Émile Gaboriau. *Monsieur Lecoq*

Goron & Émile Gautier. *Spawn of the Penitentiary*

Paul d'Ivoi. *Around the World on Five Sous* (w/Henri Chabrillat)

Rick Lai. *Shadows of the Opera: Retribution in Blood; Sisters of the Shadows: The Curse of Cagliostro*

Steve Leadley. *Sherlock Holmes: The Circle of Blood*

Maurice Leblanc. *Arsène Lupin vs. Countess Cagliostro; Arsène Lupin vs. Sherlock Holmes (The Blonde Phantom; The Hollow Needle); The Many Faces of Arsène Lupin; The Island of the Thirty Coffin; 813*

Gaston Leroux. *Chéri-Bibi; The Phantom of the Opera; Rouletabille & the Mystery of the Yellow Room; Rouletabille at Krupp's*

Richard Marsh. *The Complete Adventures of Judith Lee*

William Patrick Maynard. *The Terror of Fu Manchu; The Destiny of Fu Manchu*

Frank J. MOrlok. *Sherlock Holmes: The Grand Horizontals; Sherlock Holmes vs Jack the Ripper*

Jean Petithuguenin. *The Adventures of Ethel King*

Antonin Reschal. *The Adventures of Miss Boston*

P. de Wattyne & Y. Walter. *Sherlock Holmes vs. Fantômas*

David White. *Fantômas in America*

Pierre Yrondy. *The Adventures of Thérèse Arnaud*

Victor Margueritte. *The Bacheloress; The Companion; The Couple*